B 86

D0064900

THE
SECRET
THREAD

BOOKS BY
GRACE ZARING STONE

The Heaven and Earth of Doña Elena
The Bitter Tea of General Yen
The Almond Tree
The Cold Journey

UNDER THE PSEUDONYM OF
ETHEL VANCE

Escape
Reprisal
Winter Meeting
The Secret Thread

THE

Secret Thread

by

ETHEL VANCE
(Grace Zaring Stone)

*Theseus adventuring, risking himself amidst
the Labyrinth, assured by the secret thread of
an inner fidelity . . .*
The Journals of ANDRÉ GIDE,
Cuverville, 1912

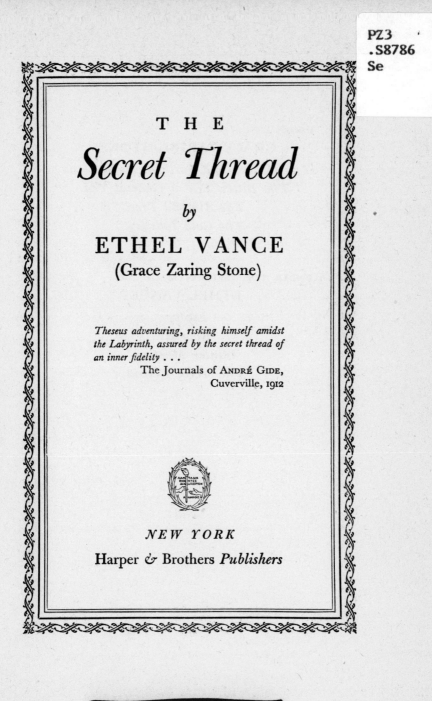

NEW YORK
Harper *& Brothers Publishers*

9-8

FIRST EDITION

F-X

❋

THIS

IS FOR

PETER

❋

THE
SECRET
THREAD

CHAPTER I

THE ship finally anchored off Quarantine, several miles from the city. It was too late for the Health and Immigration officers to come aboard so the passengers could not get ashore that night as they had hoped. They were obliged to eat their dinner in the crowded dining saloon, a curious farewell dinner, for most of them were together for the first as well as the last time. This was because it had been one of the worst crossings that even the captain—so he said—had ever made.

From the hour the ship left Europe it had been battered by mountainous seas. The feebler passengers lay in their bunks listening fearfully to the shrill whistle of the wind, the pound of the waves, and an occasional shattering of crockery in the galleys. The hardier ones couldn't find anything to do. There were no games, no gossiping on deck. All ports were tightly sealed and the smoking room was foul with all the smells of the ship, of engine grease and oil, of fishy food and toilets that were out of order.

Now this was over. The ship lay in calm water and

1

the city was beginning to sparkle, several miles away.
Through open ports came the tepid air of an early spring
evening. The racks were off the tables and people talked
to their neighbors. Excited by nearness to land and the
short time left them they tried to tell as much about
themselves as they could. They talked of what they had
been doing abroad, of how long they had been away
from home, and they gave their considered opinions on
"conditions over there." It did not matter much that no
one listened attentively to anyone else.

After dinner most of them went up on deck to look
at the city, and then they talked about where they were
going and who would be waiting for them. Tomorrow
was their concern now, and the city represented their
tomorrow.

But as they looked across the long black stretch of
water it did not seem the warm, human warren they had
been expecting. It did not seem the place where all
their land knowledge would count and all their land
appetites be satisfied. It did not seem a place in which
to bring up a family or to organize a good sales cam-
paign. It did not even seem a place where you would
see a show or get a large, red steak. It was a constellation
of light, cage over cage of unsubstantial splendor against
a dark sky. They couldn't see what supported these
glittering geometries. They were proud of it because
they felt they had made it, and it had turned out to be
like nothing else in the world; but they could not at
this moment remember the meaning of it, hcw it had
been made, and toward what end. It was an enigma, and
as they looked at it their tomorrow became enigmatic

SUBURBAN AUTOMOTIVE INC.

TOM, JIM & SAL BOIANO
PHONE 758-4444
Route 69, Opp. Post Office   Prospect, Conn.

DATE _____ 196 ___

M _____

1		
2		
3		
4		
5		
6		
7		
8		
9		
10		
11		
12	**7476**	

Plate B - CLARK SPECIALTY CO., PROSPECT, CONN.

Commisioner of M.V.

State St.

Wethersfield Ct.

06109

also. Their talk died. Gradually they went below, did their last packing, and went to bed, and when they slept most of them dreamed. But their dreams were not enigmatic at all. They dreamed of landings and customs inspections, a telegram to be sent, what to say to so-and-so, Junior waiting on the dock, and the window boxes beginning to bloom on Seventy-fifth street. They dreamed of a future as a place they already knew.

One of the passengers, a man named Cassius Terhune, after taking three sleeping pills went to bed, and he also dreamed. He dreamed of a house in the city where he used to live, which he had not seen and scarcely thought of for many years.

Next morning the bugle sounded early. Everyone got up promptly and hurried in to breakfast, and presently a launch with the Health and Immigration officials came alongside. They climbed aboard and the inspection began.

The passengers stood in two lines, the American citizens in one, the foreigners in another. The Americans exchanged jokes, feeling foolish because they were not used to questions and examinations, but the foreigners were silent. Gradually the Americans noticed this and began to look toward them as people apart. Cassius Terhune thought that these foreigners seemed like the escaping inhabitants of countries where cholera was raging, and that the Americans were conscious of them now because they feared they might carry the contagion with them. The Americans were sorry for them so long as they remained in their own countries. Here they were a danger. He remembered again the city's night aspect, the sorcery and deception of it, which were like a hoax played on this practical people out of their own materials; and, he thought, if they also are remembering it, they may feel that even their stronghold is not as solid as it was meant to be. It would be possible to become dispossessed in it as easily as elsewhere. In a moment, he thought, they will begin to look at one another with uneasiness, wondering which of their own apparently healthy bodies carries a latent sickness. They can begin on me, he thought.

As he leaned against the rail watching the city draw nearer he did not look sick in any way. It was not only that he had a fine coppery tan—two weeks in the German Alps at Grainau had given it to him—but he had also a look of adaptability that had nothing to do with a healthy color. He seemed to have the resilience and suppleness of the man who has lived all his early life under the pressure of a great, populous city and who has developed immunity to its many diseases—of body, of mind, perhaps—though he may also suffer chronically but never dangerously from others. This made his age hard to guess; he might be anywhere between forty and fifty. His handsome, thin face was both worn and smoothed by experience. Only his smile made some people feel that this urbanity was not always to be trusted. His smile was charming but at times a little foolish and deprecating, as though he remembered failures that had been absurd as often as tragic. It made people think he might not be as successful as he appeared. There was indeed always a little mystery about him because of his origins, so unmistakable in the

broader sense. The city had given him its regional
characteristics but even close acquaintances often said
of him, just what did he come from, that is, from what
sort of people, what was his background? They had many
answers, all of them quite different.

Now that the ship was well up the harbor the city
presented to the travelers another transformation. It rose
in the shadow of clouds like an upsurging of primitive
rock, stained with raw ores, pouring steam from vol-
canic vent holes. But this illusion, which seemed an
even more mocking one, did not last. As they neared
it the sun broke the clouds. All the windows shone as
bright as eyeglasses on the myriad faces of smart busi-
nessmen; the smoke represented the extravagant but
calculable expense of coal- and oil-burning furnaces.
A Staten Island ferry pulled from its slip and the passengers on it waved. "Little Old New York!" someone
exclaimed. Everyone felt reassured.

Terhune, looking down at the ferry, remembered
that on one like it he had made his first voyage and his
first return. He had been about five years old. His Aunt
Minerva had a friend living in Weehawken and once
or twice a year she went to visit her. This friend was
a retired actress rumored to have a considerable sum
of money laid by, and Aunt Minerva, who had a conviction that somehow, by some means, she herself would
come into the possession of money, didn't overlook the
possibility that if she were attentive enough about
birthdays and holidays she might be left something in
a legacy. On this occasion she hoped that perhaps little
Cassius' childish graces would have a softening effect

on the old lady's heart and she instructed him accordingly. But it was not this aspect of the expedition that interested him. It was the intense excitement of the journey: as he rode on the ferry he realized that he was leaving everything he knew, and he could not imagine going back to it. He could not believe, because of the strangeness of what was happening to him, that it would wait there for him unchanged.

In Weehawken there was a yard that seemed to him immense, a tangle of blackberry bushes and tomato vines, with chickens scratching in the dirt, and by the back porch little sour pools of bluish slop water. The yard ended abruptly in a cliff, with only a torn wire fence between him and the drop to the river. New York was all darkness and smoke on the other shore. He ate chicken and dumpling for dinner and most of the chocolates that Aunt Minerva had bought on the ferry as a present for him to give her friend. The day was endless. Finally they did go back, but in part he had been right, for the ferry, the crosstown car, the street he lived in, his house, were not the same.

As he thought of the house he remembered that last night he had dreamed about it. It came back to him now with a vividness that dreams do not generally have, except immediately on awakening. The house had been unmistakably his house, but as the dream went on it became much larger and infinitely more complex, so that new apartments were constantly forming like cells at all its outer boundaries. The light in it was neither of day nor of night, but a sort of twilight. He was in no doubt as to why he was there: he was there to search for something. What that something was he never found out, though at moments it seemed to be just outside his knowledge. The whole dream was permeated by this compulsion, and also by a need for haste, which also was uncertain and either sprang from a danger in the house or was merely a necessity to catch a train. At times his search, the meaning of which was never revealed, became so confused and intensive that the house and himself suffered a change, and it was then as though he shrank to molecular size and circulated through a vascular system or in the canals of an inner ear. Again it seemed to him that the house, with him and whatever else was in it, sank underground. But the curious part was that it was not a nightmare, not really a dream of fear, except as any compulsion has always some admixture of terror.

Thinking of it he realized it had a direct connection with his sickness, was at once a pattern of it and perhaps an escape from it. The thought made him consider again the sickness from which he felt at the moment free, so that he could look at it with a certain detachment. He knew its origin was mental. The headaches, nausea, pains, weakness, sleeplessness, all the rest, were only symptoms of the mental sickness. But such a sickness has many and deep roots, and he had been unwilling so far to try to trace them. He had been impatient of the efforts of the psychologist in Germany and impatient with himself. It would pass, he kept telling himself, with rest, a change of scene, and, above all, if he let it alone.

What happened was that at times his mind would step up its pace, go off into accelerated, intense speculations of a sort, up to now, quite new to him, but which he felt the greatest exaltation in attacking, marveling at what seemed the novelty and significance of his thoughts. Then suddenly, just as brilliant solutions were about to be reached, he would recognize the insistent jangle of machinery gone wrong, and everything would abruptly and somehow shamefully stop. His mind would move in no direction, though for a little while directions still multiplied almost mockingly around him. And finally came a dull sense of dread and anguish in which he knew he had been deceived, that he was sick, and that if something didn't stop him he would be sicker still.

The dream, as he saw it now, was a child's reconstruction, a child's facsimile of this state, and at the same time it presented the solution of a child by offering him a refuge, placing him again where he had once been secure from such dangers. The subconscious, he thought, certainly stays on the job. It's an officious little worker, but it isn't very effective. The subconscious is too gullible.

And he thought a rather minor deception would be that the house itself, the real house, probably wasn't even in existence. It was an old New York house. Such houses have short lives. In no other city is there such a ruthless tearing down. No, he thought, the house has gone; but he thought of it as he had once before, as dissolving not so much by physical means as by a process in himself.

The ship docked finally and some reporters came aboard. Various passengers were corralled in a corner of the sun deck and there was a flash of bulbs as a young

French actress on her way to Hollywood provided a bit of cheesecake, sitting on the ship's rail. Terhune was among those questioned, but on this occasion he did not shine because the first question asked him was whether, as rumored, he had had a nervous breakdown in Germany and was coming home on that account. It startled him to hear it put in so many words. Contrary to all probability, indeed to the fact that doctors had seen him and treated him, that cables had been sent, he had been imagining that no one really suspected what was the matter with him, and he began a long explanation of a strep throat infection, which he had also had, and why the doctor had ordered a change of climate. He went on almost automatically to express optimism over the re-education of the German people but he saw he was not holding their interest. This was not —he was well aware of it—his expected style. Nothing is more lamentable than an habitually dynamic man talking about his health, or a pungent one expressing a flabby, invalid hopefulness. They strayed away from him and clustered about the French girl.

When they had left him alone he told himself that anyone able to guess accurately what people are thinking about him is bound to feel ridiculous at least part of the time. And he knew very well what people thought about him, especially those who for some reason or other, frequently envy, did not admire him.

But only the successful are envied, and he had been successful. He had inherited money, not from the old actress but, curiously, from Aunt Minerva herself. Perhaps he would have been a success without it but it had certainly helped. It was not such a lot of money, not enough to put its own burdens and its own fear on him, but enough to give him an education of the sort he wanted, to carry him over certain discouragements, ease several failures, and give him for many years the underlying conviction that whatever happened he was not intended to know the worst.

It gave him freedom to follow not one career but several. Coming from the army in 1918 he studied for the law, practiced for a short while in New York, then Washington, because the woman he married, daughter of a retired admiral, thought Washington the center of the world and could not be happy in New York. Then he passed into the State Department for a temporary special assignment and from there became an assistant secretary of the Treasury, and finally the small but distinguished college of which he was an alumnus offered him its presidency and he accepted it. He had been president for the last five years and now he was simply waiting for something more important. This German business was a foretaste of what he might expect—perhaps a diplomatic post. Perhaps in the end, a Cabinet post. His friends said that eventually he would get pretty much what he wanted. They were not sure of what that would be.

In spite of his success certain things had gone wrong for him, though he was still considered by those who knew him to be very fortunate. (The troubles of the successful never cast any perceptible shadow in the minds of their friends.) His marriage, for instance, had turned out badly. Lita was a beauty, of the delicate, precise, machine-made American sort, but nervously, aridly self-centered. Always opinionated, always impervious, poised on frail, obstinate tensions and convictions, never listening, always sure, always right. Lita was the admiral in Dresden china. Lita was a bore. On the night she married again he got very drunk, not from sorrow but from relief, and he spent it in a maudlin hilarity, thinking that his private experience of her was now being shared by someone he didn't even know. Then for months after he was depressed. Not at losing her but at the waste and failure she represented.

After that the only woman who had any real place in his life was Rénée. Rénée was Lita's foil. She was reasonable and intelligent and kind. She had a gift for friendship and tenderness. He was very fond of her and he never married her. People said he treated Rénée badly, though Rénée never seemed to think so. She always said to him, we have a wonderful understanding. But in the end she had left him. She married a young newspaper man, several years younger than herself, who had developed tuberculosis and was being sent to Arizona. He was going to write a play there. Rénée went with him and Terhune never heard of either of them again.

These experiences were over. They had been over for years and to tell the truth, he didn't very often think of either of these women, only occasionally of Rénée, when a little cloud of loneliness would settle down on him at the end of a hard day. But he felt he was a man meant to be alone, trained and hardened since early childhood to be just that. He had all the techniques for dealing with aloneness, the many interests and enjoyments, the deep feeling of pleasure in order, which is impossible to achieve except in solitude, and he had the friends who at any time would people areas suddenly left empty. Yes, he got along very well—or had up until a few months ago.

The questions of the reporters still nagged at him. Of course he couldn't have hoped to conceal the fact that something had gone wrong. It was ridiculous to pretend he could. But had his friends any inkling of it? He tried to remember, for instance, just what at times he might have written to Charlie Bates, and he thought of a conversation he'd had with Charlie just before he sailed. Charlie had said, "I can see this job is going to raise hell with you." "And why?" Terhune had asked. Charlie said, "You're the guy that always wants an answer." And he had said, "I'm really not that much of a fool. I know where the only world without contradictions is. It's in the mind of a logician. And who wants to live in the mind of a logician?" Charlie looked at him skeptically and said, "Just the same, you'll hate the god-awful mess of it, and I don't mean only the physical mess. But don't go asking yourself too many questions. There are limits to what you can know." Terhune hadn't gone on with it but he'd thought: Yes, Charlie old boy, and you mean a man is only likeable, dignified, and efficient when he accepts those limits. But don't worry, I'll find plenty to do over there. Things that *can be done.*

He was on the pier before he knew it, standing under "T." The inspector ruffled through his bags. He put the seals on and a porter gathered them up on a hand truck. Terhune started after him down the pier. It was a long pier and there was an unexpected, animal, ammoniac smell about, as though elephants and their fodder were hidden behind the crates and boxes. And where in God's name, he thought irritably, do all these boxes come from, where do they go, what's in them? Who cares enough, and about what, to start the long chains of production and disposal? Just to look at them, combined with that zoo smell, made his head ache, made him feel in spite of his usual energy that there was too much in the world, too many people, too many intentions, too much credulity. He found himself thinking again of the house, of his dream. For all its complicated, ambiguous, and submerged character it had one great and simple merit. It was empty.

Anyway, here at last before him was the city. At the edge of a cobbled space he saw a row of low brick houses. An overhead driveway cast a rusty tunnel of shade, and heavy trucks made a continuous rumble on the cobbles.

"Taxi!"

A yellow cab drew up. The porter stowed his bags and Terhune got in.

"Pennsylvania Station," he said.

. As they bumped along he leaned forward and read the name of the driver. He had a feeling that the first name he saw on his return might mean something to him, be some sort of clue to the future. As near as he could make it out it was Mario Cabrini. At once it struck him as familiar. Cabrini? What did that remind

him of? No, he was thinking of Cassini. That was the
name of a boy he used to know, a little swarthy kid,
tough as nails, Jo Cassini, who played ball down on the
empty lots by the gas tanks near the river. Aunt Minerva used to say, "Do you have to play with all those
disgusting dagos? Why, we get our groceries from Cassini."

She thought it was more elegant to run a boarding
house than a grocery store. Even a boarding house for
the "profession." Even one too far from Broadway to
draw a good clientele, so that it was mostly filled with
jugglers, trainers of dogs and seals, magicians, and other
third-rate vaudeville acts from the smaller circuits. The
best Aunt Minerva ever drew were the Bounding Morellis; they were headliners on the Keith Circuit, but
they were close with their money because they had an
idiot child whom they kept in an expensive institution
somewhere upstate. But no one knew really why people
came to Aunt Minerva. The "profession" has its habits
also; that was all one could say.

Of course there was Madame Golden. She was the
star boarder and had the two best rooms, the front parlor and the back bedroom, the whole first floor. In the
parlor she gave singing lessons: do, re, mi, fa, sol, la, si,
do! Her canary accompanied her. Madame Golden also
sang in the chorus of the Met. She was, so she used to
say, the *doyenne* of the chorus, its oldest member. One
night she gave Aunt Minerva two seats in the family
circle for *Rigoletto*. Cassius was taken along because
the tickets came too late for her to get anyone else.
Aunt Minerva didn't care for opera and didn't expect

Cassius to, but she liked going. She borrowed opera
glasses from someone and wore a pair of Perrin gloves,
much too tight, that had also been given her. To her
disgust the first people she saw were the Cassinis, who
greeted them noisily. When Caruso sang Aunt Minerva
clapped her hands in polite applause, but the Cassinis
rose in their seats, sweating from every pore and roar-
ing, "Brava! Brava!" Their lack of restraint embarrassed Cass as much as it did Aunt Minerva, but in spite
of himself he was terribly moved. The golden voice, the
tragedy, which was so dim as to be only a form of sweetness, made him want to cry. Afterward, when he
thought of this fair, painted Italy where everyone sang
of love and death he compared it with the Italy of the
Cassinis' grocery store. Here there was sawdust on the
floor, smelly cheeses and macaroni in odd shapes, and
Mrs. Cassini with her harsh mustache and a garlic
breath. The first Italy, he decided, must certainly be a
fake, not so much because the facts had been altered as
because it did not produce the emotion engendered by
the other. That the Cassinis had shared this emotion
with him only went to show that people are willing to
believe in fakes if it gives them pleasure to do so. This
had dimly been his conclusion, but even then he suspected something of the true nature of illusion for he
would not give up the other Italy entirely and went on
cherishing it in his imagination.

They had reached the station. He paid the driver and
got out. At the ticket window he asked for a Pullman
to Washington for that night and the agent gave him
a lower for the midnight train. As he walked to the

Western Union desk he wondered at what precise moment he had decided to spend the whole day in New
York. Perhaps on the pier, perhaps in the taxi. Anyway,
now it was decided. And it would be to look up his old
house of course, for there could be no other reason. He
wrote out a telegram to Charlie, with whom he always
stayed: "Arrived safely. Taking midnight train. See you
for breakfast. Cass."

Crossing the station he thought again of his decision
and he resented it. He did not like these unconscious
decisions. He felt as though someone else, someone less
able to judge, had made them for him. As he followed
his redcap to the baggage-checking counter he deter-
mined that, while it was useless to change his ticket, he
would spend his day in some other way. He always
found plenty to do in New York. In the taxi he said,
"Hotel Plaza," and relaxed in his seat, trying to think
what some of those things might be.

The taxi turned up Seventh Avenue and the day was
all brightness and shadow. A sharp wind had sprung
up, hurrying clouds across the sky, and there were great
patches of blue overhead, edged with scallops of silver.
Below this magnificence the street looked wan and ugly,
a street of the cutrate, the secondhand, the imitation, a
marginal street. After the cities of Europe he was struck
again by the relentless, longitudinal character of New
York, how everything of its energy flows up and down,
confined on all sides by water. And yet even in this
ceaseless, forced direction there are occasional clots,
making little pockets where life collects and stagnates

gently. In such a pocket he had lived once, scarcely knowing that the city he was now seeing existed.

Suddenly, by the crossing of a few streets, the poverty and ugliness were gone. There were pansies in a thick carpet around the fountain of the Plaza, twenty-carat diamonds shone in the shop windows, and the trees of the Park flaunted their extravagance and their promise of leafage in the midst of stone-covered real estate which carried the highest taxes in the world. This place had something of the fascination of a vortex; you could almost hear it humming as it drew luxury irresistibly to itself, that luxury which was a result of all the multiple energies of the city and seemed here to be their sole end.

Aunt Minerva used to say, "Now if that mining stock Mr. Bolger got me would only begin to pay. . . ." Then she would go on to describe how some day they would live on Riverside Drive. In that world outside their little region this was her topmost flight. One of her boarders, a blond ingenue, had decided to let herself be kept there by some middle-aged gentleman, and after a visit Aunt Minerva never stopped talking about the gilt furniture, real lace pillows, and a butler with an accent like Charles Hawtrey. She talked of these symbols of elegance even to Cassius, as though it were a craving in her to give her love of money a more substantial form. For love of money, as Schopenhauer said, is human happiness in the abstract, and only he who is no longer capable of enjoying happiness in the concrete devotes his heart to it.

As he got out of the taxi a girl came down the steps.

He paid his fare while she stood waiting to get in, and
her red hat trembled in a ray of sun. He had time also
to see her legs, which were not at all the kind he had
been seeing lately. They were in fine nylons and exag-
geratedly tapered at the ankles, with that peculiar stiff-
ness of never having borne the weight of a burden, no
pitcher, no bundle, no baby, perhaps even no sorrow.
Fetish legs, he thought. Fetish legs for torpid and lux-
urious lovers. They were like Lita's legs. A vague dull-
ness of recollection came to him and with it a vague
prickle of desire. I need a dry martini, he thought, and
it must be very dry, very cold. The great solution: aph-
rodisiac, Mickey Finn, in one.

He had his martini at the bar off the Oak Room.
There was no one there at this hour but himself. He
sent out for a paper and read it from end to end, attentively at first because this was something else he hadn't
seen for a long time, but quickly flagging and finally
forcing himself to read what he felt he had read many
times before. The martini did not help his headache
either, but still he ordered another and even got another paper and began to read that. Then the bar began
to fill and looking at his watch he saw that it was nearly
one.

He jumped up and at once a great gust of sickness
struck him so that he could scarcely stand. He sat down,
wondering if a man could actually faint in public. The
room moved in dark waves around him. He thought, I
shouldn't have had those drinks so far ahead of good
solid food. He thought hard of a steak and a cup of black
coffee, conjuring them up and anticipating their effect

in himself. Presently he felt better. He got up and went
into the Oak Room.

There he ordered the steak and coffee and as he
waited he thought again of luxury and he thought of
hunger. He thought of a man with a fat belly looking
through the plate glass window of a restaurant, a child
keeling over from starvation on the sidewalk. He
thought of other things he had seen lately. The inhu-
man refuse of Osweiczin, the exquisite shell of Pisa
shattered. He thought of war as he had once known it
himself, and of a friend killed at his side. He thought
of the fortuitous distribution of suffering and happiness.
One hungers, one eats. One is tormented, one rides free.
One lives, one dies. And perhaps there is no answer. Or
rather, there are many answers. And if one could remain cool in it all, if one could disassociate oneself
from the noise and smell and pressure, one might find
a very good answer. It would go like this: that the general welfare may conceivably come, finally and with the
deathly slowness of time, but that this is not the aim.
The aim is understanding, of which this welfare is only
a minor, almost accidental result. We aspire toward
conscious knowledge. We surely have therefore a power
latent in us that is capable of penetrating the innermost
nature of things. Don't ask, Charlie said, but what else
should be our aim? It is not enough just to see to it
that people get plenty to eat.

The steak was thick, juicy, and as he liked it. He tried
to enjoy it. The coffee was hot and strong. He tried to
enjoy that too. But he went on thinking: all my life I
have been what is known as a successful man; success

means adaptability, and what is adaptability but reasonableness. I am reasonable, so reasonable that I know the limits. Then at what moment did I cross the line? It was not at any of the times I have been remembering.

But then he knew in himself the moment. It was the old woman, he thought. It was she who did it. She was not the worst. She was not even a part of the worst. She was not a part of anything. She had removed herself from reality into a world of shades and reflections. She was no longer living. Still, she did it.

It began on a street, one side intact, one side ruined. If you looked at one side you saw order; if you looked at the other you saw chaos. In between the two was a queer, neutral passage. It was full of whispers of dust, and as the wind blew, a door without a latch banged softly back and forth somewhere behind a broken wall. This street was quiet and plucked as bare as a bone: there were no scraps of newspaper, not a wilted flower nor a cigarette butt. There were no cats. And always the gentle banging of the door suggested not that something was about to happen but that nothing ever would happen and that the street as it was would never change.

He used to walk down this street. He didn't look much at the few people he saw but he got into the habit of saying good morning to the porter of the Jaegerhorn, who was always lounging in the doorway and who gave him the bilious smile of a fat man grown flabby and a little military salute as he passed. The porter never seemed to have anything to do and his life appeared to stretch behind and before him in endless idleness.

Then one day he saw the old woman coming. First he saw her head tied in a cloth and then her coat, which could never at any time have been meant for her, and then, as she came nearer, her shoes. They were deformed and rotting and knotted like fungus growths. They gave her an anthropomorphic appearance, as though she were partly made of roots, as though she were an ancient walking tree. She came opposite him and he saw she was an old woman out marketing. In her bag were several dried and wrinkled carrots. And finally he saw her face. He stepped hastily aside on the narrow path to give her way, flattening himself against the wall, and as her eyes turned to him he managed a gallant bow.

The old woman stood stock still. She fixed her black eyes on him and moisture gathered in the sagging red pouches of her lids. Then like lightning some proud image visibly struck her. Her ruined face broke into a brilliant and gracious smile as of recognition. She inclined her head slightly and exclaimed, "Ah! Good morning." He bowed and lifted his hat, and went on.

Farther down the street the porter at the Jaegerhorn looked at him sluggishly as he passed.

The next day and many days the same: the street, the old woman, and the encounter. Each time this moment when they met was complete in itself, sealed in its own dimension. Always it had a slight variation, a new and subtle reflection of herself which she created little by little, day by day, unhurried, and offered to him as though it were a gift of price. This moment had in it no lament, no appeal, not even an oblique acknowledgment of the present. It was herself as she had been, or even as she had wished to be, and he accepted it according to her will. But it was also deeply his own will to see her like this rather than as she was.

Once he looked up too quickly—they had their exact understanding of each move and gesture—and he saw her half a block away. She was standing at the end of the narrow walk, peering down at the covered opening of a drain. She leaned over, examined something limp and gray, and picked it up. Then she looked around her fearfully and crammed it in the bag. He bent his head, pretending not to see, though he guessed that her eyesight did not carry that far and that she could not see him. When she was opposite he lifted his hat and met her bright smile. Today it was wayward, frivolous, it had the cruel edge of a faraway coquettish triumph.

This was the day he stopped at the Jaegerhorn and talked to the porter lounging in the doorway, the porter with his plum-colored coat and a striped vest and brass buttons.

"Can you tell me who the old lady is?" he asked him.

"What old lady?"

"The one who just went by. She goes by every day. You must have seen her, you must know who she is."

The porter's face was very soft and insolent.

"Why should you be interested?" he said. "There are so many old ladies—young ladies as well."

"Tell me or don't tell me," he said angrily. "I can find out from someone else."

He took a piece of money out of his pocket and shook it lightly in his palm. The porter did not look at it but his eyes wavered. He said heavily, "She is a person who has been away for a long time. Now she is back."

"You mean she has been in one of the camps?"

"I don't really know where she has been. She is a foreigner. She doesn't belong here. She màrried here a long time ago and she has had children here and grand-children here. I only know that all of them were taken away. One by one they were taken away and did not come back. Only she has come back. The young die and the old live and come back. That's how things go."

"What sort of foreigner was she?"

"I have never interested myself to inquire." Then the porter grew suddenly flurried and wild. "I know that once they were grand people!" he cried. "Everyone had to bow down before them. Now no one bows. It is she who bows. It is the old woman who bows now!"

He stopped, looking at the money in Terhune's hand. "Who is that money for?" he asked nervously.

"It's not for you," Terhune said, and he walked on.

But then he didn't walk any more on that street. Each day when he went out he chose some other way. He knew that the old woman would expect him but he couldn't bring himself to see her. He told himself that this episode he continued to lend himself to had become silly and meaningless. What did the old girl want! She wanted what Lita in her place (if one could possibly imagine Lita stripped of everything) would want. The same ghostly narcissism would have survived in Lita, only touching just because it *was* ghostly, hanging on air, without prop or foundation. And Lita would also take to magic. Reduced to the idiocy of a savage state,

Lita would demand purgings, sweatings, bleedings, incantations, divination by entrails and the flights of birds. Lita would demand just some such ritual of the glance. The whole thing confused and tormented him. But still he stayed away.

A few days went by, and finally one day, because it was a short cut to where he was going, he went down the street once more, the street of murmuring dust and bone emptiness and the door banging somewhere in the roofless house. As he hurried along he realized it was the hour for her to appear and he stopped still at the spot where they usually met. But she was nowhere to be seen. Only the porter of the Jaegerhorn lounged in his doorway, watching a cloud pass by. Could it be, he thought, that she had never really been? With a sudden stricture of the nerves he thought, could such a solace possibly be granted me? But no, because he felt her presence. She was somewhere near, and he was compelled to find her.

He did not know where to look. He stood lost in uncertainty and the door slammed gently open and shut, open and shut, in the roofless house. Then, with the languid gait of a dream-walker, he followed the sound, climbed the steps and went through a rent in the wall. He crossed a wide, rubbly floor and there it was, the door of the inner room, a door like any other, with traces of white paint on it but without a latch. He pushed it and went through. The walls were narrow, under open sky, and a cloud, possibly the cloud the porter was watching, floated over his head.

She was hanging from a crossbeam. Her string bag,

with a spoiled cabbage in it, lay on the floor. As the
door swung her feet made a slight circular movement.

As he looked up something of her passed into him
and became inescapably part of him, and feeling this
he hated her.

CHAPTER II

HE DRANK two cups of coffee and felt almost well again. I was wrong to dodge this, he thought. There is nothing like self-examination if it is honest, without a sense of pathos or the mumbo jumbo of the witch doctor. But above all, if one has preknowledge of what one is looking for. There is something in a book I read which says that if I start to pick out a red bead from a collection of beads I must already have anticipated the red bead in my own mind. The question and answer therefore are in myself.

This obviously was the culminating point for me. It's true the breakdown had started before but it was two days after finding her that I had the attack in the bathroom of the hotel, at a time when I was not thinking about her, was in fact shaving and, as I remember it, only wondering whether or not to wear a heavy overcoat that morning. It was like the attack in the bar but worse. However, as I see it now it was not so much breakdown as the beginning of cure for what must be a very long sickness, perhaps as long as my life. It is part of that struggle which goes on between the desire for

understanding and the almost reptilian fear of understanding. And the red bead? I haven't yet the clear anticipation of a red bead. That will come. Anyway, it's
a beginning of cure.

He ordered a brandy and drank it slowly, and this
time his feeling of exaltation did not break off abruptly
but tapered gradually into a suspension of effort. He
found himself wondering idly whom the man across
from him looked like, and whether he had perhaps seen
him before. He found himself wondering, without any
special interest, why his cook could never grill a steak
properly, since it was such a simple culinary perform-
ance. He tried to remember just how alarming his letters to Charlie Bates might have been, and he thought
perhaps Charlie had spoken of them or even read them
to someone, and that might be one of the reasons why
the cable authorizing his return had come so promptly.
And he felt mildly annoyed with Charlie.

Then he tried to pull his mind together to the point
of giving attention to his future, his immediate future,
the things he had to do, making out his report, writing
certain letters which would counteract any false impres-
sions that might have got about, perhaps also taking
that rest he had been ordered to take. I am too tired, he
thought, to plunge just now into any consideration of
the *means* whereby this cure is going to come about. It
is enough to know it lies in me. I can't force the means
now but the future will bring something. Then suddenly he felt as though he saw himself in a film, sitting
at a table alone, drinking a glass of brandy, a waiter
passing by, and suddenly, as sometimes happens, there

was a hitch in the machinery, everything stopped. The glass did not reach his mouth, the waiter poised on one foot. It was as though he were being shown that, for him, there was no future.

He paid his bill, got up and started toward the door, seeing as he passed under the clock that it was half after three. He thought of his house again, but the house and the dream of it were repellent to him now. He remembered that the house had seemed underground and that there had been a warning in it, rather than a promise. He went down the corridor and stood on the side steps overlooking the Park.

These were the hours of the afternoon that are hardest to fill, and as he tried to decide what he might do—a movie, a picture gallery, a walk in the Park—he found himself thinking most persistently of sleep. It was the first time in many weeks that sleep had seemed possible to him. But to sleep was scarcely practicable at the moment and night would be soon enough. He walked over to the horse carriages and stood by them a moment. The raw wind still blew along the street, the sky was heavily overshadowed now, and it was going to rain, perhaps not before night. It was too cold for a drive. A walk might do him good. He strolled into the Park.

Presently he was in the Zoo. In spite of the chill it was crowded and he remembered then that it was Saturday afternoon, and that meant he would arrive in Washington Sunday, with all the Departments closed. What a bore! He'd never thought of that. Of course he would spend the day with Charlie, and a day of rest, if you could call a day with the Bates rest, would be all to the good. Still, he had the vaguely irritated feeling of having been stalled, and of something put off that had to be got over with.

He walked aimlessly from cage to cage in the Zoo. The animals, he thought, were sad survivals of an intention doomed from its start. If you accepted the idea of an experimenting Creator, you would say that it was unimaginative of Him not to have foreseen that they would always be too uniform according to their kind. A zebra or a giraffe is a truly elegant creature, but not in series, as though turned out by dressmakers for the Seventh Avenue trade. He looked at them listlessly for a while, then sat down on a bench, found it too cold and moved on.

He walked on as far as where the chess players sit and joined the silent ring of the kibitzers. He loved a good game of chess, which he had played ever since he was a boy. One of the boarders had taught him, to the great disappointment of Madame Golden who, on the evenings when she was at home, was accustomed to playing casino with him and, when he was older, double canfield. She hated chess because there was no luck in it. All her card playing was a simple form of fortune telling. The chances of cards corresponded to the chances of fortune. In canfield she would tell her fortune, or his, by the way the cards fell. "Now," she would say, "if the black queen turns up it means Mr. Bolger's oil stock will begin to pay." Mr. Bolger was the dashing promoter of the neighborhood, the one they all turned their money over to, when they had any. If the black queen didn't turn up she would peek under the cards

until she found it and, if she thought no one was looking, would slip it out. She understood that to be lucky
you have to cheat a little.

But now he couldn't even keep his mind on the chess.
He thought, what am I waiting for? I clearly intend to
go down and see the house anyway. Am I waiting for a
black queen? Why make such a to-do over a trifle? I'll
find the house or not find it. In either case it will only
be an anticlimax, a disappointment.

He walked to the Fifth Avenue entrance, and as he
reached it a bus came rocketing along. He stepped out,
but at that moment the light changed and a taxi made
a sudden turn. He was caught between them. The bus
screamed to a stop.

He had a moment of blankness, then the impression
that someone had been hurt. Not that he had been hurt,
but as though perhaps the film of safety that enveloped
him had been tugged from a distance, the sensation that
is described as someone walking on your grave.

But no one was hurt. He got on the bus and sat
wedged in the narrow seat. The bus was caught in stran-
gulating traffic and he knew it would take a long time
to reach where it was going. He fell into a slight doze.

He allowed himself to be carried to the end of the
line, but when he got out he was glad to have more
time to reach the place he was looking for. To have
taken a taxi, to have arrived by some shortcut, wouldn't
have done. Now that he was actually on his way he
wanted his recollections to come by degrees, without
forcing, and he wanted them, in so far as it was possible,
to be true ones. So he started to walk diagonally across

the square and up University Place. And again he realized how constricted the area of his recollections was. He had known no more than a few streets, if you left out an occasional excursion into what had been for him a foreign world: a night at the opera, a visit to Vantine's to buy Japanese gimcracks for Christmas, Siegel Cooper and the boy's outfitting department, with a soda under the golden statue, or the Eden Musée, where the Hindu widow committed suicide and Charlotte Corday leaned against the bars.

There was nothing in these streets that was a part of his old life. But as he walked a feeling of tenderness for that life grew in him and without effort he began to believe that the character of what he was seeing deepened and became more familiar. He stopped often to look at the slant of a roof, the angle of a wall, or the name over a door. He listened to the clamor, so much noisier than uptown because of the trucks loading and unloading in cross streets and the timbre of the voices in which there was often a Mediterranean density and resonance. Gradually he could almost feel that he recognized certain houses and signs, and if not actually the passing faces at least resemblances. Here was this high room and the two Cantonese who ironed shirts under a ceiling of painted tin. And the office of A. Aaronson, Bail Bonds, where a woman hesitated on the steps; the Cut Rate Drug Store; Quick Service Shoe Repairing; Benson Surgical Supplies, Belts, Stockings, Trusses; and even Missy Modes, "For the Woman Who Cares." Also La Grotta Azzura, Pizzeria—blue walls with frescoes of Capri and fluted paper napkins in the glasses. A

solitary man sitting at a table. He felt he knew something about the man, even if it was no more than a remembered saltiness of anchovies and some discomfort
or sadness of eating early and alone.

Then as he crossed the last square where children
played hopscotch on the chalked pavement, a sudden
shower of lovely notes fell through the air. He stood
still, not needing to turn his head toward the church
from whose clock they came, for these same notes had
sounded all through his childhood, through the calls
of street hucksters and children's shrill voices, through
the muffle of rain and the noises of the house, but best
of all, in the stillness of early mornings, with the pale
sky outside his window. Then they brought a moment
of melancholy that had as yet no other place in his days,
and was only a foretaste, a hint, of some subtle luxury
to come. This was his first true recognition.

There was no time to savor it, however, because at
the same instant he knew there was something queer
just ahead and his return was threatened in the very
moment of its realization. At the end of the street a
steam shovel hung out against emptiness. He hurried
toward it and just as he reached the brink an eerie
whistle blew as though a tin angel announced the end
of the world.

Indeed, the city ended here, the city he had just made
his own again. Ahead of him lay the city he had left
behind, the shambles of brick and mortar, the motionless but violent ruin. In the shock of seeing it he closed
his eyes but at once the explanation came to him and
he opened them again and saw a workman in overalls

swinging a lunch pail. He had beaten the whistle and was hurrying across the avenue toward a subway.

Terhune did not know if he was disappointed or relieved, but clearly there was nothing here for him, nothing to do now but turn away. Then his eyes fell on a signboard across the street. He could read the large lettering from where he stood: THE SEABURY TREADWELL VILLAGE. A RESIDENTIAL COMMUNITY. PLANNED IN CO-OPERATION WITH THE CITY OF NEW YORK.

The ruin had given itself a name and an explanation. It was slum clearance, a housing project. Something old and ugly gone, something new in its place. This should stir him to hopefulness. It gave the future a form and a certainty. He looked across to the bald gas tanks by the river and tried to imagine what this future would be like, tried to imagine clean and orderly apartments, with wide windows, plumbing, garden plots, playgrounds, and the people who would live here, the healthy children. The apartments would not take substance, the children were not in motion. He could not see the future.

He looked at the street number beside him, he remembered it well, and he felt as though he were at sea again and the number of the street was a marker to give him a position. Then he looked across the wasteland and saw the demolition ended about four blocks to the north. Further up and toward the river houses were still standing, and back of them perhaps his house.

He crossed the avenue. The streets leading into the destruction were blocked off. He could walk only along the rim of it, but now that he could look directly in

he saw that it was very different from the city he had
left. It was the same shapeless mass of rubble but there
was too much left behind. He saw bits of rubber hose
and lead pipe, metal lath, scrap lumber and corrugated
garbage pails. He saw an old cooking range, a piece of
brass bedstead, a shoe, a tatter of already aged bunting
on which was printed, WELCOME HOME, WILLIE COMP-
TON. There was a cat stepping delicately around an ancient boiler. Over all was thick, pale dust and a glint
of broken glass, but the place was not sad. The destruction had something lavish, playful, even comic, about
it. As though some titanic clown had put on a terrific
show, meaning no harm at all and simply for the fun
of it.

After one look no one could mistake this ruin for
the other. Moreover, even before the demolition was
complete they were beginning to clear it up and to
build again. Over toward the river he could see pile
drivers and power shovels. Here and there were heaps
of steel piling and wooden concrete forms ready for use.
Scattered through it were raw wooden contractor's
shacks. Tomorrow the whole place would burst into
noise and movement. No, not tomorrow, he thought,
tomorrow's Sunday. Everything will be quiet tomorrow.

As he came close to the line of houses he saw a street
that was not barred. Only a low sign read, ROAD CLOSED
TO TRAFFIC. PERSONS USING THIS ROAD DO SO AT THEIR
OWN RISK. He was about to turn in, so as to cut across
to the houses, when a watchman carrying a nightstick
came out of one of the wooden shacks.

"Don't go in there, mister," he said.

Terhune said, "I just wanted to take a short cut." He pointed vaguely and a voice inside the shack called, "Hey, Bill! Come here a minute." The watchman glanced briefly at Terhune. "O.K.," he said, "look out for the glass." Then he went into the shack.

Terhune passed the sign and began to walk across the rubble, picking his way carefully. Every now and then he stopped to look around him and get his bearings. Because everything was laid flat he could see to the north and west great buildings that had never been there in his day. Their vast, delicate obelisks were outlined in light streaming in long rays through the clouds. The city, as it will, even when you are in the midst of its ugliness, suddenly became romantic and the ruins changed and took on a picturesque, Piranesi look.

When he reached the houses he saw they were abandoned. Their fronts were scarred by acetylene torches where the fire escapes had been burned off. The window glass was gone. In some of them sky showed through holes in the roof. Where there had been a shop he looked into a little cage choked with fallen plaster, the twisted ends of light wires hanging starkly from the walls. On one corner was a movie theater. The wreckers had torn down the whole back section, leaving a half-dome of bright yellow with a crazy catwalk clinging to it. A billboard lay on its back: *The Harvey Girls, with Judy Garland.*

He went beyond this to the next street. Here also were houses along one side and they also were abandoned but they were in better shape. This was his street and he knew well the house he stood by. It had been a fine house, with a fan over the doorway, and he remembered the gold sign that had been in the window: JACOB COHEN. ALL RABBINICAL RITES PERFORMED. WEDDINGS.

Jakey Cohen's father, a man with a black beard and a funny hat. Jakey was the best pitcher in the district, and he could box, too. (Didn't he become a lightweight champion?) All the kids looked up to Jakey, but just the same whenever they saw his old man they used to sing a jeering song: "Holy Moses, King of the Jews, bought his wife a pair of shoes." They had a whole balladry to fit occasions when a mob craziness came over them, when their little brutal selves rose and took fire from one another, so that they had to torment something even if it was only a cat. But they never sang this particular song when Jakey was around. It was partly because they were afraid of his skill, partly because they admired him. They were willing to injure him, but not to his face. Fear, and then a shame they could not control, prevented. Two stages, Terhune thought wryly, of the formation of a moral order.

From here on he knew each house. Several doors down was Murphy's Pool Parlor. Mr. Connors and his henchmen gathered every evening in the back room. Connors was a contractor and the local boss. Everyone was afraid of him. In private he was spoken of harshly. Mr. Bolger never called him anything but "that goddamned harp," but even he, the great promoter, when he met him on the street, said, "Good morning, Mr. Connors. Fine weather we're having."

Mr. Connors was also Rosie's father. Little blue-eyed

Irish Rosie, his first sweetheart, his first love. He smiled at the falseness of it. Rosie was his first love all right, but as he thought of her now he realized she was just what Lita must have been as a child (that was Rosie's revenge, perhaps), and like Lita she had the faculty of provoking in others feelings as false as her own. Even now, he thought, even after all these years, my first feeling about Rosie turns out to be a false one. There was only one that had been genuine and it was the same that had been genuine with Lita, before it drowned itself in her perfect, chilly beauty. In Rosie's time, he thought, I guess I wasn't so fastidious, and he remembered what had happened in the area the evening of the children's party, and the blindness and urgency of kissing Rosie, in that way he had never kissed anyone before.

Unfortunately, Wakefield happened to see him at it. Wakefield couldn't get through the sixth grade but he was a whiz at Kelly pool (even the experts gathered to watch him), and when his mother wasn't around he smoked cigarettes. There was usually one dangling from his pale lips. "Every cigarette is a coffin nail"; this gave Wakefield a morbid, death's-head fascination. Each time Wakefield met him, after the area episode, he winked and said, "Hello, Buster. Does your auntie know you're out?" He could never be sure whether Wakefield's connivance glorified him or made a fool of him. Then years later, the first time he ever went to bed with a girl, he thought of Wakefield in one frightened and triumphant flash, and of Rosie, too. So *this* was what it was!

His house should be three doors beyond the red brick
school building, and here was the school now, shabby
and unchanged except for a dim gold sign: BOARD OF
EDUCATION. BUREAU OF SPEECH IMPROVEMENT. They
never had speech improvement in his day but they had
an elocution contest. He had won a prize.

Beyond it two houses were gone. In their place was
a garage. It looked in fairly good condition, painted
white, though dirty and peeling now. The gasoline
pumps had been taken away. In a broken window still
clung a sign: THE FLYING RED HORSE. The garage
threw his own house out of scale, so that at first he
could scarcely recognize it, and there was nothing on
the other side of it, either; it was the last house left
standing in this row. Beyond it was only rubble, with
a wrecking ball ready to batter it down.

And now, standing between the garage and the ruin,
his first impression was, Why, it's a fine house. It was
built of brick, narrow, with a high stoop and a door
with a fanlight. There used to be handsome iron rail-
ings and baskets which he remembered, but these were
gone. There had been fire escapes, also, a much later
addition, and these, too, had been burned off. The windows were covered with boarding, all except the delicately shaped dormers in the attic, where he could see
the gleam of old glass. On the door the brass lock and
handle were replaced by a heavy iron bar with a padlock. The house was thoroughly sealed; even if he had
wanted to go inside it wasn't possible. It stood there
with a look of mutilated elegance. Yes, he saw that it
must always have been elegant, though when he lived
in it he didn't know what elegance was.

His sense of the return curiously evaporated. The house he had come to see was not familiar to him in the way the school, the pool parlor, the Cohen house, were familiar. Perhaps it was because the garage made it seem so much smaller, perhaps the empty lots and the wrecking ball gave it a perilous, threatened look. Or even because of its elegance now, evident, which showed him that when he had lived in it he had not seen its true quality. In any case, it was strange to him. He felt he had never really seen it before and that it had been put here now to deceive him, as the houses in Arabian stories are conjured up and vanish again in the same night, as indeed this house would shortly vanish.

He was suddenly tired and he sat down on the lower step to rest and smoke a cigarette. He bent over to light it and when he lifted his head he saw a man standing beside him.

"Hello, hello," the man said briskly.

He was an old man with white hair spraying thinly from a nearly bald head. There was a silvery stubble on his jaws, and as he smiled he showed two broken front teeth. He had crafty, squirrel-bright eyes. He wore a greenish overcoat, too big for him, his shirt had no collar, and his shoes were broken out at the toes. He carried a big paper market bag.

"How's to spare a cigarette?" he asked.

Terhune took his case out hesitatingly and offered it. The old man took three cigarettes. He put one in his mouth and stuck one behind each ear.

"Never pass up a chance," he said.

Terhune offered his lighter and the old man took a

deep puff. Then he sat down on the steps and placed his bag carefully between his feet. Smoke trickled luxuriously from his lips and nostrils.

"Boy!" he exclaimed. "That's what the doctor ordered."

The stoop was narrow and their arms touched. A close, spoiled smell came from the man, a mixture of old clothes and bad breath. Terhune could feel the liveliness of his body, which had something soft but springy and fragile, like a squirrel's body. The old man turned and gave him a long, bright stare. Then he said, "Guess what I just picked up next door?"

Terhune looked down at the bag. It was printed in black letters STUYVESANT MARKET, and it was bulging with shapes.

"What?" he asked.

"Two perfectly good glass lamp shades. One has a sort of crack, but nothing serious."

Terhune said, "Quite a find."

"Oh, this place is a gold mine," the man said. "About ten thousand people were moved out of here. It stands to reason they couldn't take everything with them."

"I suppose not."

"You'd be surprised at what they left behind. Of course the really important stuff was carted off by dealers. But I can still pick up things here and there. I carry them to a junk man I know over by the river. He gives me a fair price for them. Sometimes though I sell direct to the housewife, if I think I've got something that will appeal. Women like to think they're getting a bargain."

"I suppose so."

"Of course, I have to present it right. Now you take for example china. Most breakable thing there is; the world's full of broken china. Now I find a saucer without a cup, a cup without a saucer. I combine them. If they make a match—rosebuds, gold rim, something like that—it's so much the better. Anyway, I take my cup and saucer, talk up what a fine antique it is, and ask a quarter. A woman thinks she's getting a bargain, though she could do much better at any ten-cent store."

He looked at Terhune to see how his patience was holding out, and his anxious glance, covered as well as he could with a social smile, touched Terhune. He had certainly not intended to talk to him. He was an old bum with a sharp eye for the easy mark, even if that only meant someone to listen. But his speech showed he had had some education and his present adaptation of it to circumstances had an old-fashioned flavor that made it pathetic. Even in his impertinence about the cigarettes there was still, Terhune thought, a suggestion that he remembered a period when manners were better and this was just his idea of how to get along today.

When he saw Terhune wasn't leaving him he said, "You know, you'd be surprised to find what some people do go for. Now take that friend of mine who lives over there." He pointed in the direction from which Terhune had come toward the empty, boarded houses. "He picks up things around here, too. But he don't sell them. He just collects them, and he has some very peculiar tastes."

"You mean," Terhune said, "someone lives here in this ruin?"

"Someone!" the old man exclaimed. "Why, listen.

Look at the place. It's got houses, hasn't it? Walls, roofs, doors, windows? An empty house these days is like a vacuum: nature abhors it. Plenty people these houses look awfully good to. Seeing it right now it looks deserted. Come night it's got quite a population."

"What about the watchmen?"

"Them! They're nothing but mugs with nightsticks. They can't patrol *this* place. Think of all the corners, the rubble, the chimneys, the cellars. Did you know you could walk for blocks here without ever coming up above ground? Why, there's every kind of person living down here, from a fellow who eats sterno for breakfast to a kid wanted for murder."

"Really? That's hard to believe."

"Is it? Well, I can tell you there's a kid hiding out in one of these dumps right now. He and some pals tried to hold up a service station. Got nervous and shot an attendant. He'll be picked up any day though, because he goes out all the time to buy papers and see if there's anything about him in them. Conceited cuss, really. He's crazy to make the headlines."

"Not a safe place, is it?" Terhune looked at the old man with irony. He didn't believe any of it. "Not quite the place to spend a night," he said.

"Well, I often do. It's cheaper than a flop house, it's more private, and it's cleaner. I get awful sick of paying thirty cents to sleep in one of those flea bags! And I don't have any trouble here myself. I know pretty near everyone in here. They all call me Pop. Everyone, even that kid I was just speaking of, calls me Pop. I've got so I've almost forgot my own name. Yes, I have friends and acquaintances all over. As I was telling you, there is this other fellow here who collects things. He belongs in the loony bin actually, but he's a good pinochle player. I like pinochle. We play often. Sometimes we play all night when we can get enough candles. I'll tell you a little incident. One night I went there and he was out. So I climbed all the way up to the attic looking for him. The whole place is piled with junk he picks up, but what do you think I found in the attic?"

"What?" Terhune asked.

"I found a bride lying on an iron bed. Yes, sir, flat on her back, with golden hair and a veil streaming down and blue eyes turned up to the ceiling."

"A corpse?" Terhune asked drily.

"No, a dummy. Like those you see in the windows on Grand Street. How'd he get her there? Search me. I never asked. That is, not directly. But," he smiled slyly and rubbed his finger on the tip of his nose, "I manage to refer to her every now and then in the course of our conversations, because I can see he's afraid of losing her. He's afraid they'll come and take her away. That scares him, so he always has something for me now whenever I come—a can of beer, cigarettes, maybe a dog. Very profitable. You see, you got to know how to handle people."

He winked, and his wink turned his words into something disreputable. It not only was meant to show that he didn't take seriously human experiences, such as he'd just hinted at, but it also demanded a sort of shady connivance on Terhunes' part. And the wink passed suddenly into a series of spasmodic tics, his whole face jerking so painfully that Terhune looked away.

The old man, he thought, is a bit cracked. That's how he got into this state. Also he gave the impression of an almost deliberate overturning of balance, an almost evil pleasure in it. When Terhune looked at him again he was leaning forward making invisible marks on the pavement with his fingers. He made circles running clockwise and lines back and forth like pendulums. He made spirals and used two fingers to take little jumps across them.

The tic still went on but less so, and finally it stopped. His lips formed recognizable words spoken just below a whisper. "A helix," he said. "You could hop from section to section like a flea—space and time together—a four-dimensional continuum. . . ." Suddenly he looked up, his eyes shining as though he had just given a revealing demonstration. "I'll bet you didn't think I knew all this," he exclaimed. "You just said to yourself, 'Here's some old crank showing off. But I've made very interesting studies in my day, very interesting. Matter of fact, I still do. They relate to time, of course. What else is there when you come right down to it?"

"Yes," Terhune said hastily. He started to get up but the old man seized his sleeve and pulled him back. He said earnestly, "Now just what are you doing down here?"

"Here?" Terhune said. He shook his hand off and stood up. "You mean in this part of town? I used to live here."

"That so?" The old man got up too, holding his bag. "Whereabouts?" he asked.

"Here. In this house. We've been sitting on the steps."
He turned and looked at it, and the old man turned with
him. "*This* house?" he asked.

"Yes. It's pretty nice, isn't it? Seems in good condition,
too. Better than the rest of them."

"It isn't," the old man said. His voice startled Terhune. It seemed to be a snarl of ill temper. "It isn't as
good as it looks," he said. "Inside you're liable to find
anything. And if it's nothing worse than rotting floors
and ceilings and rat dirt all over then you're lucky."

"Well, I can't get in," Terhune said.

They stood side by side, looking at the house, Terhune feeling almost as unexplainably excited and angry
as the old man. Then he noticed something he had not
seen before. The padlock on the iron hasp hung a little
loosely. It was not possible to tell from where he stood
but suddenly he felt sure that the lock was not caught.
Whoever shut it last hadn't snapped it.

He said slowly, "Maybe I'll just take a look after
all."

He drew a bill from his wallet but he didn't even
look to see what it was. He was thinking of the house
again. Half turning he held the bill out.

"Please take it," he said, "I'd like you to have a good
dinner on me."

The old man wrenched his eyes away from the house.
His anger had died. He smiled his broken-toothed smile.

"Thanks," he said, "thanks a lot." He took the bill and
put it carefully in his pocket, glancing stealthily at Terhune. "Well, I guess I'll be on my way," he said. He
cleared his throat several times. Then he picked up the
paper bag and started down the street. Terhune watched

him. When he had gone a little way the bag suddenly split, two glass shades fell through and broke into pieces on the sidewalk. The old fellow gave a shrill little cry of dismay. He knelt to look at them, and the two cigarettes fell from behind his ears. He snatched them up, put them in his pocket, and abandoning the broken glass scuttled off.

When he was gone the street was empty as Pompeii. Terhune glanced at his watch. He decided he had about fifteen minutes to give to the house. The door he was sure was open. But he hesitated a second. He took a final look at the rubble around him, at the far, tall buildings, dark now against stormy and brilliant light in the lower sky, and the strangeness of seeing New York as a ruin struck him once more. But now he felt that he actually was looking at the future, seeing with his eyes a disaster that would have someday a more terrible reality, and now the tall buildings were what a man would someday see in *his* imagination, as he remembered the towers of the lost city.

He saw that there was no one to stop him and he went up the steps. A boat hooted mournfully from the river. He felt cold and drew his overcoat around his neck. The padlock, as he had expected, was not secured. He took it off and lifted the latch. Then he hung the padlock back on the iron loop, opened the door, and stepped inside. In the little vestibule a piece of newspaper lay on the black and white tile of the floor. He bent curiously to look at it and saw that it was today's paper.

CHAPTER III

WHEN he had closed the door to the street he had a moment of vertigo. In the dim light the house stretched before him, suddenly immense and labyrinthine, as in his dream. He opened the street door, letting in a crack of outside air, and leaned against it till the dizziness passed away. Then he closed it again carefully.

The vestibule was small. It was shut off from the hall by two Victorian doors with frosted glass panes. From this side the tracings on the glass meant nothing but he opened the doors and went into the hall, and here the panes glowed winter white in the faint light of the fan. He looked out into a landscape of snow peaks and chalets and waterfalls. He used to imagine, standing here, that this was the adventurous world he was about to enter, and here it was once more, the tiny figure under a pine tree, Rudi, the intrepid Swiss guide, Major Younghusband, with one foot in Tibet—himself. Now a crack cut the figure in half. He looked closely at it but he felt no return of his happy ego; he felt only the melancholy of the crack.

The true smell of the hall had also gone, the smell that was always the first contact with the spirit of the house. What long trials had dissipated the aroma of damp umbrellas, of Irish stew, and the *Lilac Végétale* that Madame Golden rubbed into her hair? The air was flat and nothing moved in it, it had a fusty, stagnant flavor unrecognizable to him, perhaps from the cockroaches scurrying in old drains, or from the rats in their holes.

He tried his feet cautiously on the floor boards, he peered at the ceiling where long shreds of plaster hung loosely, and he shook the railing of the stair: everything seemed to be intact. These old houses were strongly made. The walls were so solid that boarded up as the structure was, it kept out all outside sounds. The more pity to be tearing down what was so obviously meant for long endurance.

He turned to the door on the left and opened it into darkness. He got his cigarette lighter out of his pocket and held it before him, shading it with one hand like a candle. This room had been curiously treated. Along the wall where the handsome mahogany doors opened into the back room were a series of flimsy partitions making four cubicles. The floor here was scuffed and worn. On the walls were the scars of old plumbing fixtures and of overhead lights. The black marble mantel remained. There must have been a stove here though, for there was a hole in the wall above it with the mark of a chimney frill showing and in the floor the marks where the stove legs had rested. He thought this had been used lately as a barber shop.

This room had once been spacious, all the walls

covered with signed photographs of singers (one could
imagine Madame Golden, the *doyenne* of the chorus,
waiting in the wings to waylay these signatures). He
could remember especially a photograph of the most
beautiful woman in the world, Lina Cavalieri, in an
evening cape of sable and lace, her name scrawled as
with a toothpick dipped in ink. There were more
photographs on the rosewood piano draped with a
Spanish shawl, and music stacked in great heaps: vocal
exercises, songs to words by Metastassio, famous opera
arias, a song in manuscript composed and dedicated
to Madame Golden by the German piano tuner down
the street and called *At Eventide*. In the corner there
used to be a couch under a Turkish canopy of crossed
spears. For this room and the one behind it and for all
meals Madame Golden paid twenty-five dollars a week.
She lived here like some minor witch of the second or
third category, who because of age and misfortune had
lost most of her powers. Music and divination often
failed her. The world was against her, as she daily complained. But he always found her comic, partly because
others did, and partly because her age and temperament
hid the root of her disappointments from him. When he
laughed at her explosive lamentations he could sometimes make her laugh with him. Often they laughed together over nothing till the tears streamed down her
face. These rooms were like the caves he sailed through
at Coney Island in the summer: they were the Fun
House, the Tunnel of Love. He looked around him
now. Only the mantel remained.

As he turned to go he saw a drawing on the wall by the

door. It was like a child's drawing except that the two figures were in a rudimentary attitude. That no one should mistake the attitude a single short word had been scrawled in a balloon from one of the mouths. He closed the door behind him.

He peered again into the gloom of the hall. He could barely see the door at the end. It led, as he remembered, into a queer, dark closet where Madame Golden had a gas burner on which she sometimes cooked spaghetti or ravioli for her noisy friends. She would sometimes forget to turn the gas off, and then the odor of suicide would leak slowly through the house. There were iron tubs, too, for laundry. Beyond was a rickety porch with a clothesline tied to a post and stretching to the ailanthus tree. The monumental undergarments of Aunt Minerva would be flapping on the line, as indecently helpless as hanged men, or as babies having their diapers changed.

He went to the stairs and shook the rail and tested the lower steps. They seemed sound. As he climbed, holding to the rail and keeping his lighter in front of him, for the upper floor was darker, he began to notice a curious thing. The dust on the rail was smeared, in places almost cleaned, as though someone's hand, lately coming down, had slid along it. This was so unlikely that it wasn't until he was near the top step, by the niche where the statue of the blackamoor holding a lamp used to stand, that he remembered the paper in the entrance hall, today's paper. He stopped and looked at the stair rail and then at the niche. The niche was full of dust. "That's funny," he said.

He stood still, listening to the house, but he could

hear nothing, not even the street noises. There is no silence quite like that of an empty, enclosed house, for unlike an open space the imagination creates there sounds of life that echo in the ear.

Then he remembered what the old man had told him. Someone's been in here, he thought. The young killer? The loony? Hardly. The old man would have warned him. More probably someone like the old man himself, who wouldn't come back, if he came back at all, until it was dark and the watchmen were easier to elude. Still, he called out, "Anyone here?"

He discovered that when no one answers in an empty house you never quite believe it. Again he imagined someone *not answering.* Then he thought, don't be a damned fool—there's no one here. Or if there is, it's some bum scared to death. Then suddenly he was convinced there was no one. He went on up.

Just at the head of the stairs had been the one bathroom of the house, with an iron tub and a gas water heater, and outside a notice to boarders relating to the regulations for bathing and washing out small laundry. Those who wanted hot water at odd times had to get it from the reservoir of the big range in the basement kitchen, because the gas heater could be turned on only at certain times. On the floor above there was a toilet but no bath. In the attic, where he slept, nothing. Each morning, before the boarders were up, he had to carry his slop pail down the ladder to the floor below and empty it in the toilet.

He glanced into the bathroom. There was a different tub but it was already old and stained with rust, a basin, a toilet with a broken chain. The toilet was clogged with newspapers and not so long ago it had been used. He turned hastily away.

There was only one room on this floor that meant anything to him but he opened all the doors one by one, turning his light into the blackness. They were empty. Then he came to the Morellis' room. Madame Golden complained of the thumping of their practice overhead and Aunt Minerva said they ruined the carpet, but the Morellis when not practicing were a mousy couple strangely quiet. They could sit absolutely still on their chairs in a way most people, who couldn't control their muscles as well, could not do. When he and his best friend, Tommy Jefferson, first saw their act—on passes naturally—he could hardly believe it was they on the stage. They wore pink tights with glittering spangles and they performed miracles of dangerous grace. When Mr. Morelli swung to his silver trapeze Mrs. Morelli stood nonchalantly with arms folded behind her back, only stepping forward to catch the handkerchief tossed from above. Toward the last part of the act Mr. Morelli came to the footlights and said a few modest, guttural words which no one could understand except that they began, "Ladies and gentlemen, with your kind permission . . ." And then, at this final, most dangerous turn of all, they missed. Coldly and with a certain air of fatality they began all over again. There was an ominous roll of drums from the orchestra but they missed again. Tommy clutched his arm and whispered, "They can't do it." His own heart pounded, he could hardly bear to look at them. But at the third try they made it. The orchestra burst into triumphant music and the audience applauded. Not loud enough or long enough, he thought, considering how hard they had tried. When he got home he told Aunt Minerva about it and she said indifferently that it was an old acrobats' trick. They missed on purpose, she said, because people wouldn't know it was hard unless they saw the failure. He watched them come home that night. They were climbing the stairs together to their room, talking German to each other in tired, low voices. Their name was not really Morelli but they took that for professional reasons. They were Austrians from Linz.

The Morellis' room also was empty. On the floor above—the last floor if you did not count the attic— there were several rooms, but it was only Aunt Minerva's room that he remembered. She lived in the front room over the Morellis. It was a bare place, all its scant furniture the discards of other rooms; not because Aunt Minerva held herself modestly nor even for economy's sake, but as a sort of ascetic preparation for the condition she always knew was coming. She used to say, "Now someday I think I'll get a big chair for that corner and an oriental rug to go in front of the fireplace, and maybe an oil painting to hang over it." In the meantime the room and Aunt Minerva waited, while she slept in an iron bed without casters and kept her hairpins in a cracked saucer. When she was in the room it seemed crowded. She was a huge, mottled woman with a resemblance to a turtle. No one saw her in motion very often but she ran the house effectively enough and she knew everything that went on, even to the last ounce of butter used and how much money a boarder had in the savings account. She knew who used too much hot water, and who had a secret illness he dared not speak of. She read the Sunday supplements about what the rich were doing in Newport, feeling that a hidden bond of omnipotence united them and that someday this would be openly proclaimed. This belief, together with her capacity for finding out what went on even behind locked doors—though actually she was indifferent to most of it —gave her a brooding, formidable personality. She was named for a goddess and she had a goddesslike indifference to all but her special purpose and function. Her greatest indifference of all was for the boy he had been. His mother had died at his birth and his father, an actor, had deserted him. There was no one else to take him. That was all there was to it. And as he grew older he became a useful sort of boy. Now he stood a long time outside her door but he felt only a tiredness. He did not even open the door.

At the end of this hall was the trapdoor in the ceiling and the ladder against it, with the chain hanging down. Aunt Minerva sometimes talked of having a stair built but she never got around to it. It was still a trapdoor, a ladder, and a chain.

Above was the attic, and this was for him the center of the house. It was the biggest room, a great, ungainly place of shadows with ceilings sloping on three sides, always looking bare in spite of the Gothic accumulation in the corners: the abandoned trunks and the hatboxes, a broken sewing machine, a sofa without legs, a Flexible Flyer with one runner gone, all the leavings of past

boarders and their children, never thrown away for Aunt
Minerva didn't believe in throwing things away. In
one corner stood his iron cot and washstand, a "chiffonier"—the oldest and ugliest in the house, with drawers
that always stuck—and more intimately his own, pictures
on the walls representing current enthusiasms: the
biggest Cunard liner, or Theodore Roosevelt in an Afri-
can hunting outfit. Also sometimes, picture postcards
that boarders on the road remembered to send back—a
grain elevator at Duluth, the Garden of the Gods,
"Greetings from Asbury Park." And finally the books.

These were on a shelf that stretched along the high
part of the wall, put there once to keep preserves or
herbs or God knows what away from damp and rats. To
reach it he had to step from his bed to the chiffonier, but
this was a great advantage, for Aunt Minerva on her rare
prowlings to see what went on up here, could not lift
herself to it at all. She said he read too much and that
it was bad for him. "He's just a dreamer," she would say
tritely and disapprovingly, "just a dreamer," and she
often called from below, "Cass, what you doing up
there? I want you to go to the store for me." All she
wanted might be a small bottle of vanilla, but anything
would serve to get him away from his books. It was true
that he read at times when he should be studying, or
doing his chores, or playing outside in the fine weather
—whenever he could manage to pass unnoticed for an
hour or so, but especially at night. And he read whatever
came his way, books, papers, magazines, good, bad, or
indifferent. He had all his accumulation on that nearly
inaccessible shelf: back copies of St. Nicholas, Henty

books, a few Dickens, Mühlbach novels, some of Dumas, Kipling, *The Sea Wolf,* a popular science book, Plato's *Republic, The Life of the Bee,* even a volume of the *Encyclopedia Britannica, P to Qa,* and a paperback translation of *Sappho.* As he thought of these he could feel even now the ache of the elbows (he always read lying on his stomach), the eye strain and slight headache from bad light, which were a delicious prelude to the gradual absorption into alien experience and thought and, finally, to an identification so complete that, remembering it now, he could not recapture the final sensation but only the moment of betrayal when, drawn back suddenly by that voice below or perhaps the church bell admonishing him across quiet streets that it was midnight, he found himself propped on the attic floor again or on his hard mattress. This was the world, this book world, where he had come closest to happiness, a world of miniatures, precise and water clear, everything in it astonishing, perfectly related, cradled in its own logic, of a flawless unity. Here it had been sealed by these four walls and, because of a nostalgia for where he had found it, always for the rest of his life he unconsciously recreated the climate of the place, in rooms of books, with height and a sense of inaccessibility and a covering of fine, bachelor dustiness.

He reached up to the chain and pulled. The ladder squeaked like a trapped mouse, swung downward from the ceiling and hit the floor. Putting out his lighter he climbed it, pushed the trapdoor open, and stepped into the attic. The ladder swung up behind him.

The attic was dark. It should not have been dark

because the windows, he remembered, were not boarded on the outside. He lit his lighter again and threw the beam toward them. They were covered with what looked like pieces of old brown army blankets, stretched across and nailed tightly at the sides. He took a step forward and saw that the attic was filled with boxes. All around and stacked as far as the slope of the roof would allow were packing cases. In the center was a cleared space, and in it a plain deal table and four kitchen chairs. From a fixture in the ceiling a long cord with an unshaded bulb hung directly over it and another cord connected with a small radio on the table. The floor around was littered with cigarette butts. The whole suggested a conference, but what sort of conference? Who holds a conference in the attic of a condemned house?

He had known from the moment he opened the unlocked front door that something was askew. The paper of today, the dustless stair rail, the lately used toilet, and something more intangible, something cynical and secretive in the air. Whatever it was, the key to it must be here.

He turned the light switch, but it only made an empty click. No light came on. He was afraid his lighter fluid would give out, so he threaded his way among the cases to one of the windows and yanked at the blanket. It came loose at the sides. He drew it up and tied it in a loop. He took his handkerchief and wiped some of the dirt from the panes. The sky was a smolder of reds. It seemed very near. He turned around and looked at the room, at the cases that glowed in the reflected light. Suddenly they reminded him of something. Of what?

For a moment he thought it was his dream, but there was nothing like them in his dream. Still, they had something familiar about them. Then he remembered. It was the cases on the pier that morning. Again he said, "That's funny," for there was at the back of his consciousness an instant connection of some sort. He began to move among them and examine them. They were almost all of uniform size, secured with metal bands, marked with black letters and numbers. They looked as though they had been exposed to soot and rain. He leaned over to see their markings. The first one he looked at was labeled LICENSED E.T.H.—C.M.D. SCOTCH WHISKY. DUMFER-LINE. SCOTLAND. The others were the same, but he found a few on which was written COGNAC. FRAPINS. SEGONZAC.

They had been stolen. He knew it, and he knew how the job had been done. He had read about something like it, about a gang caught at just this business, and the story at once came back to him. The boxes were incoming. Some checker on the pier had simply falsified the number of cases—say out of fifty he recorded only forty-five—which were delivered to the warehouse. The others were taken elsewhere. He could not estimate how many had been brought here but this was obviously a distributing point. Whoever ran the racket must have a setup with the watchmen, those mugs with nightsticks. Maybe only one or two of the watchmen. But however that was handled, the usefulness of this particular house must be nearly at an end. Already the wrecker with the huge ball was waiting in the lot next door. Tomorrow was Sunday and nothing would happen, but it looked as though on Monday the workmen would begin on the place. That, perhaps, was why the lower floors were empty. And what was piled up here the racketeers would have to move shortly, possibly tonight.

He felt a queer, dull sense of shock. Back of what he was thinking something slipped, fell out of place. He was not really alarmed by what he saw but he was shaking and he sat down on a case to rest. Actually, when contrasted with the danger he had already sensed both in his dream and in the house itself, this did not seem to be very much. He remembered how once some of his clothes had been stolen and how the thief had turned out to be the furnace man, and that he had felt only a slightly guilty pity for the poor devil's fumbling. He was caught so quickly and inevitably. The truth is that all such acts in the midst of our highly organized society tend to seem amateurish. In crime stories there is always a slick professional style and adroitness, but in fact most crime is naïve and overconfident. The first thought is, but did they actually think they could get away with it?

No, it was not the danger, if even there was danger, since nothing prevented him from getting up and leaving at once. It was more like the shock of disappointment. This conception of his return as a search for something, and a finding of course, must have been stronger than he thought. Was there really no more to be found than a lot of stolen whisky, a demonstration of what he already knew—that men will risk a great deal for very little?

But back of it was still that creeping sense of wrongness and a feeling that what he saw here could not be all. And a growing urgency began to grip him. He looked around him again and across the attic he saw on

the shelf still other boxes, smaller ones, light, like cartons, there where his books used to be. What could be
in them? What took the place of Henty, Dickens, and
The Life of the Bee?

His mind fixed itself on these boxes and the compulsion in him grew stronger. I must know what's there, he
thought. He got up and moved toward the shelf, pushing aside the heavy boxes stacked one on the other, making a crooked lane for himself.

When he came to the shelf it was still out of his reach.
After all these years he had not grown to the height of
the shelf. It was well out of the reach of any average-sized
man but this inadequacy, never overcome, struck him
as full of dark meaning. He pushed one case angrily back
on another and climbed to the top one. Then he took
out his pen knife and slit open a carton and reached in.
He drew out a slithery cellophane package. "I'll be
damned," he said. "Nylons. They go for the works."

Whisky and nylons. Stupéfiants and aphrodisiacs.
What was this about nylons, about desire, about sadness,
about a woman, about a woman in front of the Plaza,
with legs like Lita's? What was wrong about her? What
do you want a woman for—Lita, Rénee, too, even Rosie
—all of them? Only to hang in a closet and take out every
now and then as an object of vanity—theirs and yours?
Well, that's just where they hang now, he thought, like
Bluebeard's wives, in a dark closet full of moth-eaten
coats and old golf balls.

And why do I suddenly remember Mrs. Morelli, he
thought, and that cold Christmas morning? Coming
down these stairs in a hurry when she opened her door,
a package in her hand. She was dressed to go out because

they had to play four shows that day. A holiday was no holiday to them. "I have something for you," she said. She gave him the package and watched him as he opened it. It was a pair of mittens, and he knew she had knitted them herself because he often saw her knitting. Aunt Minerva said she knitted mitts and mufflers and coats for her "afflicted" child and that it was silly of her, for how would such a child know the difference or be grateful for them? Now she had knitted these for him. All winter his hands were raw and cracked from chilblains, so he was very pleased, especially as she had chosen red wool, his favorite color. When he glanced up he saw a strange, trancelike look on her face, heavy and rapt. He did not stop to think but threw his arms around her neck and kissed her. Mrs. Morelli stood still and he could feel the quietness of all her bones. He stepped back, already embarrassed by what he'd done, seeing two sticky tears trickle from her eyes. She stood with her hands behind her back, just as she stood on the stage, as though it were the only attitude she knew, but her lips began to form words, foreign words, not spoken but which in terror he guessed—"My child, my love . . ." The words were not for him. He turned away and ran downstairs.

Then the tension, the compulsion he felt turned into that fearful activity of the mind, and this time it was as though a storm were breaking around a delicate instrument that whirled and reversed and madly strained to save itself.

What am I looking for, he thought. I am looking for an order of which I can be a part. An order akin to my intelligence, discoverable by me, and this order must be a certainty. I am looking for a certainty. At this exact moment one man is composing music, another is formulating a law, another giving his blood to a fellow. Another is highjacking whisky, and perhaps at this exact moment a man is murdering a child on a lonely road. But behind them all is a fixed and stable behavior, a character, an identity. I am a part of that behavior, that character, that identity. I must discover it. Once I nearly did. The old woman hung from a beam, like this beam over my head. But I mistook for magic what was a permanent identity. So I betrayed it. And it was myself I hated. Not her.

He heard the sound of his voice, saying something, and in the sudden quiet that followed his consciousness emptied itself. He felt his mind shrivel to the size of a pea, shrivel until it was only a vestigial node rooted at the top of his spine. His body grew weaker, helpless, became an embryo, a minute cluster of cells. And then the storm took him again. He snatched at the shelf, and the shelf tipped toward him, a few cartons slipped past, and he fell.

A sharp pain broke something in him into equal parts.

"What happened?" he whispered.

After a time he sat up and saw his leg bent under him. He leaned forward and with agonizing delicacy straightened it out.

"I've broken my leg," he said clearly.

No one heard him.

He sank back and let his head rest against the floor. It was quite dark and it grew darker as he sank still further. He was in the absolute of darkness and he had time to feel some peace before it took him entirely.

CHAPTER IV

IN THE dark he began to have a gradual consciousness that somewhere there was pain. Slowly, like the light of a burning glass coming to focus, it centered in himself. Then it seemed to push him upward. He opened his eyes and saw in the dark a floating square that held the throbbing night sky of the city. His first thought was: late, it must be late.

Then he felt cold. He was cold all over and only the pain, in one leg, made a splash of hotness. He felt his blood flowing sluggishly and the rhythm was like the floor moving under him. Gradually, as he centered his attention around it, he grew slightly warmer.

He ran his hand along his thigh past the knee but he could not reach the ankle without raising himself and that he didn't even try. There was a fiery band around his ankle, like a fetter, holding him to the floor. It took him some time to formulate the actual words: "My ankle's broken." When he heard them spoken he moved another step into consciousness.

Then he lay still and slowly accepted his condition, the pain, the chill, the rhythmic flow of blood. Several hours might have gone by without him, perhaps only a few minutes, but now he had to grasp the wheel again and lock himself back into time. He couldn't hurry this recovery.

His mind seemed to be sharply clear. No matter what the state of his body, his mind—he was quite sure of it—was clear. Only it was empty. It contained nothing but the moment and there was no expectancy in it. Attentiveness but no expectancy. Each moment stamped itself on his mind but brought him nothing. Not even strangeness. He lay on the floor of his own room in his own house. Outside was the city and the night. And presently, without surprise, he heard a sound. Something gentle and cautious happening in the house. And after it there was silence again. No sound. What he had heard was the opening and closing of a door.

Then he heard a tap, tapping. Each tap was a step on the stairs. He counted them exactly—eighteen, nineteen, twenty, twenty-one. That was the first flight. They stopped a moment and the sound changed as they came along the hall. Then the next flight. Eighteen, nineteen, twenty, twenty-one. The steps seemed to tap out some signal in a code he didn't know. As they came along the upper hall, the high square of night sky grew dimmer and a beam in the ceiling above him took a faint form.

The steps stopped at the foot of the ladder. Suddenly a long white ray struck through the open trapdoor. It made an intense circle on the ceiling, cut an arc and vanished downward once more. With this light he took the final step into consciousness. He saw he was lying behind boxes, hidden from the center of the room.

Because he was hidden he felt a moment of panic, not

for himself but as though there was a danger in him to whoever was coming. The danger flickered in the dark, and surely the man below also must feel it. He heard no movement. There was a long hesitation there at the foot of the ladder. Then the ladder gave its mouselike squeak, was pulled down, and struck the floor with a thump. The steps came awkwardly up, reached the top, and someone stood in the room.

The white ray circled all around, resting for a moment on the shelf over his head, but he lay in a shadow as improbable as an eclipse. Shall I call out now? he thought. A return of panic, the panic of being hidden and dangerous stopped him.

Then he heard steps taken cautiously in his direction and suddenly he said, "I'm over here."

The steps stopped abruptly. He heard a sharp intake of breath but no one answered him. Only the ray swung in the direction of his voice.

"I can't move," he said. "I've broken my ankle. Come and look behind the boxes." He added reassuringly, "I can't do you any harm."

"Oh yeah?"

The words spoken hoarsely, half in recoil and half in derision, touched him with wonder. They hung on the air and as his ear went on listening an echo seemed to form from them, a faint and tremulous vibration. For a moment he thought he heard a boy's voice, his own voice answering him from a long way off.

Then he said slowly, "Why, it's a woman."

"Don't kid yourself," she said. "I got a gun."

This hoarse, dry whisper had no echo.

He answered sharply, "What nonsense! You don't need a gun."

She took another step forward and spoke in a louder voice, "You come out of there."

She waited, but this time it was he who didn't answer.

"You better come out. I'm going to count ten."

"Be reasonable," he said. "Supposing I wanted to hurt you. Wouldn't I have waited for you as you came up the ladder? If you've really got a gun push the boxes away and look. You're not taking much of a chance."

He heard her breathing. Then she came toward the boxes and began tugging at them. The white ray made a crazy dance. So she wouldn't find him lying flat, he pushed his elbows on the floor and drew himself up. The movement sent long, hot tentacles up his leg but he reached a sitting position and leaned back against one of the cases. When she had widened the crooked lane he'd made she turned the torch full in his eyes.

He closed his eyes and said, "Please don't," but she came nearer and held it in his face.

"You can see for yourself," he said. "If I could get up I would."

The light moved over him from his face to his empty hands, down his legs, lingered on his ankle. He leaned forward and saw it was swollen and distorted. Then he tried to see what she was like, but she turned the light back in his face and became herself only something dark with a gleam of eyeballs.

Then she said in a surprised and apparently more natural voice, "I never saw you before!"

"Of course not."

She moved backward, holding the torch in front of her, till she got to the table in the center of the room. Then she reached up behind her and turned the light switch. It clicked several times.

"No use," he said. "I tried it. Isn't the electricity turned off?"

She didn't answer but put the torch, still lighted, on the table, opened a drawer and found a fresh bulb. She changed the bulbs quickly and turned the new one on. The room sprang into a bleak and dusty pallor, with angular blocks of shadows heaped around it. She put her torch out and drew a chair toward her, pausing with one hand on the back to see if there was anything more that she must do. Suddenly she saw the blanket tied up over the window. "Hey!" she cried. "What you been doing?"

As she ran to the window her coat slipped from her shoulders to the floor. She didn't notice it. She caught the blanket and began pulling at the knot that he had made.

"I wanted more light," he explained.

"Well, you leave things alone around here."

It took her several minutes to get the knot undone. Then the blanket hung a little crookedly and she had to jerk it into place. She came back finally, stopping to pick her coat up off the floor and sling it across her shoulders.

She sat down in the chair, facing him, leaned her elbows on the table and stared.

She seemed no more than fourteen. There was no one to compare her with but she was very small. Her waist and stomach—he'd seen them when she tugged at the blanket—were so flat it was hard to imagine her ever eating a square meal. Yes, fourteen, he thought; then as he went on looking at her he changed his opinion. Fifteen at the least, maybe sixteen. She was wearing a costume so curious it might have been a masquerade: checked slacks over pear-shaped buttocks and a sweater with the sleeves rolled above her elbows. Over her shoulders was the coat, with some sort of catskin collar—a "sports" coat. On the other hand, she was wearing evening slippers with fantastically high heels and open toes. Her hands were large, capable looking, except for long red nails. She had thickly coated her round face with powder and her mouth had been enlarged by lipstick into a false Negroid bloom. Her eyebrows were nearly invisible; where they should have been were two faint ridges like wave markings on sand. Because of the paleness of these eyebrows he thought her hair natural; it was a fine, silvery flaxen color, the true platinum blond, falling in waves to her shoulders and drawn up to a lofty pompadour in front. The skin of her neck was milky white—it looked bluish in the shadow—but there was an adolescent pimple on her chin. He saw that whatever of her physical self she had not been able to mask or damage was tentative, hesitant, still tenderly malleable, and that in spite of this her air of assurance was not entirely precocious. And he saw also that she had no gun.

They stared at each other for several moments without speaking. If she had been really frightened at finding him she did not show it now. Her expression was so calm

it gave him an immediate impression not only of control
but of hollowness, as though in the ingredients that
made her something expected was lacking.

"O.K., you can spill it now. How'd you get in here?"

"Why," he said slowly, "by the front door."

"Yeah? Where'd you get the key?"

"You know that padlock," he answered. "It wasn't
caught. I just walked in."

"You didn't jimmy it?"

"No, I found it that way."

"What about Gus? Was he here?"

"Gus? Who's Gus?"

"Never mind who Gus is. I said, was he here?"

"No. No one was here."

"So you just found the door open and walked in. But
no one was here?"

"No one."

"Didn't Gus come at all?"

"No. I tell you, no one has come, unless they came
and went while I was knocked out."

"Oh, you were knocked out, were you?"

"I told you I've broken my ankle."

"And that knocked you out?"

"Yes," he said sharply, "it knocked me out."

She looked incredulous. Then he saw on her face a
faintly humorous anticipation, not unfriendly, as though
by agreement they were going to lead up to some still
distant joke. This disconcerted him. He tried to make
his position clear to her, speaking in short, simple sen-
tences, partly so she would understand more easily,

partly because he was breathing in short, uneven breaths.

"I've told you how I got in," he said, "but I suppose you want to know why I came. Well, I used to live in this house. I hadn't seen it for years, so many years I'd almost forgotten about it. Then, when I was in New York for a day, I thought I'd like to see what had become of it. So I came here. The door was unlatched and I walked in. I only meant to look around but I fell in the dark and broke my ankle. I passed out. The first thing I knew, you were here."

When he had finished, her faintly humorous look was tinged with irony. She said, "You left something out, didn't you?"

"Of course I left something out. But it's something I'm afraid I can't tell you."

"I'll bet," she said.

"I only meant I couldn't make you understand."

"Maybe you better try anyway."

"What will you do if I don't?"

"Sit here," she said, "if you can sit here—I can sit *here.*"

She reached into the pocket of her coat and got out a packet of chewing gum, stripped off a piece, and stuck it in her mouth. Then her jaws began to move in a maddening and monotonous rhythm. She crossed one leg and swung it gently. Her eyes left him and became abstracted.

"If I try to tell you," he said, "will you stop that chewing?"

She didn't answer but her eyes fixed on him again.

Then she flicked the gum into one cheek with her tongue and her face was still.

He said, "The reason I wanted to see it again was because of a dream I had."

When he spoke there was always a pause before her reply. Now the pause was longer.

"A dream?" she said.

"Yes. Do you ever dream?"

"No."

"You don't dream at all?"

"Nope. I don't dream at all—well, if I do I forget."

"Usually I forget, too. This time I didn't. That was what was different about it, that I remembered it."

She considered a moment and said, "Then what?"

"Then I thought, any dream has its interpretation. I don't mean dream book interpretations. I mean a dream itself is a form of memory. Your unconscious mind is functioning, not, say, as reasoning, but as memory. There is bound to be a logic in it, a shape behind a shape. A meaning, in other words. Well, I came to find out what it was."

She leaned her elbows on the table. "I don't get you," she said.

"I was afraid you wouldn't."

When she saw he wasn't going to say any more she said, "That's your story?"

"Yes."

"Want to know what I think?"

He nodded.

"I think it's a lot of crap."

Even this was not insolence. It was rather a good-tempered summing up of his efforts. Her line, evidently, was: be very calm, be very practical and keep within certain limits; above all, don't take any wooden nickels, and if things get confusing be jocular. This, as he saw it, was the formula, and he had to come over to her side, even if it gave him the vertigo of standing with each foot in a separate dimension, neither of them stable.

He said, "What I was really trying to tell you was that I'm harmless."

"Yeah?" she said drily. "I got that part."

"I'm still a surprise to you," he said.

"You sure are."

"But you must be getting used to it by now. Here I am, harmless, as I just said. Tell me what you think?"

She narrowed her eyes and a cynical gleam showed in them. "If I didn't see it, I wouldn't believe it."

He smiled. "Anyway, you do see it."

She didn't answer and he made an effort to conceive of how he must appear to her. The flickering sense of danger came back, but no more precise than it had been. And she wasn't afraid of him, really; she only thought him spurious and perhaps comic. She didn't believe in him, just as he didn't believe in her. Neither was yet real to the other. This, he thought, was probably better for him. Gus, when he came, would surely conclude only too quickly what he was.

"You can surely see I need your help," he said.

"Oh, yeah?"

"Supposing instead of finding me here you'd come on me lying in the street?"

"I didn't though."

"No. But look at it this way: I might just as well have broken my ankle *outside*, and if I had and you'd found me you'd have done without question what I'm going to ask you to do now."

"What's that?"

"To go somewhere and call a hospital. I don't know what hospital but dial the operator. She'll know. Tell them to send an ambulance. Tell them it's an emergency. I'll be out of here before you know it."

Again she waited. Then she said, *"That's* all I have to do!"

"Yes. Will you do it?"

"No."

"Why not? But I don't understand you."

"That makes it fifty-fifty," she said. Then she added, "You must think I'm pretty dumb."

"Dumb? Why?"

"Well, who the hell are you? You haven't said. Maybe you'd make trouble."

"Trouble?" He looked around at the cases. "You mean all this?"

"Yeah," she drawled, "that's just what I mean."

"This is pretty important to someone?"

"It's not peanuts," she said.

"No. It's a lot of money. But if that's what you're thinking of, get me out of here before this Gus of yours comes and I'll make it worth your while."

"Yeah? How?"

"Why, how should I? What do you want me to do? I'll do whatever you want."

"Supposing I don't want anything?"

"If you don't it's because you haven't thought about it. It's because the world is bigger than you know and there's a lot in it you might want."

Her good temper vanished suddenly. Her round face became reproving. "You better get another line," she said briefly.

The rebuff made him flush, not only because he wasn't used to rebuffs but because he felt it was deserved.

"Let's take it another way then."

"Let's don't," she said.

"You don't want to talk at all?"

She folded her arms across her chest. As a gesture of disregard for him she began to chew again. "You and me'll just wait for Gus," she said.

"All right. Evidently we wait for Gus."

She said coldly, "I'll give you a tip, too. Gus is no pushover. If you tell him what you've told me he won't go for it any more than I go for it. I'm telling you—you better get another line." She chewed for a minute, then she said, "Besides, he's nervous."

"Nervous?"

"Yeah, nervous. He acts on impulse. But maybe you already found that out?"

"I wish you'd get over the idea that he's been here. You seem to think he's come in, actually broken my ankle, and for some reason left."

She nodded, chewing.

"But my dear girl, what is this Gus, Gargantua? You don't break a man's ankle like that."

"In a scrap you might."

"Well, there's been no scrap."

"Maybe not," she said. Then she added, "Maybe there won't be one—if you're smart."

"What if he doesn't come?" he asked.

"Then we wait for Mort."

She made no more attempt to explain Mort than she had Gus. She was like Annie, the Irish immigrant girl who cooked for Aunt Minerva. Annie talked of her friends and relatives back in County Cork, told anecdotes, quoted sayings, but never explained anyone. People must know them because she did.

"Mort," he said. "Now we've got Mort. And who is Mort?"

"He's the big shot." She raised her invisible eyebrows as though to say, "You didn't even know that one."

"So Mort's the big shot. Tougher than Gus, then?"

"That's right." Her face grew more solemn, warning him out of her private knowledge that on this subject it was not for him to get funny. The joke, if there had been a joke, was all her own. "They don't come any tougher," she said.

"Good!" he said, exasperated. "Then in Mort at least we reach the ultimate."

"The what?"

"The ultimate. Than which there is no further."

"Wise guy!" she said. "Say, listen. I'm telling you, whoever comes, cut out the double-talk. They won't like it."

He felt himself that it was double-talk and that it was leading him nowhere. And suddenly he had the immediate need to make some familiar gesture, one that would restore him to his habits even if only of body. He reached in his pocket and found his cigarette case. He'd lost the lighter in his fall but he had a paper clip of matches.

"Mind if I smoke?" he asked.

"Go ahead."

He lighted the cigarette and inhaled deeply. It made him feel queasy but still it was a comfort to him. It touched him with the assurance of the known returning, and the sensation of unreality became less disturbing.

It is stupid, he thought, to feel that there are degrees in reality. Anything that happens is real. There are only degrees in certainty. I am uncertain about a thousand things, even about myself, which ought to be what is most intelligible to me. And here I am confronted with a creature who, as nearly as it's possible to be, is certain. She is all imitation; her manners, gestures, humor, solemnity, whole style of being, are imitations, but she is quite certain of the necessity for them. She simply doesn't know any others. The thing about her that comes nearest to being an uncertainty is her sex, which isn't made yet. The imitation has reached a completion but the sex hasn't. (Why else did I think I heard a boy's voice?) One good look at her shows me that there is an unformed mouth under the lipstick, an unformed bosom under the sweater, a pimple under the powder. Because her sex is in this tentative stage the "I" of her doesn't yet know itself for the "I." It's still part of a collectivism of childhood and instinct and ignorance. Why, she hasn't even become conscious enough of separation to imagine that I might misunderstand her! She only knows, vaguely still, that she doesn't understand me. I am about to be her first real uncertainty.

"What's your name?" he asked her.

She looked surprised. The question must have suggested some impropriety. She shook her head.

"You won't tell me?"

"What for?"

"Convenience. Everyone has a tag. I want to know what tag to put on you. If you won't tell me I'll have to make one up."

"Well, make one up then."

"You mightn't like it."

"What's yours?" she asked.

"Mine is Cassius Terhune. Do you like it?"

She didn't answer.

"You don't. Tell me yours then. Maybe I'll like yours."

She still hesitated. Finally she said in her low voice, her self-conscious voice, "It's Edna."

"Edna?" he said. "Just Edna? Nothing more?"

"Just Edna."

"Edna," he repeated. "It's a lovely, suave name. It sounds like cream. I don't know whether it suits you. In time maybe it will. Now tell me how old you are."

"Say, what is this?"

"Old enough to have a boy friend? Is Gus the boy friend?"

She made a little grimace. Then she said, importantly, "Listen, Mr. Wiesenheimer, Gus is my brother."

"I see. That explains why he is so big and tough. And is Mort a big, tough brother, too?"

"No," she said, "he's not." Her face was wary. "Say, you got your nerve asking all these questions!"

"I've answered all you wanted to ask."

"Yeah—and how!"

"The best I could."

"Oh, you're screwy," she said.

"You don't mean that. What you mean is you can't quite believe in me, or that our being together here like this is real."

"I never saw anyone like you," she said, deliberately. "You're in a spot, a tough spot, and I guess you know it. But you act like you're thinking about something else."

"I am thinking of the spot," he said, "I'm trying to. But you're right. It's not quite real to me either—and you aren't." He smiled at her but she looked stolidly back. "What makes a thing that is real seem unreal?" he said. "Mightn't it sometimes be only because of an unexpected illumination, a light that shows us more than we are accustomed to see, so that we can't immediately relate it to what we knew before? Don't we have to accustom our eye, our inner eye?"

A faint uneasiness showed in her face. With a long, manicured finger she scratched her temple at the line of moonglow hair. It was almost a gesture of troubled thought. For the first time she seemed to lose full control of the situation.

Pain and the excitement of talking and the constant effort at realization were exhausting him. Sweat formed

on his forehead and trickled down his face. He reached
into a pocket for his handkerchief and he felt a bottle
there. It was his sleeping pills. That morning, just as
his baggage had been taken from the cabin, he'd noticed the bottle on the washstand and put it in his
pocket. He took it out now and looked at it, wondering
if it would help the pain any to take two of them. He
shook them out on his palm.

She watched him and her eyes narrowed. "Say, *that's*
not smart," she said.

"They're only sedatives," he told her, "and my ankle
hurts badly. These were prescribed by a doctor. They're
harmless."

"I'll bet!"

"You think it's a drug."

Her unease grew stronger. Obviously a doubt had
entered her. What was this all about anyway? Maybe it
wasn't so simple and maybe it wasn't so funny. She said,
"You better watch it."

He put the bottle back without taking any.

"What's going to happen when they come?" he asked
her.

"I wouldn't know," she said evasively.

"Yes, you would. You told me I might make trouble.
Will they think that too?"

"Sure they will." She twisted her leg around the leg
of the chair. "But I was just thinking," she said, "that
if you wanted to, if you were smart, maybe you and
them could get together on something."

"On what?"

"On what? Why, I don't know your angle."

"I have no angle."

"Well, you better get one then. They'll sure ask you a lot of questions."

"I won't have any answers. I can't tell them why I came. I can't make it sound believable. Anyway, I'm here, and they can't afford to have me here."

He stopped and as he looked around him the place became for him a whole shimmer of deceptions with nothing as he had yet seen it, not the attic, the girl, or his own hand holding the cigarette. His present state became a bubble reflecting something that was to come, a bubble that in a moment would break, leaving nothing.

"Why," he exclaimed, "do you think they'd actually kill me?"

He put his cigarette out slowly on the floor. She followed his gesture with her eyes, then shifted them to his face. She stared at him as though her doubt had become a more acute anxiety. He felt her whole attention seize him, and he thought that he, Cass Terhune, little Cass, who used to sleep here, play here, read books here, even here already preparing to die because he had been started on the process by being born (as the Morellis, Madame Golden, and Aunt Minerva, and the old woman hanging from a beam, were now all dead), he too would soon be only one more blob of death in the midst of the world's dead. And the girl was simply realizing that she looked at death for the first time.

Then he couldn't concentrate on it. In his exhaustion he lapsed into a half-doze, like the dozes of train travel, when the words of a book just put down jounce in the head to the rhythm of rails, or perhaps a pain somewhere in the body. Words like "pondering the events of the evening," "pausing to take stock of the situation," "waiting for Death, the Grim Reaper."

He roused himself and thought, I won't die yet. Not till I find what I came for. Not till I know. . . . And his mind refused to accept his death. This was the mind that ceaselessly examined his own experience and, no matter how many times it was frustrated, went right on looking for solutions. For it was, he must remember, a tough, agile, and well-blooded instrument. It was used to variety and the impossible. Besides, it didn't always fail. Not only was it capable of understanding an objective order of right and wrong, of entering into the beauty of a mathematical theorem or the music of Mozart, but it could also on occasion settle a dispute between two members of the faculty and, if it came down to it, devise a way to get rid of a plague of moles in the garden. This mind, for all its many past frustrations, now working under pressure could surely get him out of this.

And especially, he thought, with this simple creature to work on.

"Wouldn't you rather I got out alive?" he asked.

The question shocked her. He could see it in her face. A minute ago she had looked on him as death seen for the first time. But the fact of death, so nearly realized, made the fact of life also more real, and he was becoming a living man to her precisely because she had recognized death in him. But it was his livingness that disturbed her, not his death.

She looked at him for the first time with a personal antagonism. "Why do you keep talking like that?" she asked.

"You mean why do I talk as though I knew they'd kill me? But first you say I don't see the spot I'm in. Now that I do you don't like it."

"But what's the idea of saying they'll bump you?"

"So it's you who didn't see! Or perhaps you saw but didn't think it meant anything to you. Maybe death is just a word you've heard. Now it's not a word. It's someone you're looking at and have talked to. And worse than that, you'll have a part in it."

"You could make a deal," she said obstinately.

"Nonsense. You know I can't. You don't want to admit it. But the decision of whether I live or don't live is up to you."

"I got nothing to do with it."

"That's not true. You know it. That's why you could hate me now. You do hate me. How we hate those who force us to decide. It is so much nicer to let others do that for us."

Her face flushed. Where the powder was thinnest on her lids the fair skin grew darker. "You oughtn't to of come," she said.

"But I did, and that doesn't let you out."

"Listen. Get this straight," she said. She began to talk loudly, emphasizing each word. "I don't specially want them to do anything to you. But I got nothing to say about it. What do you think I am? I'm nothing but an em-ploy-ee here."

"You work? That is for them?"

"Not even for them. I work, or anyway I used to, in the beauty shoppee downstairs. I gave the manicures. I got paid just like anyone else."

"It wasn't a barber shop, then," he said. "It was a beauty shop."

"That's right."

"Then it was run as a front naturally. Did you distribute the nylons from there?"

She ignored this question. "I'm an em-ploy-ee," she said. "That's all."

"A stooge!" he exclaimed. "A dummy, a piece of window dressing."

"I got paid for giving manicures."

"Then what are you doing here now?"

"Now? What's it to you? Well, anyway, maybe I better tell you. They're my friends, see? So sometimes, like now, Mort asks me a favor and I do it. Like he told me to get ahold of Gus. I couldn't find him anywhere so I left word he should come here. I think maybe Mort's on his way here, too. Anyway, one of them will be here. And from then on it's strictly up to them."

Her husky voice was hard. She breathed quickly.

"You aren't worrying on their account?" he asked.

"Why should I?"

"There's a difference," he said, "a difference between stealing whisky and selling it without a license—and a murder rap."

"They can look out for that."

"Are you sure of it?"

"Yeah," she said briefly.

Her conviction was that they were big and tough and

strong and she had no fear for them. Also she wished they would come and take this thing out of her hands.

He said again, "But wouldn't you rather I got out alive?"

It all came to this: first, she had to see him as a living man—that was already happening though she still resisted it—then she would have to see something to be saved. But there was no time to stir her imagination, which was obviously sluggish and unprepared. It would be difficult to deceive her into believing there was any value, or even a charm, in him worth saving because the truth was (though it takes imagination also to see the truth) that he was a man with nothing to offer her but danger.

It seemed so hopeless that he smiled, and seeing this smile she became angry. Her whole face lighted with anger. "You're sure dumb!" she cried. "How many times I got to tell you it's not up to me. Gee, but you're dumb!" She twisted in her chair as though she were tied and trying to get loose.

"You could take the chance," he said. "They couldn't. I'd have to promise not to talk. Right? But they couldn't believe that. Only you could believe it."

"Me?"

"You're not afraid as they'd be. You could believe me, because already you know me a little."

"That's great!" she exclaimed. "First you say you have a dream. You walk in your sleep. You come and fall down and you break your leg. I'm supposed to believe that! And now you say if I get you out you won't squeal. And I'm supposed to believe that, too."

"Can't you?"

"Oh, you can screw for all I care," she said savagely. "You're nothing to me. But I got my friends to think about. Anyone can make a promise, anyone can welsh on it afterward."

"You'll have to judge whether I'm a welsher or not. Haven't you ever trusted anyone?"

"Mort," she said.

"Only Mort?"

"Yeah, only Mort."

"What did it take to make you trust him? Have you tried him out for years and years? Have you put him to tests, each one a little harder than the one before? And have you reached a conclusive test that settles everything? Is that why you trust him, because you have achieved a final and rational and self-limiting experience? Why, there is no certainty like that! If you look for that you could never trust anyone."

She said in a whisper, "Well, I don't trust you." The anger had left her face, her eyes looked out at him from a child's world into one that was amorphous, full of reflections and mystery. He remembered faintly, and from a long way off, how he had once seen people and things, and he felt again the first dread and longing to understand as he had felt them in their pristine freshness and pain.

"I don't want to deceive you," he said. "If you trust me you'll risk a great deal. What makes children trust? They trust with their bodies, they open their mouths for food, and they're secure in their instinct that tells them that what they need will be given them. But it doesn't stay like that. Later it's *you* who have to give, and I'm afraid nothing less than a piece of yourself is ever enough. Once you do that your safety is over."

"I wish I'd never seen you," she said.

"I know exactly how you feel. But I'm afraid you're in for it. The worst of it is that I have nothing good to offer you in return. There is no completion in life. What you feel must be there you don't find. Still, you must trust life. If you don't the penalty is worse."

After a moment's silence she gave an ugly little self-conscious laugh. "You're screwy," she said. "Anyway, I don't get you."

"That's because I'm talking about what I haven't learned myself. I'll tell you what happened to me once. I knew an old woman. She was so old she didn't really want anything more than a look she and I gave each other when we met. She wanted only a shadow of something, a happiness that maybe never was. It was no risk to me, except that even that look and that shadow meant giving a part of myself. It meant trusting the whole of life outside myself."

She glanced up at him quickly and in her eyes he saw a startled question she wasn't aware of: what was the strange, shadowy happiness he had to give?

"You'd think," he said, "I wouldn't have refused?"
She didn't answer.

"Well, for a while I didn't. Then all at once I couldn't give it. I never saw her again—not alive."

She raised her eyebrows, trying to show she didn't care. She started to chew her gum. Then she took it out of her mouth and stuck it on the underside of the table. "What happened?" she asked huskily.

"She hanged herself," he said. "See what you can get into?" He looked at her lightheadedly, because at this moment the dream sensation came back. The house was the labyrinth and the danger was near. It was coming. Mort and Gus were coming. Hurry. Hurry. The end was coming. The end of frustration also. But the end.

"It's too late, isn't it?" he said.

Then this passed. There was no one coming. They were alone here. She was trembling on the edge of decision. Part of his mind saw that clearly. One word might force her. Without thinking he said, "Edna, I guess I'll have to haunt *you* now. Would you like that?"

Her eyes raised to his were already haunted, and he added quickly, "I'm ashamed of what I'm saying. Don't listen to me. It's all mixed and impure. I'm saying it for myself only. Don't listen. Do what you like."

In the long silence she slowly lowered her eyes and her head bent so he could scarcely see her face. She didn't even move when they heard the street door opening. It was shut with no effort at caution and a man's footsteps sounded from below. He felt no fear and no hope, only numbness, as though those sensations he had no use for any more were leaving him. But as his eyes fixed themselves resignedly on her face, accepting what was to come, a change broke in her. Some acute rush of feeling swept her so fiercely it was like watching a spasm of pain. Then she was calm again, the callous adolescent, a little hollow for lack of vital material, deliberately humorous in the face of the fact. She made a little signal to him with her forefinger, got up quickly and lightly, and came across the room. She tugged at the cases and pulled them back across the open space she had made.

"Get back in there," she whispered. "Lie still."

She pulled other cases, listened to the steps coming up. As he let himself slide back to the floor behind the piled up cases he had time to see her secret, resolved smile. He dragged himself behind the highest pile of cases and lay quietly. Then he heard her tiptoe back to the table and sit down.

He heard a click and thought it was the light switch. It took him several seconds to realize that darkness had not come. The room above him was still bright. The man's footsteps had reached the floor below. Then a soft explosion made a puff of sound in the room. It diminished at once, fanned out into the tinkle of a piano playing boogie-woogie. Edna had turned on the radio.

A voice came sharply up from below. "Hey, that you, Edna?"

After a pause Edna said, "Yeah."

CHAPTER V

THE ladder swung down with a thump and the man came up. He walked with a slurring, uneven step across the floor.

"Hi!" he said.

"Hi!" Edna answered.

He pulled out a chair and sat down. Neither of them spoke. The piano played with the dreaminess of distance. Then one of them turned the dial to a voice giving out the news, to a band, a bit of a Brahms symphony, finally to the voice of a crooner singing something about "melodee" and "memoree." The man said, "Jeez, do we have to listen to him?" and it went back to the far tinkle of the boogie-woogie.

Terhune lay absolutely still behind the boxes. The numbness passed and an acute sensitiveness took its place. He was so conscious of himself lying there he could not believe he was hidden. Then when he saw he really was he could not believe it would last. He tensed all his faculties for that moment when the man's eyes would fall on him.

But as the music went on, the unearthly piano with its pulsing, hypnotic bass, it seemed to spread a thin

veil of sound over him. It covered his breathing, tiny
involuntary movements of his body, a nerve jumping,
the pain in his ankle, his mind's activity, everything
that cried out, "I'm here. Come and find me."

And as he saw that he remained hidden other things
seemed to protect him: the air of habit and of easy,
worn familiarity between Edna and whoever this man
was, and even the man himself, who curiously appeared
to help him in his effort to make of himself an emptiness, a nothingness in the room. The man's blindness
and deafness spread from him like a deliberate web.
He and the man were like two spiders in opposite corners manufacturing together this unawareness.

He heard Edna say, "Mort wants to see you." And
he knew then the man was Gus, and that it was better
it should be Gus than Mort, but still, when they began
to talk, he tried not to listen too intently because his
listening might be obscurely felt by them.

Gus said, "Yeah. That's what Louie told me."

"You saw Louie?"

"Yeah. He said you'd been in looking for me."

"I was. Mort called and said did I know where you
were."

"What'd you tell him?"

"I said I didn't know."

"You're a big help!"

The piano gave a spurt of loudness. Edna raised her
voice over it. "Well, I didn't know."

"So then what?" Gus asked.

"Then he said, when would you be in?"

"What'd you say?"

"I said I didn't know."

"Jeez! What you mean is you didn't know."

Their voices were alike. They had a muffled hoarse-
ness, something muted that suggested the croaking of
nocturnal birds. The long pause between question and
answer he had already noticed in Edna. It showed they
were not used to actual conversation but only to ejaculations, brief, surreptitious remarks. They had their
same style, strained and mannered, rigidly conven-
tional, meant to attract attention, but if not that then
to save pride.

"So then what?" Gus asked.

"So then he said for me to get in touch with you."

"Yeah."

"And I talked to Louie and he said maybe you'd be
in later. So I said when you came in to tell you to come
here. But I thought Mort would come. If he don't come
in a minute we better scram."

"Yeah, we better."

Gus yawned. He rapped on the table with his fingers,
making a clever counterpoint of rhythm to the piano.
Terhune could feel that he was preoccupied. Something
held all his attention and it was this as much as anything that gave his unawareness an air of being deliberate.

He was beginning to listen to them in spite of himself, feeling by degrees that he was safer. But what they
said did not yet make a continuity or have any meaning
for him.

Edna said, "I been everywhere looking for you. I
went to Louie's first, then I went to Joe's place and to

Casey's and even to Negrelli's. Then I went back to Louie's. Then I went around some more. Where were you?"

"Oh," he said vaguely, "places. Say, do you really go for this stuff?"

"Yeah, I like it."

"Well turn it lower then."

"It won't go any lower. How long you think we ought to wait here?"

"Maybe nine. After that we better blow."

Gus made the sounds of taking out a pack of cigarettes. He struck a match and a ghost of smoke drifted to the ceiling.

"How's to give me a cigarette," Edna said, "or haven't you got anything but reefers?"

"How many you had today?"

"What's the difference?"

"I said, how many?"

"Oh, six—seven maybe."

"Chain smoking. Listen kid, you want to stunt your growth?"

Edna either smiled or did not smile but Gus threw her a cigarette. Another match struck and another coil of smoke trickled upward.

Gus twitched in his chair for a while. All his movements showed uneasiness. He couldn't sit still. Edna could. There was no sound from Edna. Then Gus said, "It's kind of hot in here."

"Yeah, it is."

His voice rose suddenly. "Say! Who's been monkeying with that window?"

"What window?"

"How many windows we got? *That* window. Someone's been monkeying with it."

He jumped up and walked over to it with his sliding,
uneven gait.

"Not me," Edna said.

"Well, someone has. The tacks are out. They're lying
all over the place."

"Well, why don't you fix it?"

Gus stood still, examining the window, and no one
spoke. In their silence Terhune scarcely breathed. With
Gus moving around the room his ability to stay hidden
had changed sharply. If Gus moved a few feet in one
direction or another his eye would fall on him. But Gus
stood where he was, his back turned. His inattention
began to have something obstinate about it. He said to
Edna, "Gimme one of your shoes."

"What?"

Edna did not move. Terhune felt she was afraid to
move. She counted on the denseness of her own personality as part of his covering, and her immobility was
a part of that.

"These are my good shoes," she said.

"So what? You and your good shoes."

But Gus slipped off one of his own. "I have to do
everything," he complained. He hammered at the tacks
for a moment, came back and sat down.

There was a slight difference in their voices after all.
In Gus's there was instability, even a fine threat of always imminent hysteria. Terhune wondered how many
reefers Gus was in the habit of smoking, if he took any

other dope, if he drank, if he was merely a delinquent like Edna or something worse.

"Been here long?" Gus asked.

"Not very. Say, what time is it?"

"Ten to nine."

A slight noise of Edna moving in her chair. "Say," she said, "that's some watch. New, isn't it?"

"Yeah, it's new."

"Where'd you get it?"

"It's a present."

"Who gave it to you?"

"My public, kid. My fans."

"I'll bet."

"You like it?"

"Yeah, it's nice. Who gave it to you?"

"Say, have you a one-track mind!"

"I'll bet Gloria gave it to you."

"Well, quit betting. You're liable to get into trouble."

"How about you getting into trouble? You think Mort'll like Gloria giving you watches?"

"I'm telling you, cut it out."

Gus's voice took such a sharp rise that Terhune felt a thrill of anxiety, not for himself but for Edna. Edna ought not to bait a man with a voice like that. Then he thought, after all, she knows him. Perhaps now she's only stirring up a minor tempest to cloud the atmosphere.

Gus scraped his chair backward and tilted it up on two legs. He said angrily but with a note of confusion in his voice, "No one gave it to me. I bought it myself.

That was just a gag. But you got no sense of humor. Jeez, what a dumb cluck!"

The radio went off with a sudden snap. The silence seemed larger than the space of the attic and as though it stretched out deep on all sides. And in the silence Terhune could feel the quarrel building itself up between them. But Gus could not endure silence. He was not sharp enough to know what actually went on in it, though he was sharp enough to know that something went on.

Then he said in a voice that was suddenly cajoling and placating, "I know a certain little lady who is going to get a present herself."

"Who, me?"

"I'm not kidding."

"What is it?"

"Wait and you'll see."

"Why do I have to wait?"

"Because I said so."

"Well, who's going to give it to me?"

Gus didn't answer. He began to whistle softly. His air of good clean fun was completely false. He was simply responding to Edna's present falseness with his own, just for instance, just in case, not yet knowing why. Edna's falseness was calculated. His was not.

They were alike but they were also different. Terhune saw them as both pale, almost albino in coloring; he even saw their hands, large and active, their undersized bodies. But Edna was the dense one, Edna had strength in her. Gus was a weakling, a self-pitier; he was transparent as a jellyfish.

Edna said, "It's a trip to Atlantic City."

"What's that?" His chair legs struck the floor sharply. "Say, who's talking about trips to Atlantic City?"

"Well, I just said it's a trip to Atlantic City."

"I heard you the first time. What trip, whose trip?"

"Just a trip."

"*You're* going to Atlantic City?"

"Why not?"

"You and who else?"

She waited long enough to tantalize him and then said, "Mort."

Terhune could almost feel the weak but violent impact of Gus's eyes, pale, no doubt, like Edna's, full of anger. But he would be helpless until things went too far, for that was the trouble with Edna. She couldn't be merely shaken; nothing short of the extreme measures would ever do. It struck Terhune that already he knew that much about her. And he knew something about Gus, too. He knew that because he was the weaker he was the more dangerous. In spite of himself he was knowing them both. In spite of himself he was beginning to follow their narration with the closest attention. It unreeled before him like a movie in a dark theater, showing as white pantomime in the midst of his mind's darkness, which was a part of the darkness he lay in, of the night outside, of the obscurity of what would happen.

When Gus spoke incipient hysteria showed more openly in his voice. "So Mort said he'd take you to Atlantic City?"

"That's right."

"He *said* he'd take you."

"Oh, well," she murmured indifferently, "he pratically said so."

"Oh," he mimicked, "so he just *pratically* said so." Then his fury burst through. "Listen, bird brain!" he cried, "he never said so! He never said he'd take you anywhere, and if you know what's good for you, you won't say it either—not so as anyone can hear you, but especially not so's Mort can hear you. Because he's not going to like it, see? He's not going to like it a-tall."

Gus got up and pushed his chair back. He took two or three lurching steps up and down the room, stopping to snarl at Edna, "I just wish you had a looking glass in here. So's you could see that face, and them clothes you got on, and that shape. Only you got no shape. Why, if you was to give it away for free, who'd want it? Get wise to yourself, kid, get wise."

He paced up and down, always lurching as though at any moment he might take a long slide across the floor. His anger seemed to Terhune more and more excessive. He seemed to hate Edna for not being more attractive. He'd have liked to use her, perhaps, if he'd thought there was anything he could use. Either there were the makings of a pimp in Gus or he was covering something.

Then he sat down, pulling his chair up to lean nearer to her, to have it out. He said weightily, "You better begin to understand a few things. You're talking about Atlantic City. Well, you've never been there, have you? But *I* been there. And I know what happens there. First, Mort takes a soot in the Fairvue Avon. It's got

big davenports and floor lamps and a Capehart and
baskets of glads tied with ribbons at thirty bucks a
basket. It's got cases of champagne and Scotch whisky.
It's got bellhops running in and out with ice. Service
every minute. All anybody can eat and drink. And
finally, it's got dames. And it's the dames that you ought
to know about, because these dames I'm referring to,
they got class. What I mean, class! They got sophistica-
tion, they got glamor. And then they got something else,
kid, that you haven't—know what I mean?"

He stopped and Terhune could feel his eyes on Edna,
and a deliberate flickering cruelty in them. "Say," he
drawled hoarsely, "I guess you'd like to be there at that.
Because, come to think of it, I noticed quite a few
things lately, quite a few things. But you better forget
it. Sure, Mort thinks you're a funny kid. He likes to
kid you along, he gets plenty of laughs out of you. But
just the same, don't go getting ideas. Because, like I
said, he wouldn't like it. And if you really want to know
what he thinks about you, let me tell you a little incident that happened the other day. We're all at Louie's
and Mort is talking to a fellow of the name of Joe
Nathan, who just flew in from Chicago, and this Nathan
says, 'Where'd you get that midget I see you talking to
outside?' And Mort says, 'That's Edna. I found her one
morning under my bureau and I figure if I can find
three more I'll have an act.' "

"Oh, veree funny," Edna said. But her voice shook
slightly and it was obvious she was hurt. "I suppose it's
Gloria's got all the class," she said. "I suppose it's *her*
Mort takes to Atlantic City. Well, he won't when he
knows she gave you a wrist watch."

In the silence it seemed that Gus hovered over Edna. His chair squeaked on two legs as he leaned toward her. Then the dull impact of a blow rang in the room. Perhaps it was only a hard slap, but Terhune felt the danger he had felt when Edna first came into the room and stood in the dark listening—a danger from himself. He realized how accurate that feeling had been. It *was* he who had brought danger to her, and this was the first sound of it, like a distant clap of thunder on a sultry afternoon.

Edna did not move. Finally she said softly, "Don't you ever hit me again, Gus."

"Oh, for Christ sake!" Gus exclaimed. His chair dropped back again, as though the blow had taken all the strength out of him.

"Well, don't you ever do it again, you hear?"

"For Christ sake," he repeated petulantly. "You had it coming to you. Yapping all the time about that watch."

"You can stow that watch," she said, "I guess you know where."

"Aw, cut it out!" he cried. "For Christ sake, try to be a lady, will you?"

But he sounded extinguished. There was nothing but self-pity in his voice. He got himself another cigarette from his pack. He lit it, but he didn't offer one to Edna. Terhune could imagine him sitting despondently, smoking with jerky gestures, his eyes not quite focusing. And Edna he saw with her hand held against her cheek, or perhaps leaving it exposed to redden slowly under Gus's shifting glances, looking at him all the while with her unblinking eyes.

Then the radio went on again. The dial jerked back
and forth, bringing out queer wedges of split sound,
the crooner, the Brahms symphony, the band, back to
the piano.

"What you trying to get?" Edna asked.

"News," Gus answered.

"Well, it isn't nine yet."

He kept turning the dial.

"What was the present?" Edna asked.

She sounded quite neutral again, neither amiable
nor angry, back in her familiar habits. They were making their hoarse, night sounds, their ejaculations of
birds calling across the dark.

"What present?" he asked, absently.

"That one you said."

"Oh, that." The radio gave a sudden bleat. He
turned it down. "It was Gloria's coat."

"What coat?"

"Her beaver coat. She's through with it. She's got a
new one. She said she'd give you the beaver."

"Well, I don't want it."

"All right. So you don't want it. You want to keep
on looking like a crumb. Go ahead. Only, don't expect
me to take you anywheres."

"You don't anyway."

"Is that fair? Right now, when I came in, I had it all
set to take you out for a beer and hamburger. When'd
you have your dinner?"

"Six o'clock."

"What'd you have?"

"Beer and hamburger."

Gus tittered. "We gotta vary your diet. Someday I'll buy you a steak, only just now I got no time."

"Gee, that's tough," Edna said, sarcastically.

"I wonder if my watch is slow," he said. "Say, here's the time signal."

A voice said, "Nine o'clock Eastern Standard Time," and another voice began to sing a commercial.

"What's eating you?" Edna asked.

"What's eating me? Nothing's eating me."

"Something's eating you. What is it?"

"Nothing's eating me."

"You've got the jitters. Tell me, what's the matter?"

"Listen, flannel mouth, the day I tell *you* anything—"

"You might as well," she said, "I know something's happened. What is it?"

"Say, oblige me! Just keep your trap shut, will you? I got plenty on my mind without you."

"What am *I* doing?"

"You're trying to get me in bad with Mort, that's what you're doing. And just at a time when he ain't feeling so good anyway."

Edna said, "Well, I knew when he phoned something was wrong. Now I can tell by the way you act. But how'd *you* find out? Who told you? You were with Gloria all afternoon."

"Have I said anything? Have I?"

"Did Louie tell you?"

Gus didn't answer.

"Then Louie must of found out something after I was there. Because he didn't know."

"That's right, Sherlock. Go right ahead. Pretty soon you'll hit something."

"Did Louie say not to tell me?"

"Say—who'd ever mention your name!"

"Then why don't *you* tell me?"

But he kept silent and she didn't press him. She could endure a silence but she knew that in his present state Gus couldn't take it long. A voice said, "Recommendation for a Coal Authority is announced by the International Bank for Reconstruction and Development . . ."

Gus said abruptly, "It's damned funny Mort would tell me to come here."

"He didn't. *I* told you."

"That's right. You did. Why didn't you just wait for me at Louie's?"

"I don't like Louie's."

"How long were you there?"

"Just a couple minutes."

"Then *you* didn't hear anything?"

"No. What would I hear?"

"I don't know," he said. His voice was high and sharp. "Louie didn't know. But something must of went wrong at the docks."

"Yeah? What?"

He began to talk excitedly and quickly. "That damn fool. He always has to be checking up on everyone. He's always got no confidence in anyone."

"What damn fool?"

"I'm telling you—Mort. He takes a truck down to Pier 92 this afternoon, just to see how they're making

out. I says to him, I says, 'Mort, leave good enough
alone; ain't everything going O.K.?' And he says, 'Yeah,
maybe you're right. I think I'll just get in a little hand-
ball at Casey's,' he says, 'and maybe have a massage. I
gained five pounds last month.' But after I left him he
must of went."

"But what happened?"

"I don't know what happened. All I know is Louie
tells me that Bill tells him he spots a G-man with the
longshoremen down at 92, and the minute Mort drives
up Bill gives him the high sign and Mort gets it all right
and drives off. But this guy climbs in a car and tails
him. And now I don't know *what* happened. And
neither does anyone else, because Mort ain't been seen
since."

"He phoned me at seven," Edna said.

"Where from?"

"He didn't say."

Gus said, "Well, maybe there was nothing to it." He
was sorry he had spoken, but he obviously wanted to
share it with Edna. He even wanted to frighten Edna.
Terhune guessed that he didn't have much luck with
that as a rule.

The radio voice said, "A saving of four billion eight
hundred thousand dollars to wage and salary earners
and their employers was practically assured . . ." The
voice seemed quite natural, as though the announcer,
invisible as Terhune himself, had decided to join the
group in the attic and take his part in what went on.

Edna was making small movements and Terhune
couldn't guess what they were till Gus cried irritably,

"For Christ sake leave it alone, will you? A dirty rag won't help. Try washing it some time." Evidently she was making up her face. She finished deliberately and put whatever she had used away.

"Mort oughtn't to have gone," she said finally. "Too many people know his face. Specially—"

"Listen!" Gus cried.

The voice said, "The body of a man found riddled with bullets in a car at the foot of a dead-end lane in Astoria was identified as that of an F.B.I. agent. Police are looking for a man driving a truck that left Pier 92 this afternoon. He is believed to be head of a ring operating on the waterfront. The weather for New York and vicinity—" The radio snapped off.

There was a long silence.

Edna said, "Gee!"

Then Gus said, "Well, it's the business."

Then neither of them spoke.

They seemed to be considering, each in his own way, what they had heard. Terhune could not tell in their silence which was more affected and whether they were frightened or not, but he knew that Gus twitched and Edna sat quietly. The smell of Gus's cigarette began to make the air heavy.

"What do you do now?" Edna asked.

"I don't know." Gus's voice was querulous with complaint. "That's what Mort'll tell us. But if it's Jersey— hell, I hate Jersey in the spring."

"Yeah. Gloria won't be there," Edna said coldly. "But what about the stuff here? Scrap it?"

"Sure. It's too hot to move. If they could put the

finger on him like that . . . Fact is, more I think of it, *we* oughtn't to be here."

"Yeah, that's right. Where'll you go?"

"Casey's. Mort, sure as hell, is sitting in Casey's right now."

"And after that?"

"After that maybe you won't see me for a while. But I'm not saying so. You go home and keep your trap shut, and whatever you do, don't hang around—like at Louie's—asking questions. And don't try to get in touch."

"I wish I could go with you."

"Say, are you nuts? Use your brain. Stay home and *don't talk*. Now just remember what I said, will you? Because if you don't, the Department of Sanitation is liable to fish you out of a drain some morning—in pieces."

"O.K.," Edna said. Her voice, still low, showed relief. "O.K.," she repeated more briskly, and then both chairs scraped back. They stood up. "Let's go."

It's over, Terhune thought. In one moment they'll be gone. A whole flutter of new things seemed to wait just outside his attention. But let them get away first. Already he could feel relief from the heaviness, the pressure of their human presences.

They started toward the trapdoor and Gus suddenly stopped. "Say," he said, "better get some of your stuff. What's the use of leaving everything? This may be your last chance."

It was in Edna's silence that Terhune realized what

this meant. Edna's "stuff" was the nylons, and they were just over his head.

It was the end, after all. He felt a violent shock, curiosity perhaps, stronger but sudden and piercing as the pain in his leg. *What's it like to die?* In a little while I'll know.

Gus started to walk back to the cases. He took five or six steps and kicked a case. "They're all jammed up," he said.

Terhune heard a few staggering steps and a thud as Edna fell back in her chair. "Oh, Gus! Come here!"

"What's the matter?" Gus's voice was shrill. He wheeled around. "Don't *do* that! I feel nervous already. What's the matter?"

"I'm sick."

"*You're* sick!" He went back to her with his lurching step. "Say, what is this? Jeez, you *look* sick." He shook her. "What's the matter?"

"My head," she said. "It feels awful. Maybe you hit me too hard."

Gus shook her again. "It's something you ate," he said. "Snap out of it, will you? Listen, this ain't a time to be sick."

"I want to get home," she wailed. Then her voice came muffled, as though she had put her face in her arms. "You take me home, Gus."

"Why, you're scared!" he exclaimed. "Jeez, you're just plain scared. I never thought I'd see it."

"Well, I'm sick."

"O.K., O.K., you're sick. Well, get going. The hell with this stuff anyway. What's a few nylons? Come on."

He helped her to her feet. "Think you can walk?"
"If you hold onto me."

They stood a moment, and while they didn't speak
Terhune felt a doubt in Gus's mind. Perhaps it came
from a change of expression in Edna, a look that meant
she was putting something over on him, to make him
ashamed of hitting her, or just to get him away for some
reason he couldn't guess. His doubt burned in him like
a hot wire. Then the pleasure he felt in her apparent
fear made him believe in that. His doubt went out.
They began to move toward the door.

"I'll find a taxi," he said.

"You going with me?"

"Like hell. I gotta get to Casey's. Jeez, I forgot the
light."

He ran back and turned it off. The sudden dark was
pierced by the white ray.

Terhune heard them shuffling at the head of the
trapdoor.

"You go first."

"No, you go."

Edna went first.

Gus said, "O.K.?" and her voice came from below,
"O.K." Then he followed her. He closed the trapdoor
behind him, and when that was closed there was no
more sound.

CHAPTER VI

AND that was all there was to it. He was alone. Exactly as before. Alone in the attic. What had happened here seemed a compressed lifetime of many emotions, false and true, of errors, misuses of intelligence and will, even flashes of revelation—all over now as abruptly as though death had indeed ended them, and once over, diminishing, shrinking into a few hours of the night. He looked around the attic, which now held only obstacles of an order easily dealt with, nothing but inorganic matter in fact, matter ruled by laws that had nothing to do with his own, neither hostile to him nor benevolent. He took a deep breath of relief.

But first, he thought, I must wait fifteen minutes at least to make quite sure they have disappeared. I have to make sure just in case I didn't dream the whole thing after all, that Gus doesn't come back for something, that they don't meet Mort on the way out and all come back. But he thought neither of these would happen. Mort, supposing he existed in the flesh, couldn't possibly risk it. Gus had come because of Edna's message; it was all her idea, and as soon as his dim wits grasped the situation he had left. Mort at this moment was sitting in the back room at Casey's, for if the stuff here was hot Mort himself was hotter. On second thought, he more probably was already on his way to a hideout in Jersey. No, Mort, old boy, he thought, you and I are not intended to meet. That's obvious, so I don't need to worry about you. And you can exist or not exist and be damned to you.

And when I get out of here—in about ten or fifteen minutes, he thought—it will be hard to decide whether or not even Edna existed. Even now I can't remember what she looked like, I can't remember what she said, I can't remember why she did what she did for me, or what I thought I saw in her at that last moment. All I can remember is her voice, which is now only an echo of an echo of my own.

But can hours that seemed to hold so much evaporate like this? Can I actually anticipate in myself what time will slowly do? Then with Edna it will be the same. She will go back to being the miniature gangster's moll, the little virgin of the wisecracks, safe in ignorance, only momentarily troubled, unseeing, except as now and then she sees a joke. And I'll be one of the jokes, slightly acid but still funny, the joke she played on Mort once, because he wouldn't take her to Atlantic City, where champagne flows and gladiolas bloom in florists' baskets. An echo and a joke. That's what we've become.

Well, he thought, the fifteen minutes are up. So now it's time to put the end to it. I must go to work, step by step, methodically, patiently, unemotionally, and with respect for the nature of the obstacles: wooden floors, boxes, ladders, stairs. And the first step is to feel stronger. After that I will push the boxes aside, crawl across the floor, and open the trapdoor, let myself down the ladder, crawl along the upper hall, somehow get down the stairs. Do this once over and reach finally the front door. Why, nothing can go wrong, he thought. This is all purely physical and experiential. There is nothing metaphysical about it, unless you pretend that that first step of feeling stronger involves something of the first principles of being.

His leg, almost forgotten in the tension of remaining hidden, began to send out streamers of pain. And yet this had its usefulness. It was a constant reminder of at least one reality, his own body. It would remind him not to let himself drift again toward dreams of one sort or another, for that had so far proven to be only a drifting toward death. It had for a time apparently led him into the role of victim. There is the rational and the irrational resolve, and the mind is capable of undertaking opposites at the same time. Everyone knows how in the midst of a determination to succeed, some part of us is also preparing to fail, how in the midst of despair we already begin to hope. So if he had allowed himself to become the victim it was also at the same time the victim who was to escape.

And now that returning strength, which was the first stage, suddenly lifted him up. He sat up again and putting his arms around the nearest case pushed it out of the way. It moved slowly and heavily. Edna, he thought with surprise, had managed the same thing with a few tugs. But Edna was young and well and had not broken an ankle. He pushed another. Still another. The way was open, but he couldn't do any more for the moment. Already he had to rest again. He longed for a swallow of whisky.

Before crawling out of this penned-in space he might, he told himself, find his lighter. When he fell it must have been thrown some distance from him. While he rested he felt along the floor. He touched a few scattered envelopes of nylons but the lighter was not here. It must have lodged in a crack, or between boxes. The useless search began to irritate him. Obviously the damn thing lay there waiting to be found. Or did it? Was it hiding? Was it against him? His contest with the inanimate already seemed less simple.

He began to push himself slowly over the floor. The pain in his leg grew with each movement. He was physically weaker than he had thought himself to be, so much so that he did not dare to foresee how he was going to get himself down the ladder and the stairs but only how he would reach the trapdoor.

It was a long journey across the floor. He could see nothing in the blackness but he had an ant's feeling of the room and perhaps it was also an ant's sense of the hostility of things that he felt as he crawled.

A sudden heavy patter sounded all through the darkness. It was rain beating on the roof, lashing at the closed windows. Its subdued roar filled the attic and sent arrows of pain and expectancy through him. He stopped to listen. What does *that* mean, he thought, is there to be a change? What's it a sign of? It was a sign

of nothing except that the clouds had finally broken
and the city was being drenched. The gutters outside
were running water and people were standing under
awnings, calling and whistling for taxis. Overhead, even
through the rain, he heard a plane thunder by. Perhaps
the first lightning of spring flashed around it, for he
heard through the noise a sharper clap, another kind
of thunder. How brilliantly the plane would shine, wet
and glistening, in a lightning flash, plunging again into
stormy darkness toward some distant landing field! All
the world outside, planes, lightning, streaming water,
shrill taxi whistles—all the noise and movement—were
one unsubstantial cloud. Only this attic, where the smell
of dust mysteriously stirred, was real. He lay on the floor
until the rain's onslaught quieted. It settled into a subdued rustling, like leaves in a forest.

Then he started again toward the trapdoor. His
fingers, stretched ahead of him, touched the unmistakable mark on the floor. He leaned over to feel the
outline and through the noise of rain he heard someone
walking on the floor below.

That would be Edna.

Edna, who had become, so he believed, only the echo
of a voice he might sometimes remember, at once took
shape again. The girl in the slacks, with silvery hair, and
the round, pale face, whose expressions changed from
the stolid to the humorous, to that suddenly warm,
piercing look when she had sprung up to hide him, and
finally the resolute, secret smile. Edna was coming back.
He could hear her steps. Edna—no echo but a creature
full of the movements and eccentricities of the living.

Her steps came slowly, as though she moved confusedly in the dark, and he wondered if she'd lost her torch, or for some reason given it to Gus. Just at the foot of the ladder, he heard a match struck, and a low exclamation. It didn't sound like a woman's voice, but Edna's voice often didn't. The steps moved away a bit and stopped. Another match.

It wasn't Edna. This person didn't know the place, and the steps when they came back were not the tap, tapping of her high heels. They were shuffling, heavy, and hesitant.

He waited there and whoever it was waited below.

But this time he wasn't going to be caught like a trapped rabbit. A fury of impatience to act for once, not to think but to act, seized him. He moved himself carefully to the side of the crack. He heard the chain being fumbled with and a series of low mutterings, and suddenly he thought, Gus, and Gus is drunk; he has come back for the nylons, or for something, but he's drunk. Or maybe it's even Mort. Perhaps he should try to hide again. No, it was too late for that, and besides, he was through with hiding. The ladder thumped down and someone was coming up. There was a fumbling at the trapdoor, another low exclamation, and the door pushed upward.

He could see nothing, but he felt cooler air from below and a bad smell came with it.

A voice near him whispered urgently, "Hey!" then a match struck over his head and instantly it fell from the hand that held it to the floor, giving him a flash of trouser legs and wet, old shoes. He caught at an ankle and jerked it forward. The man fell half across his body, half down the open trapdoor, giving a whimpering sound of fear. The darkness broke into radiating pain and light and he let the man claw at him and scramble back.

He felt him lean over him to see if he was breathing. Then he clutched at him again, feeling for his throat. But the man pushed him easily off and rolled aside. He stumbled across the room, bumped heavily into the table, and said, "Hell!" He was sobbing with fright and indignation. He reached the light and turned it on.

The room was chalky white again and the old man stood in the middle of it. "You god-damned ape!" he cried.

Terhune sat up and stared at him, and the old man stared back, making distracted, indignant sounds, putting his clothes to rights, smoothing his hair. Then he collapsed suddenly in one of the chairs, breathing with his mouth open like a fish out of water.

"You pretty near killed me," he gasped.

Terhune began to laugh. His laughter shook him from head to foot. "It's Pop," he said. "Hello, Pop. I'm sorry."

"You better be," Pop said, "you better be!"

Terhune went on laughing. But Pop looked at him angrily. "Watch it," he said, "watch it now."

Terhune stopped. He saw the difference in their positions and he felt shame for his weak laughter and for the whole futile, absurd attack. He straightened his own clothes. "I thought you were someone else," he said.

"Fat chance you'd have had with someone else!"

Terhune said again, "Well, I'm sorry." The shame of his behavior was heavy on him, and the power of the old man to criticize and reprove openly made it heavier. He said, "Could you help me to a chair? I'm tired of being on the floor."

Pop looked at him dubiously. "Planning any more jiujitsu?" he asked.

"With you? Certainly not. Anyway, I've got a broken ankle. I can't really do anything, as you've already seen."

"O.K."

He came over to Terhune and helped him lift himself. Leaning heavily on the old man Terhune hopped on one foot and made the distance to the nearest chair. He sat down and Pop pushed up another chair and laid his leg straight along it. The pain was almost more than he could bear but at least he was upright like a man at last. Even the room looked different, smaller and emptier. He got his cigarette case out and took a cigarette. By concentrating on every movement he managed to light it and take a puff or two.

"Well," he said breathlessly, "so *you're* here."

"Yes, I'm here."

"What does that mean? Did you just come in to sleep? You certainly picked the wrong place."

He held out his case to Pop and the old man took a cigarette with none of his former joking servility. He lighted it with one of his own matches.

"It looks like you picked the wrong place yourself," he said gravely.

"That's true. And you warned me, didn't you? Did you know about it?"

"Oh, a little."

Terhune smoked for a minute. By leaning half against the table he could sit up, but not for long. This dizzy balance of being at man's height again could not, he felt, really last.

"Then what are you doing here?" he asked.

He knew from the way the old man looked at him that he was surprised by the physical change in him, that even his voice must be sounding very weak. And he didn't like to think of what must be going through the fellow's head.

"Well," Pop said, "I guess you know why I'm here."

"No, I don't. Tell me."

"Edna sent me."

"Edna?"

"Sure, Edna."

But who else could have sent him? Since Edna had been the only living creature who knew he was here.

"Tell me about it."

"Not tonight. You don't look so good. You better try to get some sleep."

"Sleep? You're crazy. I can't possibly sleep. I've got to get out of here."

"Well, you can't get out tonight."

"Why not?"

"Because Edna's got to figure it out, and she hasn't had time. What did you think, that she sent me back here to put in some phone calls for you? To have a lot of ambulances and police wagons out in the street? Hell! We've got to get you somewhere where you can be picked up."

"Where?"

"I don't know yet. It's up to Edna. I told you she hasn't had time to figure it out."

"But I can't stay here!"

He felt he was talking so faintly that the old man wouldn't hear him. He felt as he had when he began to take gas at the dentist's. He felt the little crepitations in himself and the clinging to a single theme, and the fogginess all around.

But the old man heard him and answered him. "You can stay here, all right," he said.

"Mort may come."

"Mort's busy. He won't come."

"Or Gus?"

"He's busy, too. Besides, he's hopped to the ears by now. Don't you worry about them. Get your rest."

"My rest—!"

"Yes. Edna says you'll be O.K. for tonight."

"What if she's wrong?"

"Then we're all up the creek!"

Terhune reached in his pocket and got out his sleeping pills. He looked from them to the cigarette in his other hand. But he couldn't finish the cigarette. He laboriously ground it out on the table. Then he shook out four pills. He put them in his mouth, made saliva around them, and swallowed them. He leaned sideways against the table, looking at Pop, who swam toward him and back again, still like a fish seen through an aquarium wall.

"It's awfully hot in here, isn't it?" Terhune said.

"It's kind of close."

His head drooped sidewise on his arm. He felt he must say something that would hold the situation unresolved. He was not consenting to this; it must be left open to change.

He said hazily, "I'll be with you in just a minute."

That wasn't what he'd meant but it didn't matter.

He went to sleep.

CHAPTER VII

H E HAD an impression that someone moved close
to him, that hands touched him, then that someone went out and came in again, and it was
later that the sunlight shone in his eyes. He opened
them straight into a long, dusty beam. A man was staring
at him from the shadow, waiting to tell him that he had
overslept. He felt, through the mustiness and luxury
of a drugged sleep, the pain of his broken bone and he
tried to push himself backward into sleep. But it was
no use; sleep drained away, leaving him high and dry.

There was a pungent, clean smell close to his nose.
He lifted his head and saw on the table a little pan of
coffee, bubbling on a sterno. Beside it were two rolls in
a split paper bag. There was an opened can of coffee,
an unopened can of beans, two paper cups, and a quart-
size milk bottle half full of water. Across the table, just
under the beam of sunlight that came from one of the
high windows where the blanket had been tied back
once more, was the old man. He was sitting in his shirt
sleeves in a tattered vest, his overcoat behind him. When
he saw Terhune was awake he leaned forward into the

sunlight and blew out the flame of the sterno. The top
of his head was bald and there were black spots on it like
flyspecks.

"You sure can sleep," he said. He poured coffee into
one of the cups and pushed it across the table. He
pointed at a roll. "Go ahead. I've had mine."

"Thanks," Terhune said. He slopped the coffee
around a bit to cool it and then drank it all.

"Have some more?"

"Please."

The old man filled the cup again. Terhune drank
more coffee. He ate the roll. Then the old man reached
in his overcoat pocket and brought out another package.
He opened it with a satisfied expression. "I think of
everything," he said. It contained a razor and a tube of
cream, some blades. "I thought you'd want to shave."

He had not brought a mirror and he told Terhune
there was no water but that in the milk bottle they had
given him at the drugstore, and he intended to save that
for coffee. Terhune managed to shave without it, not a
good job but better than none. Pop helped him with his
makeshift arrangements. In the morning light Terhune
felt keenly the indignities of physical disability but the
old man didn't seem to notice. Indignity of this kind
was an old story to him.

When Terhune lit a cigarette he took a pipe from his
pocket, a brand new one, and a shining, oiled silk pouch.
He looked up slyly as he filled the pipe, then struck a
match and settled back in his chair to enjoy it.

"How do you feel now?" he asked.

"Rotten," Terhune said.

"Wait till the coffee gets to working. Want another cup?"

"No, thanks."

"An accident like yours," Pop told him, "upsets the stomach. It upsets the whole nervous system. That's why I didn't fix the beans for you. Later on you'll be hungry. I guess beans aren't the best thing at that but it's Sunday. I had to go to a delicatessen and a drug store. This is the best I could get."

"I owe you for all this," Terhune said.

Pop smiled. "Oh, no you don't. I took some of your money."

"Good," Terhune said. "That's fine." Though he wished to sound hearty it came out false. It was Pop who had all the air of being at ease in the midst of circumstances he thoroughly understood.

After a few puffs Terhune said, "You say Edna asked you to come here."

"That's right."

"I'd like to know a little more about it. I'd like to ask you a few questions."

"Go ahead."

"To tell the truth, I don't know where to begin. But before I ask you anything maybe I'd better make one thing clear. I came to this place with no knowledge of what was in it—you didn't tell me, by the way. I was quite ignorant, and in a sense I expect to remain so. I mean that after what Edna has done for me I have no intention of making any move that will get her into trouble. You believe that, I hope. I tell you because I assume you're a friend of hers."

Pop went on smoking. Like Edna he seemed to see something comic ahead, but Terhune felt his joke would be of an entirely different order.

"I looked at your passport," he said.

"Oh, you looked at that."

"Sure, I looked at everything. I guess it's about like you say."

"Then we understand that."

"Oh, sure. We understand that you mean no harm to Edna. Well, she believes it already; so I will, too, until I see something that makes me change my mind."

He had an almost natty air of self-assurance, sitting there deciding what he would or would not believe. "You're lucky," he said, "you're sure lucky it was Edna you ran into. She's just a kid. You could easily talk her into anything, a fellow like you, all this air of the great world and so on, and not bad looking either." He squinted up his eyes at him. "And maybe with some of the good old moxie, too. Well, anyway, whatever you said to her, it worked. But the gang here—that would have been different, very different."

"Tell me about the gang," Terhune said. He felt an acute dislike for the old man but it wasn't possible to give way to it. "Tell me, is it a big racket or small-time stuff?"

The old man stroked his pipe with mottled fingers, the gesture, Terhune thought, of some nice old guy full of homely philosophy. "Depends on what you mean by small time," he said. "Everything's relative. They're no Costellos or Lucianos, or even Adonises or Phil Kastens or such. The big time is in the gambling rackets, slot machines, and so on, the dope or the vice rackets. No, there's no one here owns any expensive New York real estate or swanky night clubs. You can't flatter yourself that you've fallen into the hands of the big time. They're a pretty second-rate bunch of crooks. There's only one of them with any class at all, and that's Mort." When he spoke the name his voice bristled with contempt and irritation.

"Edna spoke of Mort," Terhune said. "She told me Mort was the big shot. And she told me he was tough. But what else is he? Is he intelligent?"

"Intelligent!" Pop exclaimed. "What a question! Why, he hasn't the intelligence to understand the most elementary proposition. He couldn't make an accurate calculation of the simplest sort, say even relating to probability and chance, his material so to speak. But of course a fellow can get along for quite a while on much less than he needs, especially if the people he deals with all have less, too, and Mort's got a sort of bounce that's carried him just this far. In fact, I wouldn't be surprised if it hadn't carried him right up to the hot seat!" The old man cackled with pleasure. "The hot seat," he repeated, "yes, sir."

Terhune had no impression that his glee was because of seeing a criminal on the way to justice, rather that he had an intense, personal animosity for Mort.

"Still, he's tough?" he asked.

"Oh, he's tough. All except the center of his head. The center of his head is soup. Not good, rich soup, either, but the kind that's been made in ten minutes out of cabbage leaves and a chicken wing. It must be kind of funny, when you come to think of it, to have all that weight of muscle and bone, all that sort of projection—I suppose it really is—and nothing to direct it but a watery mass. Just the same," he said, his malicious smile directed at Terhune now, "*you* couldn't stop him."

"But where does his class come in, and what do you mean by 'class'?"

"Why, I mean style, just what a woman means by style. If short skirts are the rage, then she wears a short skirt in a certain way. She *believes* in a short skirt, and she wears it like she believed in it. In Mort's world they believe in being very, very tough. To be soft is like wearing a long skirt when short skirts are in. And Mort believes in his toughness. It's natural to him to believe. It isn't necessarily so with most of them. Just as only a few women really believe in their style. It's not enough for a man to be dumb, to be tough. He's got to have will enough to keep from getting scared. Most of them scare easily, they're scared half the time. Not Mort. He's got a savage, natural will and he believes in it. He always believes in his will, if you know what I mean. It's so natural to him he can even be kind of careless and easy at times, kind of slushy at times."

"What's his career been? Nothing but the rackets?"

"Nothing that I know of. He began by being the protege of a fellow called Big Bill Dwyer. Ever hear of him?"

"I think so. I don't quite place him."

"He had the biggest rum-running ring in the history of prohibition. Mort was a longshoreman when Big Bill picked him up. And pretty soon he was one of the defendants in that big '27 rum-running case. You remember that?"

"Vaguely."

"Mort was about nineteen then. He was sent to Atlanta. I don't really know what all has happened to him since. But usually a man like him dies young. Mort's over forty."

"But still in the small time."

"Oh, not *too* small. He's well fixed. He just hasn't got enough brains. He's got as far as he's going."

"What's the answer to his being able to hang on to this place? They must be going to tear it down in a day or so. But the electricity is still on. All his stuff is here. People come and go."

The old man said, "Now I wouldn't be able to tell you that, but it oughtn't to be too hard to guess. You might remember that if the racket is big enough it can tell the Tammany politicians where to get off, it can appoint a Justice of the State Supreme Court. You think a little electric current couldn't be arranged, or a little absent-mindedness when someone goes up the street? It would make you sick if you had any interest in society. But then I haven't. And to tell the truth, I haven't much interest in Mort either."

His shining eyes entirely belied his last words. But Terhune didn't go on. He thought, neither have I, at least not now that I know I won't have to see him. He's just a name to me like the rest of them: Adonis, Luciano, Costello—Italianate, almost Shakespearean names. Even Big Bill Dwyer has a faintly Merrie England ring. And "Mort" means death, he thought, though he probably doesn't know that. A name for a bull, for a bull-like man. Perhaps he is that. Not just a pathetically amateurish wrongdoer, but a man who has in him the ultimate fierce maggot of evil, blind to all but itself, never denying itself. That would really be what Pop meant by "class." Well, whether he has it or hasn't it, I'll never know.

The old man fussily relighted his pipe, and Terhune, looking around the attic, saw it was more as he remembered it by day than by night. This was because, except for the long beam, the place was in shadow and the beam was simply the one he had always seen on sunny days, cut into panes in just the same way as it fell on the floor, swarming with the same dust motes like little worlds in a system. It brought back an association of sounds and he thought he heard the remote, sad tinkle of Madame Golden's piano, playing not boogie-woogie but faded, melancholy songs—*At Eventide,* and Tosti's *Good-bye.*

And even Pop, he thought, does not seem entirely out of place here. He might be a broken down old actor. He has the vanity of one. And at the moment he is certainly half playacting. He is acting the superior man, which he thinks he is, talking to an inferior, to one who can somewhat understand him. He enjoys this role so much that he is holding his latent craziness in check for as long as he can. He is being dignified. Terhune wondered how long he could keep it up. He felt sure that Pop's breakdown, if it ever came, would be, to say the least, unseemly.

He said, "You must have run into Edna last night shortly after she left here. How did that happen?"

"Why," Pop said, "I was just coming along the avenue

when I saw Edna sitting on a fireplug. 'What's the matter, honey?' I ask her, and she says, 'Listen, Pop, I've just taken an awful chance on someone.' Then she begins to tell me all about you being up here and what she's done. She tells me the whole thing, and pretty soon I recollect how I met you outside here and I tell her about it. Then I say, 'Look out, Edna. That guy's a phony if I ever saw one. He's liable to pull a fast one.' But she says very snappily, 'Never mind that,' and before we get a chance to argue she says, 'Now listen what I want you to do. You go back up there and keep an eye on him, don't let him out of your sight, and don't let him make a move. And I'll be around pretty soon, after I've figured out what to do.' So then she gives me the key and just then Gus comes up with a taxi."

"He didn't see her give you the key?"

"No, Gus didn't see. He was thinking of something else. He was hopped up, too. Gus is sick. He's got T.B. in a bone somewhere. That's why he walks the way he does, like a dancer. That stretch in Leavenworth didn't help. Maybe he got it there, or in the army. Anyway, he keeps himself hopped up."

"He was in Leavenworth?"

"Yes. He was in the occupation army and he got into some trouble, black market probably, over in Berlin, Germany. They sent him to Leavenworth."

"And you haven't heard from Edna since last night?"

"No, but I will. I only went out long enough to buy some food and tobacco, and if she'd come while I was gone she'd have left a note or waited, or woke you up, or something. So I guess there are reasons why she hasn't come yet. But she will."

"You think she's prepared to get me out, or let me get myself out, if it can be done so it won't cause any trouble to the gang?"

"That's right. But it turns out it's kind of complicated. There's a business about Mort. Do you know about that?" He looked intently at Terhune.

"Why, no," Terhune said. The question had startled him because he realized for the first time just what his knowing about Mort should have meant to Edna. It should have made him even more of a liability to her. She must have been thinking, when Gus talked and the news came over the radio: why, *he's* listening to it all! He had said himself that there was a difference between stealing whisky and a murder rap. Now the murder had actually happened and he knew it. But she hadn't given him away, even when it would have been easiest, just by letting Gus stumble over him on his way to the nylons. After all, she needn't necessarily have known a man was there. A little shriek of female surprise would have settled that. Instead she had pretended to be sick and had gone out and told Pop to look after him.

The mind of man, he thought, is pretty well understood, better, perhaps, than the pancreas or the liver. The mind has certain definite, ascertainable functions, one of them being to observe, another to deduce. In an act of faith the mind rejects its own powers. That can only be because the need for faith is stronger than the mind, and that the mind itself accepts its limits. But that need for faith implies still another instrument, as yet in embryo and perhaps never to be realized. But if it were realized it would be to the mind what the telescope of Palomar is to the telescope of Galileo.

"The thing about Mort," Pop said with relish, "is that he's in what you might call trouble."

"Is he?" Terhune said. "How did you find it out? Did Edna tell you?"

"Not exactly. She just slipped in a word that she was worried about him, and that it wasn't a good time to be taking chances. But the fact is, I knew a whole lot about it already."

"You did?"

"No one actually came out and said it, but I did hear *something*. I pick up lots. People are accustomed to see-ing me around. They don't always pay any attention, they just say, 'It's that old bum; he's nuts anyhow.' They say things in front of me they wouldn't say in front of others." He spoke with a gleam of pride as though it were a personal triumph of his to be able to pass as senile, or even invisible, when he wished. "I went into Louie's last night (once in a while I get a free drink there) and I sensed an atmosphere. Matter of fact, I heard something over the radio there, and then there was lots of coming and going. Two or three plainclothes men wandered in to look the crowd over. And finally when Edna told me she was worried about Mort, I put two and two together. I know what Mort's trouble is, all right."

Terhune thought: and the most curious part is that I never even worried about Edna, I never thought until now that my knowing about Mort would change her.

Her faith in me seems to have made me also irrational, though I am much more difficult and resistant than she and, as she said of Gus, no pushover. Still, I never doubted her at any time.

"Is it wise for you to know about Mort?" he asked. "I shouldn't think he'd feel very safe, knowing you had such a thing on him."

"Why, listen," Pop said, "you've got no idea what I carry around in my head." He tapped his forehead and his smile showed his broken teeth. "I know enough secrets to write a book. I know enough about human nature to make a weak-headed man blow his brains out. I know enough," he said, his smile turning malicious again, "to be pretty certain what's going to happen to Edna, too, taking all this trouble over you."

Terhune said, "I promised I would do nothing that could bring any harm to her."

"That's right, and you needn't be so god-damned holy about it. I don't mean you'll run to the cops. You promised, and you might keep your promise out of some funny notion that would be about the same as liking to wear a clean shirt. That would be *your* idea of style. But of course, while she don't realize it yet, that's not Edna's idea—the clean shirt one I mean. That's not what she meant when she said she'd taken an awful chance. She's got an idea she don't know herself yet. Why, you ought to have heard the way she described you to me! I said, 'What's he like, Edna, what sort of a fellow is he?' and she said, "Oh, he's not like anyone.' I could tell right then by her face as she said it. When I said I thought you were a phony—and I do, too, in a way—and was liable to pull a fast one, she was mad. But it still wasn't the cops she was thinking of."

"What are you trying to say?" Terhune said angrily. "Are you actually pretending that I made love to Edna?"

"Oh, no," Pop said, "oh, no, indeed! You wouldn't have to do that. You wouldn't have to go near that far. But that's just the trouble, see?"

"No, I don't," Terhune said. "What I see is that Edna is practically a child, certainly to me, at any rate."

"Yeah?" Pop said derisively. "Nice alibi for you, isn't it? Well, she's not a child. She's an ignorant, uneducated little tyke, but she's got some brains and she's sure seen some funny kinds of people, and, come to think of it, she may not be quite as ignorant and uneducated in some ways as you. You look to me like you've lived a fairly sheltered life, and anyone who has lived a sheltered life hasn't only been protected but he's known how to protect himself. You've seen these women that keep an innocent eye till the day they die, and everyone they know has entered into a conspiracy to protect them? Don't kid yourself! Their ignorance is made of steel. Well, I don't say you've gone that far, and I don't say you don't know a thing or two, but I do say you've been able to protect yourself. Edna can't protect herself at all."

Terhune thought: he's right. Edna in the end can't protect herself. I'm the one who can protect myself. Last night I was ready to forget Edna, to reduce her to something absurd and lifeless that I could put out of my mind. He thought of her with horror, as of a creature he had already betrayed. But the betrayal wasn't fixed and unchangeable, indeed it was only a shadow, a warning of what might become true.

The old man watched him with sardonic eyes that had in them sparks of calculation. "What did you say to her?" he sneered. "You sure must have handed her a line. What was it? Well, it don't matter. She fell for it. But just remember she's already fallen for Mort's line, and she'll fall for the next one comes along. People," he exclaimed, clenching his pipe hard in his teeth, "they make me sick! They've been living together for a long time, two people, ten, a hundred million—society! There's only one thing you can count on about society— it don't *work*."

Terhune didn't want to talk about Edna with the old man. He made an effort to appear interested in this digression. "Yes," he said, "society. That's right."

"Man is a social animal," Pop said, "but also an anti-social animal. Right?"

"Right."

"*Why*, for Christ's sake? Why don't we leave him alone? Let him fight it out by himself. Let either part of him win. One will, anyway: I don't care which. I say," he cried, "there is no problem, there's been no problem for the last five hundred thousand years. Why? Because for the last five hundred thousand years men have been obsolete."

Plainly he had forgotten Edna.

"You get along," Terhune said. "You don't bother with society. You're a happy man."

"Happy. There's a word for you! I won't even ask you what you mean by it. I have an idea it would make me

vomit. Well, damn you, I might be happy in my own way
at that. If they'd let me alone, if I could protect myself
like you do. Oh, yes, you want to be let alone, too. How
do I know? Why by your face when I talked about Edna.
And you manage. You've got dough and I haven't, and
you know how to keep people out of your hair. I try—
yes, I try. But they won't let me alone. They persecute
me." He ran his hands through his sparse hair and wild
tears stood in his eyes. Suddenly his tic broke out and
the tears were shaken violently from his lids. He put his
pipe carefully down and the spasm lasted a minute, end-
ing in lessening twitches. Then he got out his grimy
handkerchief and methodically wiped his face. He leaned
forward and said in an entirely different voice, calm and
confidential, "You know they've had me up in court
twice just in the last month. Know why?"

"Why?" Terhune asked.

"Well, the first time a fellow I know got stuck with a
lot of rotting tomatoes, so I borrowed a pushcart and
began to peddle them up East Broadway, and first thing
you know they pulled me in. Peddling without a license.
Two bucks. Then the second time I loiter—that's what
they say—I loiter—ten minutes maybe (I had a belly-
ache) in the gent's room at the Fourteenth Street subway station. Ten days. I'm entitled to notify my friends
and relatives free of charge, but it's still ten days. What
the hell? What am I supposed to do? In both cases I try
to explain to the judge. It's a very simple problem. I
have no money for a peddler's license and I do not care
to answer the call of nature on the sidewalk. But would
he listen? No. And why?"

"Why," Terhune said.

"Because he's sitting down and I'm standing up. Half of society is sitting down and the other half is standing up. You can't have a reasonable argument that way."

Then his face gave a few more twitches but perfunctorily, as though he were merely signing off. He gave an immense yawn. Then he said, "You play pinochle?"

"No."

He picked his pipe up again. "I wouldn't have believed there was a living man didn't play pinochle. The sheltered life! Well, . . ." He looked around the attic, searching for distraction. Then, bored and petulant, he turned on the radio. "What do you like?" he said. "Classic I'll bet. Well, me, I don't care much. I just like noise." He searched until he found a band that satisfied him. The sweet slow rhythms filled the room with drowsiness. In a moment his eyelids began to flutter. He fell into the light sleep of old age. Terhune watched him a moment, then he also leaned against the table and dozed.

CHAPTER VIII

THE bar of smoky sunlight shifted, slanted toward the left. The day passed. Pop heated the beans on the sterno and made more coffee. The two ate and drank. They smoked. But Edna did not come. Every now and then Terhune said, "You still think she'll come?" The old man said, "Yes." The repeated question finally made him cross. "Why don't you take it easy?" he exclaimed. "Most people would enjoy a day of rest."

Terhune was tempted to throw the radio at him. Actually he had been thinking all day that it wouldn't be impossible, now that he was more alert, to get the better of the old man, and he was almost ready to try. The pain in his ankle was no better and the anxiety of waiting grew worse as each hour passed. But his troubles meant nothing whatever to Pop. He liked to talk and he'd found a listener, even if he wasn't a willing one. He talked about himself and his concerns. When he was forced to speak of anyone else for very long, or answer a question that didn't interest him, it was always with a fretful undertone. He spent most of the day building up the picture of himself as he would like to appear, a mysterious genius, full of secrets. There were a great many more hints of that "problem" he was working on. He never said what it was, though he referred, not quite slightingly but still condescendingly, from time to time to the "static concepts of geometry" or "the science of mere causation," of "causal relations," as though, while highly thought of by certain minds, they could only fall into some lesser category of what occupied him. And Terhune, not really listening, wondered vaguely if his "problem" would not turn out to be some fantastic contrivance like a "time machine," and if his whole scientific smatterings had not perhaps come from a reading of adventure stories of the future world put out by certain magazines.

But while the old man pictured himself as a sort of mage, and in the closed space of the attic with this prisoner-listener his sense of power was growing always more grandiose and confused, he also at intervals broke down into anecdotes of his personal encounters, querulous if involving the law but malicious if he talked of the people he knew whom he had got the better of, or at least got wise to, even if by rare chance they got the better of him. Fortunately for Terhune he took many short naps. He leaned back with his mouth open, breathing quickly and shallowly, his eyes only half closed so that Terhune could see a line of white. A gummy moisture formed on his lids, sometimes his face would contract and he would make a whimpering sound as though something threatened him in a dream. Terhune, seeing him more defenseless, was always tempted to give him the knockout blow. But in the end an attack on an old man, especially asleep, remained beyond him. And then there was still Edna.

So he managed to doze himself at intervals, leaning sidewise on the table, his head on one arm. His pain made a constant nagging accompaniment and shortened his naps as the twinges became too severe. He dreamed of old pains, old illnesses, old toothaches, a broken collarbone. He even dreamed of an accident he'd had, when in the shock of his fall he lay on the floor for a moment, feeling what he thought was the pain of a shattered bone. That pain suddenly evaporated, for the bone was not broken at all, scarcely bruised even. This was when he fell from the trapeze, here in the attic. After he and Tommy Jefferson had seen the Morellis' act they decided to be acrobats. They practiced until finally they gave a circus one rainy afternoon, charging five pins admission. But at the moment of his most difficult trick something snapped in his mind and he lost control and took a bad fall. He heard Rosie scream, "Oh, he's killed!" and then instantaneously came the pain. When he got up and found himself uninjured he was furious with her and himself. To ease his humiliation, so that he would appear not to have been incompetent but only overly daring, and also to give some authenticity to that sensation he had had, he pretended to be hurt "internally." He sat doubled up on a stool for the rest of the show, sternly refusing advice and consolation.

The next day in school whenever he saw Rosie looking at him he winced and Rosie shook her head at him sympathetically, and he felt again that he actually had suffered and his hallucination seemed plausible. The trouble with Rosie was that everything that was false worked with her. She was like a proving ground where all shady experiments were successful, a little piece of raw, tempting, female material, inviting every possible dupery and deception, every tyranny. Rosie offered, within these limits, the completest satisfactions.

With her still in his unconscious mind he dreamed then about the birthday party. The Connors gave it for Rosie and the children all had to bring presents. The neighborhood broke out into a perfect rash of subservience to the Connors. Even Aunt Minerva, who was not generous, gave him a dollar and told him to go to the store and buy one of those red satin heart-shaped boxes of candy that were left over from St. Valentine's Day of the week before, and had been in consequence marked down from a dollar and a quarter to ninety-nine cents. Then she scrubbed him and put on a clean shirt, smelling of soap and the slightly burned odor of freshly ironed linen. He took his dollar and at the same time extracted fifty cents from his pig bank. Why? To make Rosie's present even richer? Or because already some urge toward a recklessly experimental and conquering act was forming in him? Anyway, in the shop where the candy was he came upon a valentine. It was a comic valentine showing a hideous hook-nosed woman looking in a glass. The hook nose gave her a slight resemblance to Madame Golden, but the yellow curls she was pinning to her head were Rosie's. Then he read the verse,

> When in false curls you are arrayed
> You think yourself so fair and fine,
> But you are just a poor old maid
> And will be no one's Valentine.

It cost a nickel and he felt an itching anticipation as he paid for it. He did not buy the candy. Further down the street he stopped in the hardware store and bought himself a two-bladed horn-handled pen knife for a dollar and thirty-five cents. In the Connors' parlor, with all the children assembled, Rosie in white with a pink sash and Mrs. Connors in a refined and creaking taffeta, he felt a moment's panic. But when they laid their presents on the table, hair ribbons, pink celluloid combs, a box of writing paper, candy, he saw Rosie looking at him with a proprietary, complacent pride, a look that reflected somehow the maternal gaze of Mrs. Connors; and when his turn came he laid down the valentine. His turn was last because everyone expected something special from him. He was Rosie's beau. Wasn't it scrawled in chalk on the brick walls of the schoolhouse, or sometimes by a wag on the blackboard: CASS LOVES ROSIE, but more often: ROSIE LOVES CASS? So now they waited, ready to giggle, but when they saw the valentine there came a long silence. Even Mrs. Connors was at a loss. Then Rosie's face began to pucker into tears and a low murmur, half commiserating, half derisive, spread through the room. The triumph of his ego was complete. No. Instantly it was not complete. Something lacked. He took out the pen knife and carelessly laid it on top. There was silence again, then someone tittered. In that sound was envy and sudden understanding, for plainly this was the way to treat the girls: be unpredictable, be lavish if you must, but always basically indifferent to their best interests. Rosie's face relaxed. She smiled. Mrs. Connors said, "Why, Cass, what an *unusual* present," and all the children were suddenly infected with a wild, orgiastic merriment. They joined hands and made a twirling, shouting ring around the table. It was later, in the areaway, that he kissed her.

He woke up and saw that it was dusk, and he thought Edna was beside him. But it was only the heavy shadows of the room, crowding to the little patch of pale light where the table stood.

The old man was deep asleep, now breathing heavily.

"Wake up!" Terhune said. "It's dark. Edna hasn't come."

Pop started up, bewildered.

"What's that? What's that you say?"

"I say it's dark. Edna hasn't come."

The old man looked around him blinking. Then he straightened up. "Well, I can see she hasn't," he said testily. He reached for his pipe and put it down again. "I better close up first," he said.

He got up and went to the window, still a little groggy with sleep, and fussed with the blanket. He let it down and with many groans and exclamations got a shoe off and hammered the tacks in. Then he put his shoe on, groped his way back, and turned on the light.

A cold, stifling fear struck Terhune. With the light on it was night again and everything was as before. The house stretched out into a thousand passages, and the horror of the labyrinth was that no matter how the ways multiplied, not one of them led anywhere. This thing would never end!

Terhune half rose on one leg and his hands moved across the table. The old man, seeing the wild intention in him, pushed backward out of reach. "Now listen!" he cried, "now listen—take it easy."

He waved one hand up and down in a fluttering gesture of defense. "What's got into you all of a sudden?"

"It's dark," Terhune repeated. "Nothing has happened."

"Well, don't be impatient." He reached one hand out to snatch his pipe and then jerked back. "Give the girl time," he said. "She'll get here, I know."

As had happened before, it was he who now seemed reasonable and Terhune who was unbalanced. He cried, "What makes you think you know? What makes you think you know about her?"

"Why," Pop said, fumbling for a match, his eyes fixed alertly on him, "haven't I known Edna since she was knee high to a duck?"

"No!" Terhune was amazed. He hadn't expected an answer to his question and the directness of it diverted him, roused his curiosity. He sank in his chair and let his hands relax on the table. "Is that true?"

Pop saw he had gained his attention and he smiled complacently, convinced that once again he had been too smart for an adversary. "Sure," he said easily, "I knew her father and mother, too."

"Why, I thought—" Terhune said, "well, I don't know what I thought. Just that you must have run across her lately."

"Not a bit of it. I knew her father and mother and, like I said, I've known her since she was a baby."

"Her father and mother!" Terhune said. "How extraordinary!"

But why was it so extraordinary? Simply that for him Edna's reality still fluctuated. At moments she was something fictitious and in the world she sprang from her parents would be fictitious, too. At those moments she needed no explanation.

"Who were they?" he asked.

"Well," the old man said, and Terhune felt he had read his whole mind in this and would take special delight in giving him all the particulars of his error, "her father was a printer. When I moved to New York his place was next to mine. You know your neighbors down there just like in a small town. But the fellow didn't last long. He was tubercular and passed away, and that left this woman and these two kids, Gus and Edna."

He could take his time now the danger was past, so he lighted his pipe, puffed on it several times, and moved closer. "Gus," he said, "was about nine and Edna was about two. Gus was already running around with a tough gang and getting in and out of Children's Court and then being lachrymose about it. And the woman was pretty lachrymose herself. She sold out the little business and got next to nothing for it. She had to work but she had no one to leave Edna with, so she got into the habit of bringing her into my shop and leaving her there. Edna had a kind of harness the woman would tie to the leg of a chair. Edna wasn't much trouble at first. She had curls all over her head and looked kind of cute. People would drop in and speak to her. People go for kids like that, especially if they never cry and Edna never did. She never cried."

"You must have gone for her yourself," Terhune
suggested.

Pop shook his head decidedly. "Oh, I know what
you're thinking," he said. "You're thinking I'm going
to make a beautiful sob story out of this, and for two
bits you'll sob with me—and then forget it and go about
selling your papers. Well, I'm not. I'm going to give it
to you exactly as it was. I simply didn't object much to
Edna, so long as she behaved."

"All right," Terhune said. "How long did you look
after her?"

"Oh, quite a while. And finally it got to be a god-
damned nuisance. This woman was like most people.
Do one thing for them, they expect more. She began to
lead the kind of life that made people talk about her
but not to her. The neighbors dropped her one by one.
Then Edna got too big for the harness and she'd walk
in by herself. She'd sit and watch whatever I was doing,
or play with something I'd give her. I'd have to send
out to the drugstore for milk and sandwiches when she
got hungry. She'd be there pretty near all day. She
wasn't so cute then, either."

Pop leaned both elbows on the table and tilted his
head, looking across at Terhune. Suddenly his eyes
grew brighter and slyer, and at the same time there was
fright in them. "Funny thing happened to me about
then," he said, "but I don't know whether if I was to
tell you you mightn't misunderstand it."

Terhune didn't speak but the old man intended to
tell him anyway.

"People began to act in a way I didn't expect," he

said, "people I knew. First I thought they were just
trying to be 'nice.' 'Nice' people naturally interfere,
they just naturally like to butt in. For instance, someone would run in to see if I'd had my supper. Maybe
I hadn't, maybe I was busy. Someone else would ask if
I'd remembered to send my wash out, or some such fool
thing as that. Well, maybe I hadn't done that either.
Then it got so that when I talked they'd look at me in
a funny way. . . . Of course I was busy. I was occupied
with my problem. I worked on it most of the time. I
had a sort of colleague, not really a helper but just a
fellow I talked over certain points with every now and
then. He was a chemist and I didn't have time for *all*
the details connected with it, so sometimes I used what
he knew. But even he began to act funny. He said peculiar things to me. One day he asked me why I didn't
take an inventory of my stock. 'What for?' I said, and
he gave me some line about it being convenient if I
wanted to take out a new policy or maybe to sell. 'Why
in hell should I want to sell?' I asked him, but he had
no answer for that. I used to see this fellow a lot. We
talked about this problem. No use telling you what it
was, you wouldn't understand. But neither did he, as
it turned out."

His voice was growing shriller and Terhune moved
back a little. Pop caught his sleeve, as though he were
able to get up and leave him. "I was only a little run-
down," he said, insistently and shrilly, "only a little
nervous, a little tired. But do you know what happened?
I got into an argument with him one day, with this
fellow I'm telling you about. I can't even remember

what the argument was. We were sitting in my kitchen there in the back, where it's warmer by the stove, and I'd made two sandwiches to go with some beer we had, and in this argument one thing led to another and suddenly he just looked right at me and said, 'Why, you're crazy, aren't you? You've been crazy a long time.'" His eyes blazed. "That's what he said to me! Can you imagine it! I just picked up the knife and went for him—" Suddenly his face broke into its convulsion of tics. Terhune had to watch it for several minutes because he didn't dare look away from him. He thought it would never stop this time but gradually it diminished. There were three or four slow spasms and it stopped altogether. The old man got his grimy handkerchief from his trouser pocket and again wiped it all over his face. When he put it back his face was calm and even cheerful again. "Well," he said, "when I came back she was gone."

"Who was gone?"

"Why, the woman was gone, Edna's mother."

"Where'd she go?"

"I don't know. But a fellow turned up and it seems he wanted to marry her, or anyway, he wanted to take her away. She was a pretty woman, blond, like Edna, but prettier. She was plump and good-tempered and sexy, the kind when you look at her you can't make up your mind whether she belongs in a kitchen with flour on her elbows or in a cat house. But of course this fellow (I think he was from out West) wasn't so crazy about her he was ready to take the kids. And she was sick and tired of those kids herself. She told everyone she had relatives upstate who would care for them and she'd made all the arrangements. So off they went—took a powder—vanished. Only it turned out the relatives weren't having any. They came down and had the kids put in institutions. Gus ran away but Edna was too little."

"Edna was brought up in an institution?"

"That's right. At least, she was for a while. Then a woman got her out and put her to work."

"What woman?"

"Oh, a woman who ran a hamburg joint near the foot of Brooklyn Bridge. She was some kind of a foreign woman, Polack I think. It was one of those all-night joints, taxi drivers and truckmen went there, and Edna washed dishes and helped in the kitchen half the night. During the daytime, whenever the truant officers got after her, she went to school. You'd of thought she'd have died of it. Well, she's runty, but she must be tough."

"You mean to tell me an institution would turn a child over to someone like that?"

"Not if they knew. But they didn't know. What happened was they turned her over to the woman's sister, who had a farm in Jersey. This sister made a kind of racket of getting kids by adoption—nice country home to offer, chickens, cows, healthy life, etcetera. It looked great. Then when she got them there she'd work them like animals. You know how those foreigners work in the country, especially the women. Well, Edna was sick all the time. She had fevers, she told me, and every time she drank that country milk she threw it right up. I guess drugstore milk suited her better. Regular city rat, Edna!" He chuckled, all in his best humor now, and then said, "So the sister sent her up to New York and her health was fine there."

"And how did you find her again?"

"Well, I wasn't around when her mother left. When I came back I had other things to think of besides Edna. I lost my business," he said, airily waving a hand as though brushing away smoke. Terhune thought this should have brought back his excitement, but he had passed through that. His business apparently had ceased to interest him, if it ever had. "I had lean years," he said, "very lean years. But it was during those lean years, my friend, that I learned the most. I had lost my regular occupation, my friends, my responsibilities. The mind," he said fatuously, "was free."

He stopped again as another thought struck him. And this involved not memory but calculation. He began to frown. His eyes went all over Terhune, taking some new account of him. Then he said, "What about you? Got any ties yourself?"

"Ties? What sort of ties?"

"Loved ones—wife, children, that sort of thing."

"No. I've been married, but I'm not now, and I have no children."

"Widower, then. A childless widower."

"Yes."

"Is that so! I'd have thought a man your age—well, well." He allowed himself a moment of unspoken comment that was obviously, by his smile, of a nature purely carnal, then he repeated, "Well, well."

"Now about Edna," he said, "as I recall it, I ran into her one day on the street. Yes, that's just what happened, and what's more, I recognized her, believe it or not. At least, I knew I'd seen her somewhere. I have a great memory for faces and that pale coloring of hers and something about her eyes struck me. We stopped and looked at each other and finally she said, 'It's Pop,' and then I knew her."

"You saw her again after that?"

"Oh, yes, we ran into each other pretty often."

"She was working for the foreign woman?"

"Yes, she was."

"But what about Gus? How did she catch up with him?"

"Oh, she made inquiries about him. She caught up with him in no time. I don't know how pleased he was, because once she'd got hold of him she began to boss him. She began nagging him to get her a job, and damned if he didn't finally—with Mort, or you might say with Mort, anyway with Mort's floozie, this Miss Gloria."

"But what about the Polish woman?"

"She ran away from her."

"And the woman didn't try to get her back?"

"Not that I know of. Maybe she couldn't stand to be investigated, maybe she thought Edna was getting too sassy to have around. Anyway, Edna got her job, and the next thing Gus knew Edna'd found two rooms for them and was getting his meals and washing his shirts, and pretty soon she was right in with Mort, too, just getting along fine. That girl doesn't stop at anything.

There's something in Edna goes right through. She wants something, and the harder to get the better." Suddenly he broke into a laugh. "You know, I shouldn't be surprised if someday she doesn't turn out to be the president of a ladies' club or something."

Terhune smiled. But he thought how right he had been, though at the time it was only instinct that prompted him, when in giving Edna her choice he had made what he hoped she would do seem difficult instead of easy.

"Does Gus treat her well?" he asked.

"Well, no, he don't actually. Gus is a no-count. He's got the mind of a chimp, and its instincts. The only difference is he's sorry for himself and I don't think chimps ever are. If someone were to squash Gus out, it would be a damned good thing."

"But does Edna love him?"

"Love him? I don't see why she should," he said crossly. "She would have to be like that woman I read about the other day. There was a fellow killed a cop and several of the passengers in a crowded bus, and when they caught him it turned out he'd served time for larceny, felony, indecent exposure, and rape. And when his wife turned up they asked her if she'd known about it. Sure, she said, but she figured he didn't have anyone to love him but her!"

"What about Mort?" Terhune asked.

This time Mort's name produced a gravity in him. He stared steadily at Terhune, who got the impression that he was beginning to calculate again on some other level. "Mort is different," he said.

"What's their relationship?" Terhune asked.

"You mean has Mort seduced her?" He held his pipe firmly in his teeth and spread his hands out flat on the table. He made one or two sounds as though he were breathing deeply or about to say a word. Finally he said deliberately, "I've sometimes wondered myself. But I'd say no. I think I'm right, too. I think the answer is no. And the reason is just that he didn't want to. With a fellow like Mort there wouldn't be any other reason."

"Why wouldn't he want to?"

"Well, first because he's a conceited cuss and he wouldn't think she was good enough. But no, that's not the real reason. He thinks a lot of her, in his way." Pop frowned, trying to disentangle threads that turned out to be unexpectedly delicate. "You have to remember the first time he saw her she really was a child. He saw her when she was tagging around after Gus. Oh, I don't mean to give you the idea that he ever had, or has now, any pure, sweet feelings about her, just that the feelings he did have have had time to stick. Mort has made a certain kind of a thing out of her, the way you do make a special character out of someone you know, and he still likes her that way. I hardly know how to tell you what this is. A sort of pet, I suppose, a sort of stooge, too, though she don't know that part at all. Edna was always independent, she always tried to go her own way, and she always answered back. But he's got a great sense of humor, and when he once gets a joke he likes to hang on to it. Edna was a joke, and he and Edna have got lots of jokes together, too. He likes to kid her in front of people and then have her crack right back at him, and he smiles to show that he may be tough but the kiddies go for him. Then once I heard him say she brings him luck. He says ever since she's been around he's got all the breaks. He's superstitious, like all those mugs. Sometimes he calls her his mascot. 'Edna,' he'll say, 'keep your fingers crossed: I got a deal on.' It makes him feel good to think he's enough of a big shot to keep her in the way those kings kept jesters, or maybe a hunchback they could touch every now and then for luck."

Terhune said nothing. Pop's words had saddened him. They showed him Edna as she had seemed to him when he first saw her. And that Edna also had been real. She *was* like that. That she couldn't possibly have been otherwise (and what Pop said made it very clear) didn't help any. If I get out, he thought, and Edna never does? . . .

The old man made drumming noises on the table, and he still frowned. His mind concentrated again on his calculations, and Terhune knew what the calculations were. He was pretty transparent for all his wiles. Quite simply, he was fond of Edna. All through his story of her Terhune had caught, in the midst of depreciation, the overtone of the doting parent (that-little-devil-certainly-can-handle-himself tone). He wanted to help her. Vaguely he knew that all the problems he posed himself were never actually submitted to test. This one would be. It would have to *work*. And yet, all that was seasoned by misery in him, all that was dark and wayward and without hope told him it was no use.

"How old is Edna?" Terhune asked, "about sixteen?"

"She'll have a birthday soon. She'll be sixteen."

"You know her birthday?"

"Sure I know her birthday. She'll be sixteen. Some girls are married and have a kid at that age. Her mother did. Hell, what's youth? We're all young once. Nothing to it. And some never grow up. Don't want to. Don't want to be treated as anything but kids. But not Edna. She wants to grow up."

"When is her birthday?"

"Seventeenth of this month. And now you know you can give her a cake. Oh, boy! Cost you five bucks maybe," he said jeeringly. Then his face clouded over. His eyes looked into something beyond the walls of the room. "I gave her a cake, once," he said.

"Yes?" Terhune said. "When?"

"Oh, when she was twelve. It was after I came back. She hadn't gone to live with Gus yet. She was with the Polack woman."

"How did it happen?"

The old man didn't answer for a moment, then he said dreamily, "I met her on the street that night. It was funny meeting her, because she worked nights. There she was though, and she was a sight. Sleeve torn half off, black marks, scratches, and a shiner as big as a silver dollar. Seems the old bag she worked for had promised her a cake for her birthday but Edna had busted a plate, so she didn't give her a cake. She gave her a licking instead. How do you like that? And because Edna sassed her she locked her in her room. Only Edna was always very independent and climbed down the fire escape and got out. Then she was scared to go

back. Well, she told me about it and she began to cry."
His eyes became wider and more reminiscent. This was
different from his other stories. Like them it might be
apocryphal, but he wasn't telling it out of his flighty
humors or from a desire to show off judgment or skill.
He was telling it out of sadness and for no audience but
himself. He repeated, "Yes, she cried."

"Children often cry," Terhune said.

"Not Edna. Didn't I tell you she never cried? Not
even when she was little. Why, once in my place a heavy
clock fell on her thumb and broke it. She looked surprised but she didn't cry."

"Well, what did you do about it?"

The old man shook his head. Terhune thought,
maybe he doesn't remember, or his invention doesn't
run to this kind of story. But Terhune himself could
imagine it, either as it was or as the old man made it
seem. He saw the street they had met in, one of those
downtown streets, eerily empty at night, perhaps under
the shelter of the El. And a bare, colorless, odorless sea-
son between heat and cold. And probably the sound of
boats on the river, and maybe even the sound of a juke-
box, muffled by walls, to give the shut-out feeling of
knowing there were people nearby, close together, sitting at tables, talking, warming themselves at each
other's lives, sharing themselves—for all that sharing
seems no burden when you stand outside. Then he saw
Edna drifting down this street like a small ghost, exiled
from the hell of her own life, and meeting another
ghost, so ancient he was almost past the knowledge of
being one. And they exchanged the dry, ironical greet-
ing of ghosts. And that was why she had cried.

The old man began to talk again, even more inwardly, but with such confidence that Terhune thought, why it's true after all. "I said to her, I said, 'Listen Edna, you come back in half an hour and I'll see you get your cake!' So I went to a place I know that's always open and I hocked a watch fob I still had, an agate seal with a ram's head, set in solid gold. And then I went to an Eyetalian place I knew and said, 'I want a supper and a birthday cake for a kid that's got nowhere to go.' Those Eyetalians, they always fall for a thing like that. I took Edna there and sure enough, they had the supper and the cake, too, even with candles. They brought it in and everyone in the place sang Happy Birthday to You. It was some party, all right. It was some party. I got stinko on red wine and passed out, and I never did find out if Edna got home that night or not."

The cake, the red wine, the constellation of candles, were reflected in his eyes. He looked content. Then, looking up and seeing this content shared by Terhune, he changed. His mouth twitched with sudden, savage irritation. "You know there are times I can't even stand that kid," he exclaimed.

Terhune shrugged his shoulders. They didn't talk any more but sat in silence under the thin glare of the unshaded bulb. Terhune closed his eyes. He didn't sleep, but his mind formed a sort of atmosphere around Edna. She floated in it, a child with silvery hair, and her flesh had the exquisiteness and slight disgustingness of a child's flesh.

Presently the old man scraped his chair back and turned around. "Here she is," he said, "here comes Edna."

CHAPTER IX

THE ladder went down and her steps mounted slowly and carefully. When she appeared she said nothing but gave a small salute with one finger and walked sedately across the room. She was not wearing slacks but a very short-skirted black suit with an exaggerated ruffle of white blouse showing at the neck. She had the same high-heeled evening slippers and her face was thickly made up, her pompadour towered as before and there was a white, artificial camellia tucked in it. The suit was too thin for the chilly weather, too tight fitting. It was a hand-me-down, or else one she had outgrown. The blackness gave her hair and skin a peculiarly pale and sober but luminous uniformity, and the cut of the suit, the clownlike collar, made an amusing contrast, bizarre and rakishly elegant.

Pop exclaimed admiringly, "Some outfit!"

She carried a shiny patent leather purse and a package under her arm, and a roll of Sunday newspaper in her other hand. She laid them on the table. Her expression was composed.

"Hello," she said, not glancing at either of them and beginning to undo one parcel.

"What's that?" Pop said. He leaned forward. "What you got there?"

She took out three sandwiches, wrapped separately in waxed paper, and a bottle of whisky.

Pop whistled. "Say, what's this?" he exclaimed, his eyes dancing. "What goes on here?"

"It's for him," she said. "He needs it, but you can't have more than a drop."

"Oh, come now," he protested, "I need it, too. I've had a hard day. Oh, see here now, Edna."

"Just a drop," she said.

She put a sandwich in front of each of them and the bottle in the middle of the table. Then she sat down, and in the manner of a hostess said, "Well, if you're hungry, just go right ahead."

Pop picked up the bottle. "Where'd you get it?"

"Out of Gus's closet. He'll never miss it."

"Let's hope he don't." He opened the bottle, poured some in his paper cup, more than half filling it, and passed the bottle to Terhune. "Here's how," he said.

Terhune said to Edna, "I suppose you don't drink?"

Edna glanced directly at him for the first time and answered politely, "No, thank you. I wouldn't care for any."

Terhune poured some in his cup and raised it in salute. Then he took a deep swallow.

It was the best scotch. It warmed him instantly and blurred the sharp edge of pain in his ankle. "If you knew how *I* needed that!" he exclaimed.

Edna moved the bottle across the table, still within his reach but very pointedly where Pop would have to lean across to get it. Then she unwrapped her own sandwich. "It's ham," she said. "I hope you like ham."

Terhune unwrapped his. Pop, after a disgusted look at the position of the whisky bottle, opened his, examined the sandwich, and began to eat noisily.

Edna took small, neat bites, chewing them carefully. When a crumb dropped on her frill she daintily flicked it off.

Pop, with a full mouth, said, "Where is everybody?"

"I guess you might as well know," Edna said, "that Gus and Mort are over in Jersey."

"That's just where I thought they were," he said.

"You did?" She looked at him critically. "How'd you find out? You been snooping around. You picked it up somewhere."

"That's right. Old Pop—sees all, knows all."

"Well, you keep it to yourself," she said.

"You bet I will. But tell us some more. Are you sure they're there?"

"Yeah. Anyway, they're on their way."

Terhune said, "Then no one is coming here?"

"No. Nobody. Mort decided last night."

"He's abandoned this stuff?"

"That's right."

"Whereabouts in Jersey?" Pop asked.

"Oh, a place over there. A farm somewhere."

"Boy, will they love it!" he exclaimed. "I can just see it. A nice, quaint, little, quiet farm. With roosters in the morning and maybe a lonesome dog at night. Before they've been there ten minutes the place will stink, just like New York. How long do they figure to stay?"

"I wouldn't know."

"They better not stay too long. They got nothing to do, nothing to talk about. They'll start to shooting each other." He took another drink.

"Say!" Edna said reprovingly, "go easy on that liquor, will you?"

"There's no doubt then that they've gone?"

"Oh, no. I saw them go."

"And the others?"

"They're around somewhere but they won't come here. Mort said for everyone to keep away."

"Good. Then we can take our time."

"That's right. We got to wait till pretty late, anyhow. I guess till some time after twelve."

"See!" Pop said. "What did I tell you? It's a cinch. Edna's some girl."

Then he unrolled the paper and got the comic section and began to look at it. His eyes went over the pages with the dispatch of a man who is accustomed to get his journalistic pleasure hastily, from papers picked up in subway seats and park benches.

Edna chewed a moment in a refined way and then said, "There are some things though we got to talk about."

"Naturally."

"You see," she said, "there was a piece about you on the radio."

"What!" he exclaimed. "You mean they are looking for me?" He thought of Charlie in Washington, of the breakfast waiting, of the gradual build-up of uneasiness when he didn't come. (*What do you think happened to*

*him? Should we call New York? But where? Where
would he be? Could there have been a train wreck?
Shall we call the station and find out? He did say this
morning, didn't he? And finally, he's sick, you know.
Maybe we'd better call the police.*) It was proof of the
power of compulsion that had brought him here that
he had never thought of any of this! Once here the
outer world had practically ceased to exist.

"What did they say?" he asked.

"Why, they said who you were and where you had
been and everything. And then they said they had been
asked to broadcast a description, because they were
afraid you might have been 'stricken with amnesia!'
They said, too, they weren't overlooking the possibility
of foul play, because you'd got crank letters while you
were in Germany from someone in Yorkville. They said
a whole lot about you."

She looked at him wonderingly, as though the very
words she quoted stiffly and with a careful accent, almost as though they were foreign words repeated, had
added to his strangeness.

He exclaimed impulsively, "Now you know I was
telling you the truth."

"Yeah," she said. "I know. But last night I believed
you."

Their voices sounded so unexpectedly tense that both
of them could say no more. They stared at each other.
The silence seemed long.

Then Terhune said, "I didn't thank you last night.
I had no chance. But I thank you now."

Pop's voice said drily, "I'd do that." He had glanced

up from the paper. He wasn't interested in who Terhune was, or he was pretending not to be.

His voice brought a frown to Edna's face. It spoiled
the moment for her, before she even knew what it had
meant. She said constrainedly, "Oh, that's O.K." Then
she brushed the remains of the sandwich back into the
waxed paper and crumpled it into a ball.

Terhune offered her a cigarette. She took one and as
he leaned forward with a match she kept her eyes down
and he saw her jaw muscles stiffen. Seen this near she
was not nearly as composed as she had seemed. And he
himself did not feel composed. He wanted to talk to
her, not about what was on the radio or how he would
get out, but about herself and about himself, about
what was happening in both of them. The old man
seemed to be making them self-conscious and he could
think of no way to get rid of him. But he wondered, if
they were alone as before, what would happen, and
whether he could ever give what he felt any true, natural expression.

He smoked in silence, looking at her. She held her
cigarette between thumb and forefinger, inhaling am-
ateurishly in little puffs, a slight frown on her face because she knew she was being watched. This time, he
thought, she is imitating, not the gangster's moll but
the competent young secretary with a serious purpose
in life. He smiled at the image, and suddenly he didn't
want to be serious at all. He wanted to tease her serious-
ness. He remembered Pop saying that Mort was always
kidding her. Edna, no matter what role she took, in-
spired something playful: her miniature size, her as-

surance and toughness, and an undertone of genuine
good spirits, were all engaging in a puppyish way. As he
looked at her his self-consciousness began to leave him.
He began to feel actually lighthearted.

But Edna was still constrained. She said, "Now about
this piece. It makes things kind of complicated."

"Yes?" he said, inattentively. "Why?"

"Just that they're going to want to know a lot of
things."

"Who, the police?"

"Yeah. They're going to ask a lot. And the papers will
want to know, too."

"I suppose so."

"You see," she said solemnly, "you're a celebrity."

For a moment the word irritated him, then he
thought: don't be a pompous ass. After all, why do most
people I know treat me as they do; simply because,
while they don't use that word and aren't nearly so im-
pressed by the fact, they feel the same way about it that
she does? And I must remember: last night she had no
idea who I am.

"Everyone's going to want to know where you been
all this time."

"I suppose so. What about amnesia? Won't that do?"

"Maybe. But you been somewhere even if you can't
remember, and how'd you break your leg?"

"Yes, I see there are points we'll have to get clear."
But he found it hard to put his mind on it. "Can't we
just say I had an attack of amnesia, fell over some of the
rubble, and broke my leg?"

"But where?" she said. Her self-consciousness also was

leaving her. They began to smile slightly as they spoke, each recognizing that what they said was not what they were thinking about.

"In some place where I couldn't have been found right away. Say the garage next door."

"Who's going to find you?"

"Not you," he said promptly. "I don't want anyone to see you."

"Oh?" she said, vaguely.

"I can get downstairs with your help," he said, "yours and Pop's. You can leave me in the garage. I'll do the rest."

"Someone's got to find you," she said.

What *was* this change in her, he wondered. Would a few clothes, a manner suitable for dealing with a grownup who was also a celebrity, account for it? No, of course not. One difference was that now she was more visibly at the edge of change, the edge certainly —he noticed it for the first time—of beauty. All her physical qualities were like immaculate petals that hadn't come together yet to form a whole of beauty (and when they did it would already be the beginning of the decline, because they would have reached their own intention).

"I can find him!" Pop exclaimed.

They both started at the sound of his voice, though it was only a moment they'd forgotten him. He put down the paper and repeated, "*I* find him. Everyone knows I come and go here as I like, so I find him. Then *I'm* a celebrity!"

"You'd sure love that," Edna said. Her eyes brushed

him with a cynical appraisal. She was on to him, but she was gentle about it. She was fond of him. Terhune thought he knew why she was fond of him. Partly for his strange kindnesses and partly because he was old.

He remembered Pop had said Edna wanted to grow up, and that most people didn't. They were afraid. When they were afraid of understanding, what did they want? Why, they wanted aptitudes, skills, means, and especially those that would protect them against understanding! But, truly, Edna was different. Something in her leaned toward maturity. That he had felt in her from the beginning. That was why her puppyishness was endearing, why her near beauty was so touching: they were part of the risk she took.

"Edna," he said, "what does it feel like to be young? I've forgotten, but you almost make me remember."

She looked at him, surprised. "I don't know," she said.

"Of course you don't. No one does when he is young. Can you imagine me as young, very young, as young as you?"

"Sure," she said. Her smile was like the old look of seeing irresistible comedy in the unexpected contrivances and appearances of life. "Sure," she repeated. "I bet you were kind of like a boy I used to know in school."

"You think so? A boy that you knew in school, someone like me? Tell me about him."

"Oh, he was just a boy. He read books and he sort of said those things you say."

"Did you like him?"

"I kind of liked him."

"But not much."

"Well," she said, still amused, "he was an older boy, and he was kind of, well, different. His name was Sammy Levine."

"Sammy Levine!" Pop exclaimed. "His father ran a hock shop, didn't he?"

"Yeah, he did." She added severely, "And clean up that mess you made, will you?"

"Oh, sure, sure."

Pop, with a wink, began to brush crumbs off the table. He made a great business of straightening everything, laying what was there in rows and patterns. The shaving brush and razor he gathered up with ostentatious modesty and put in the pocket of his overcoat hanging on the chair. He was trying to attract their attention. "I remember Sammy," he said. "Great big eyeglasses." He looked derisively at Terhune. "Sammy was no beauty," he said.

"I didn't say he *looked* like him," Edna said, animatedly, "I only said he *talked* like him."

"You mean he talked over your head," Pop said. "You couldn't understand him."

"Say, listen." She turned to him, her whole manner quite lively and natural now. "You always say people don't understand anyone. You really mean they don't understand *you*. That's because you like to say words that make one kind of sense and inside you're making another all for yourself. You think that fools people. Well, that's O.K., if you like it, but maybe it would be nicer to say things you really mean, so people would get it."

"Do you get what *he* says?" Pop asked, pointing at Terhune with his pipe.

"Sure," she answered confidently.

"All of it?"

"All of it."

"That's fine," Pop said sarcastically. "Maybe he likes teaching little girls." Then, seeing she wasn't really paying attention to him, he leaned over, got the whisky bottle, and poured himself another. "What happened to that Sammy?" he asked. "Didn't he have an accident or something?"

"He got killed," Edna said.

"Oh, I remember. He fell off the platform of the El. He got run over."

Edna tapped her ash onto the floor with her little finger. "It was a terrible accident," she said. "He got dizzy. He was absent-minded and his eyes were bad. He was reading a book. He always went around reading a book. It was too bad."

"Oh, it was too bad, wasn't it?" Pop said. "It was too bad he couldn't grow up to run a hock shop!"

Edna said reproachfully, "It was screwy. It didn't make sense."

"Lots of things don't make sense to you. But they're a law just the same. They're a law you can't get away from. One of them is wastage."

"You and your laws! You and those things you can't get away from! What did that have to do with Sammy?"

Pop addressed himself to Terhune, shaking his finger

at him. "See," he said, "that's what they always say. Even if they can recognize a law they always say, 'But what's it got to do with me? This is different,' they say. Well, for one thing, if your eyes are bad you oughtn't to read books on the platforms of El stations. That's one law. But for another thing, it don't matter. Did you," he turned to Edna, "ever look at the moon through one of those telescopes the guy has up around Forty-third and Sixth Avenue? On clear nights you can see the moon and the rings of Saturn."

"Yes," she said.

"Well, just imagine you're looking at the earth from a telescope on the moon."

"So what?"

"So it would look like a star," Pop said. "But what is it? It's just one big garbage disposal plant."

"It's also a generating plant," Terhune said. "You can take your choice."

"See!" Edna exclaimed. "That's what I mean about you. Why do you have to say a thing like that?"

The marsh light gleamed in Pop's eyes but he looked irritated. Terhune saw with amusement that he was becoming jealous.

"What did I say?" he exclaimed. "I only said there is wastage because it doesn't matter that there is wastage. Why were there dinosaurs for fifty thousand years? There's wastage for you. That's all I said."

"No, you didn't," Edna answered. "You said it don't matter what happens to people."

Pop shrugged and winked rakishly at Terhune, but Edna looked up at Terhune hopefully, expecting him to say something. When he didn't she leaned back with a disappointed sigh.

But she couldn't stay disappointed long. Her face almost at once settled back into her gay, calm little smile. "Oh, well, you're just an old sorehead anyway," she said. "Any time I want to know I ask somebody else. Or maybe I figure it out for myself. I guess in the end you got to figure things out for yourself anyway."

Pop said, "It's positively excruciating to have to listen to platitudes like that. Figure it out for yourself, but spare us, will you?"

Edna ignored this. She wasn't even angry with him. She turned to Terhune and said, "You know, it's funny about this house here. I always kind of liked it. I don't know why. When I worked downstairs I always liked to come here. Even up here in this attic it's not so bad. I never thought I'd meet anyone here like you."

"I always liked it, too," he said. "It's the first place I ever knew. I thought I'd forgotten it but I'll never forget it now."

"When you said about coming back here, somehow it didn't sound as screwy as all that," she said. "I guess if I'd lived here I'd have wanted to come back, too. Now they're going to tear it down. It seems mean."

"Old houses," Pop mumbled, "the hell with them." He took another swallow of whisky. He turned half away from them and made movements with his mouth as though he were about to experiment with ventriloquism.

Edna looked around the room. "It's really nice up here," she said dreamily. "Isn't that funny?"

"It's you who make it nice," Terhune said. "It wasn't nice before you came. Not even in my dream. It was a sort of underground house. I was cooped up in it like a prison. You got me out."

"How?" she said, her face half serious, half smiling.

"By a brave act, a creative act. And you got me out of more than the attic. You got me out of a more horrible claustrophobia: out of myself."

She said nothing, but looked at him for a long moment. Her eyes were so clear, so full of happiness and the untroubled, immediate acceptance of happiness, that it gave him a thrill of doubt. It was so long since he had been able to take what came without thought, to take the experience purely. Every experience was weighted for him by fore and after thoughts, and he remembered too much of all of them. He remembered that one should be doubtful, one should be wary, of happiness that has nothing to support it. He was not as liberated as he had told her he was. But that was his fault, not hers.

Edna said, "Mort told me this house was swell once. Was that when you lived here?"

"No," he said, "that was long before my day."

"Why? Weren't you rich?" she asked.

"No, no," he said, "not at all. I was a poor kid, very poor."

Again they smiled at each other, recognizing that their words had only a light, oblique, relation to what they were feeling. He was thinking that at least it made him content to tell her he had once been poor. It was almost as though he were poor now, not in a momentary poverty of the attic but literally possessing nothing she could not share. He longed so much to wipe out between them his own experience and thoughts, and it almost seemed as though that might be happening, as though they were losing weight and meaning, becoming floating, ambiguous, empty, as though he were very nearly in the condition of youth.

"But how did you get educated?" she asked him. "You must of went to college."

"Yes, I went. But it all happened in a curious way. Would you like to hear?"

"Sure."

"Well, it was like this. I lived with an aunt. My parents were gone, and she ran this place as a boarding house. Yes, a run-down, cheap boarding house. She was poor but she loved money. That's really all she did love. She loved it in a special way, not for what she could get with it (though getting things represented money so she liked that, too) but out of a sort of abstract delight in it, as though money were—well—say mathematics, or philosophy. It occupied her so completely that she lived an ascetic life, like a mathematician, like a philosopher."

"Gee, that's pretty funny," Edna said. "I feel sorry for your aunt."

"So do I. Well, there was a man who used to come to see one of her boarders, a man named Bolger. He was a promoter. Do you know what that is?"

"Sure. You get people to put money in things."

"Exactly. And this Bolger fellow looked like a promoter. He looked like the kind of promoter who gets

you to put your money in a company that doesn't exist.
He wore a flashy suit that you knew hadn't been paid
for, a diamond ring that wasn't real. A ten-year-old child
looking at him would have said he was bad news. But
still, my aunt gave him her money to invest. All her
savings, little by little, went to him. He invested it in
things like a woven rubber tire company, and all sorts
of projects that never materialized. He always lost it.
But she went right on giving it to him."

"She sounds kind of peculiar."

"Well, she was. But also she was so in love with the
idea of money that she was unworldly in the ordinary
sense, and that gave her a kind of clairvoyance about it
that a person more cluttered up with normal worldli-
ness wouldn't have had. Anyway, he finally bought her
some stock in a gold mine. I believe it was the Bullfrog
mine of Tonopah, Nevada. An acquaintance of his, Tex
Rickard (he'd done him a favor once, so he said) let
him in on it. And what do you think happened?"

Edna looked at him to be sure this was to be answered. Then she said slowly, "They struck it rich?"

Pop, not turning, muttered, "Oh, you've seen the
picture!"

"Yes, they did strike it rich. My aunt made a lot of
money. She gave up the boarding house, this house,
and moved to Riverside Drive, where she'd always
wanted to be. And—she sent me to college. That's the
story."

Edna gave a long sigh. "Some story!" she said. "So
she got it first and then you got it, and it all just came
to you like that. I like that story."

Pop turned around, grabbed the whisky bottle and poured himself another drink. His face was flushed now and his eyes suffused. "I'll bet you like it," he said. "Sammy's story was screwy, but this one is just dandy. What do you like about this one, Edna?"

"Because it turned out right," she answered.

"And because it turned out right you don't have to think about it, and that's the way he meant you to like it."

"What do you mean?"

"Well, there's a truth in both stories. In the one he told you he let the truth slip in by mistake, but he was trying to tell it like a fairy story, the way you tell something to fool a kid."

"Well, it's true if he says so," she insisted.

He stopped to take a long swallow and said, "The truth in both stories is the same truth. As I said before, if a guy has bad eyes and gets dizzy he shouldn't read on the platforms of Els. If he does he'll fall off and get killed. The other truth is that the old girl was smarter than she seemed, that she knew exactly what she was doing all along, because she understood money and investment. He thought you wouldn't notice that. And by the way, I wonder how *he* came to inherit in the end? I'll bet he wasn't half dumb with auntie either."

"You're trying to spoil it," she said indignantly.

"Not a bit of it. I'm just trying to clarify it. I can't spoil it. It's a fairy story. You can't spoil a fairy story. Why, honey, this is *your* fairy story. Don't you see? He's telling you it's yours. It's only just begun, too. Isn't that right?"

Edna clenched her hands. She looked confused. "Now don't say it," she said. "I don't know what you're talking about, but don't say it."

"I'm talking about wonderful, wonderful life," Pop said.

Terhune was beginning to see the old man's point and he would have liked to wring his neck before he could put it into words. "I told it to amuse her," he said. And also, he thought, to show her that his money, whatever he had that she had not, was no part of him. But beyond that for still another reason. "You talk too much," he said angrily.

"Why, what's wrong? Why are you two ganging up on me?" Pop put on a look of injured innocence. "Hell's bells. Edna gets some of the dough, don't she? Or am I wrong? Oh, come now. She's earned it."

Terhune said, "Don't listen to the old fool, Edna. Of course you can have anything you want."

He had said this before and the words were only a bad repetition. She remembered them, too. He saw that in her face. She remembered also that she had said then she didn't want anything. She had said it from loyalty, from pride. Now she murmured again, "I don't want anything," and he knew she only meant she didn't want what he seemed ready to give. What was it, after all? Put all together in one heap, money, education, security. What did it come to? Respectability. In exchange for faith, for courage: respectability.

"Isn't it peculiar," Pop said, "how people hate to hear the truth? It's not so peculiar that Edna should hate it, because she's a kid. But she likes to have things turn out right, and she wonders why sometimes they don't. You might have explained that to her, but you didn't. You could have told her a little about cause and effect, but you didn't—it's simple enough, God knows. Instead, you hand her a line."

"Stop all this rot," Terhune said. "I was telling her a story. I was trying to entertain her."

"She was entertained, all right. She was downright beguiled. Why, it's a nice little religion you handed her, cheating and all. What's more beguiling than that? In a religion anything can happen because the world's being made every day, and the plan—if there is one— can be changed every day: by someone saying a prayer off in China, by someone else wearing a dead rat around his neck as a charm."

"Oh, Pop, cut it out," Edna said.

He turned toward her savagely. "Listen!" he cried. "You don't get the point but you better. The point is you're all the beneficiaries of something that just happened that way, auntie, him, and you. No logic in it, so no one owes anything to anyone. *And that lets him out.*" He shook his finger at her. "That's what the story is. No obligation. The world is only what it is *at the moment.* The man is logical—that's what's funny about this—and he knows all about himself. And one thing about him is that he likes to play it alone. He don't want to get involved. He'll do something for you. Sure. But then he'll take a powder on you and you'll never lay eyes on him again. Why, look at him—you can see it in his face!"

Edna looked at Terhune and tried to smile. But for

one moment he was admitting to himself that what the old man had said was true. That was why he'd told it. He had meant that there could never be a permanent, a rational, basis for what they felt between them. He meant this lightness of heart, this illusion of happiness, could not last. The feeling of release could not last. It would not be happiness or release presently but a burden. Very soon he would have to protect himself again, save himself once more. He would forget even. It was hopeless. He forced all this from his face and from his mind, but it was too late. Edna's smile failed. Even under the powder her face showed its paleness.

When he spoke his voice was dry and without life. "I'm sorry you had to hear this, because it isn't true. It might have been, even a moment ago when he told it, even then, it might have been, and he's just smart enough to see it. But it isn't true now. Believe me. You believed me once. Try to believe me again."

She didn't answer. She went on looking at him and he saw this time she did not believe him. Her look said: no, you aren't generous, you are afraid, you save yourself, you take no risk. You are *old*, like he is. You've only been trying to fool me, all along.

Then she put her elbow on the table and leaned her head on her hand. Her face looked tired and resigned. Terhune thought with a pang that this might even become her permanent expression, when she herself was old. He reached out for her hand, which lay on the table, but she drew it away before he could touch it.

"Oh, that's O.K.," she said wearily.

CHAPTER X

THEY sat in silence. The old man gurgled whisky noisily down his throat. He was getting very drunk, but it didn't matter. He'd done his worst by them already. But as so often happens, Terhune thought, he'd done it at a time when he really hoped to do his best. He wanted to prod Terhune into a strict conception of his responsibility. But since he had himself long ago repudiated all such conceptions he had no idea now how to go about it. He was like a man who has renounced the church undertaking to persuade another to become a Jesuit.

As for Edna, Terhune thought, I suppose I *have* let her down, though not in the way the old man is afraid of. And if I have been fooling her, I've also been fooling myself. I've been illusioning myself and dis-illusioning myself over a whole lifetime. But what the hell!—I want to discover the permanent, the true identity, but can't I do that without risking the failure of the false identity? To find it, do I have to move amidst a cloud of subtle and often ridiculous deceptions, stumbling after legendary marsh fires, mistaking them for fixed lights, falling into mud holes that may even be fatal? Can't I discover it without being willing to become a part of it, to give myself over to it in its entirety, losing everything along the way, even reason, and perhaps with it the knowledge of *why* I must find it?

It's curious, he thought, that out of all I could remember I should suddenly at this moment remember old Bill Babcock. We used to call him Smutty, because he had the gamiest tongue I ever knew. And what was there *we* had in common? Well, the life of the last war, with all the trappings—mud, tedium, danger. We spoke the language of that life, which was like a dialect in its limitations. We shared nothing spectacular, no rescues, no dragging of each other over No Man's Land. I can't remember anything except that he was my buddy and I was his. And that we got wounded in the same hour, almost in the same way, were sent to different base hospitals, and never saw each other again. After the war we wrote for a while. Bill was a car salesman in Saint Jo, Missouri. We were always going to meet in New York. Boy, oh boy, Bill said, would we have a party! But we never did. And finally our wives remembered to send cards at Christmas. And then that stopped, too. So what did *that* actually mean? And what will this mean? Only another experience on the way to final understanding?

Then what about Edna? What'll it mean for her? Well, Edna has a long, long life ahead, and in the course of it she will find out more what people can be. She already knows how evil they can be but she's got to know something harder still, which is how weak they

can be, how easily they tire, or are diverted, how will-
ingly they are deceived, what an obstinacy of weakness
and confusion and acidia seizes them when they are
confronted by any realization of their true purpose. We
cannot stick to *any* purpose, most of us, and least of all
the purpose of being happy—which is now her purpose.
But, he thought in astonishment, *I* was happy! I was—
for that little while.

Then he heard Pop talking again and his words were
all beginning to slur together. "A good thing about
this," he said, in a reasonable but drunken voice, "is
that it gets you, once and for all, out of that mess you're
in."

Edna was sitting with one elbow on the table. With
her fingers she pushed her soft, loose pompadour up
and down as though she had a headache. She turned
her eyes indifferently to Pop. "What mess?" she said.

"Don't be *too* dumb," he said. "There are limits.
Mort's the mess I mean."

"Lay off him," she said wearily.

"I won't do it," he said. "It's time you and me had a
talk about him, a real serious talk."

"I'm telling you to lay off him," she said.

"He's gone," Pop said, "but that don't mean he won't
come back. Oh, no! That don't mean he won't come
back." He looked wisely from her to Terhune and to
her again. "And when he does you'd better be far, far
away."

"Yeah?"

"I said far, far away. I mean that. Get me." He hiccoughed loudly.

"You're tight," she said.

"Maybe I am, but what of it? I'm still making sense. I say you better be far, far away."

"Don't say it again," she said, "because I'll be right here, waiting."

"Not if I can help it you won't. If I can help it you'll never see that great big ape again." He turned to Terhune. "Is that right, fellow, or is that right?"

"Shut up," she said, "and don't ask him anything." Her face flushed. "It's none of his business. Mort is *my* friend."

"Friend! Ha!" He slammed a hand down on the table. "Some friend. What's he done to make him your friend? He gives you a handout every so often. He slaps you on the fanny and calls you Baby. Are you dumb enough to fall for that?"

Edna's face grew darker. "I'm not kicking," she said.

Terhune said, "Let her alone for Christ's sake. You've done enough to her."

She gave him a hard look, a cold and measuring look. He had nothing to say to her. The words he could offer were all shoddy, secondhand, palm-worn. He had no new words for her.

Pop sprawled with his arms out on the table. Leaning toward her he said, "You're in love with him. I can see it. In love with that great big ape, a kid like you—"

She shrank back from him and her face remained hard.

"Someone ought to tell you about that," he said. "I don't think you know exactly what that means. This Mort—what is he? A great kidder, so they all say. And

a killer, too, according to what I hear. Oh, I guess you
know as well as I do what he is. But it's love you don't
know. Love is what someone ought to tell you about.
Someone ought to tell you what it would be like to be
loved by a big ape like Mort."

Edna said coldly, "Oh, be your age, Pop. I guess I
know more about that than you do."

Pop stared at her with his mouth open. He started to
turn to Terhune again, then he looked quickly back.
"What do you mean?" he said clearly.

Edna's eyes were as suffused as his and they looked
blind. "Just what I say," she said.

Pop banged on the table with both arms and roared at
her, "Why, you little scut! You're trying to tell me he's
loved you already. That great big ape has loved you
already!"

"So what?" she said. "I guess he's good enough for
me."

Pop gave her a wild look, full of doubt, of disgust, of
fury, and suddenly he dropped his head on his hands.
Edna stared over his head into the shadows of the room;
then she reached out mechanically and turned on the
radio.

At first there was a noise like the sound of a football
game heard at a distance, husky roars came in waves.
Suddenly an excited voice sprang into the room. "New
York. Mr. and Mrs. Stanley Stuyvesant are lullybying,"
it said. "Congratulations, Stan. . . . Flash. Washington.
Henry Wallace, not yet confirmed as Secretary of Com-
merce, threatens to carry the issue to the people. . . .
Connecticut. Governor Baldwin will appoint Admiral

Hart to fill the vacancy in the Senate. Insiders on the case say the murderer of Don Rocco gave Mrs. Rocco eight fur coats to keep her from talking. . . ." The voice took complete possession of the room.

Maybe there'll be something about me, Terhune thought. But he didn't care.

He felt sick. All his sickness of mind and body came back. Oh, Edna, it's not true. Why did you say it! It's not true. But then he knew it must be true. The circumstances all made it inevitable. But it wasn't only that. Why, he thought, I've just seen in her the complete knowledge of love, the ultimate knowledge, which is that the object of love is never worthy. And it doesn't matter. What matters is only the need to love. I don't feel sorry for Edna, he thought. I'll never know what Edna knows.

The voice had just said something but he caught only a word about "congratulations," then it snapped off.

Edna was staring at him. "Hear that?" she asked.

"No. What?"

"They picked him up."

"Who?"

"Mort. They picked him up at Newark airport. Only he didn't say it was Mort."

"Well, who did he say it was?"

"He said the man who ran the racket. He said the man who killed the G-man in Astoria. He said the police were to be congratulated."

"He must have meant Mort."

"Yeah."

"What's this?" Pop exclaimed. He lifted his head from the table. "I hear something about Mort?" he asked. He looked as though he had been crying, or asleep.

"Yes, you did. It seems they've picked him up. Edna heard it just now on the radio."

"I didn't hear they'd picked Mort up. I only heard they'd picked up a prominent racket man, the one who bumped the guy."

"Then that's Mort."

"Maybe." Her intent and questioning eyes didn't leave Terhune's face. "You think it's him?"

"Why, it must be," he said.

"But it was at Newark airport."

"Yes. Well, what?"

"They weren't going to Newark."

"You don't know, Edna," he said. "He may have changed his plans."

"No. They were driving through the tunnel, then west across Jersey. And Gus was with them. There were the two of them," she said. "Gus and Mort."

"Maybe they separated, or maybe, since Gus wasn't the killer, he wasn't important enough to mention."

"But they didn't go to Newark," she repeated insistently.

"How do you know?" Pop cried. "Did they give you their exact itinerary?"

She paid no attention to him but went on looking fixedly at Terhune, as though he should be the one to answer.

"Well then, that's Mort, isn't it?" he said.

"I don't know."

"But he killed a G-man. He was going to Jersey."

"Yeah, but it didn't say his name."

"It must be, though."

She seemed to be in a torment of doubt. "I don't get it," she said desperately. "What's it mean?"

"It means they got the great big ape," Pop said. "That's what it means." He rubbed his hands together and his voice cracked with excitement. "They got him. That's what it means."

"I think he's right, Edna."

If she loved Mort her face was not that of a grieving woman. It was all rigid with the effort to grasp something, something they couldn't see.

"He wasn't taking any plane," she said.

"Listen, Edna," Pop said shrilly, "you got to believe it. You got to. They picked him up, and it's the best thing ever happened to you. It settles everything."

And Terhune felt as he did. An elation he couldn't control was beginning to well up in him. Mort, the tough guy, the big bully boy, was caught. The helpless old man and the man with the broken leg had got the best of him. And as for Edna, he'd never put a hand on her again. He felt himself smiling, an idiotic smile of victory, but for Edna's sake he made his face serious again.

Pop seized the bottle and poured himself a drink, and Terhune thought, in a minute he'll pass out. But he didn't care. Let the old guy get blotto if he wanted to, let the final scene in the attic be a small orgy, a fantasia of triumph, too easily earned perhaps, but then in dreams nothing is earned and no one really pays for anything.

Edna said, "It's funny. It's funny they were picked up so easy."

"Oh, what the hell!" Pop said. "You just hate to think he was trying to put one over on you. I'll tell you what I'll bet. I'll bet Mort was off to Canada or Mexico. I'll bet that's what he had in mind the whole time. Only he got caught. Say, wouldn't I like to have seen his face!"

Edna pushed up her pale, silver-gold pompadour and leaned her forehead on her open palm. "Oh, I wish I *knew*!" she said.

Pop, having swallowed half a glass, gave a great, gasping belch. "You know, I suddenly remember something," he said. "It was that time I gave Mort a piece of my mind. Based on a tip someone gave me. Pop—sees all, knows all. How'd he take it? 'Pop,' he says, 'you talk too much.' Then he cracked my two front teeth in. The big ape—" Suddenly he clasped his hands together and gave a long, crowing sound of jubilation. "Oh, boy! Oh, boy! Oh, boy!"

"Listen," Edna said. She sat up straight, her eyes shining with concentration. "Listen. I want to tell you something. Gee, why didn't I think before? We gotta get out, and get out quick. That *wasn't* Mort they picked up. But he'll hear it. He always listens to the news. He's got a radio in the car. And when he hears it he'll think he's in the clear. And listen, maybe he heard it hours ago. Two or three hours. Maybe they'd just got started when he heard it. He maybe had time to turn back and get a good dinner somewhere. And then he'll come here. To get the stuff out tonight. Why, maybe he's right outside."

That was it. Terhune recognized it with all the shock of truth, and Pop recognized it, too. He got up without a word and staggered across the room and leaned over the trapdoor. He made reassuring signs back at them, then leaned over again. He put his head down and abruptly drew it back. He held his finger to his lips. "Ssh," he said. "Don't talk so loud. They're down there now. I hear them walking around."

In the silence they listened, but they heard nothing.

Pop tiptoed unsteadily back. "What'll we do?" he whispered.

"I don't hear anything," she said.

"Neither do I," Terhune said.

"They're there, I tell you. I heard someone walking. I heard someone shutting a door."

Terhune said, "He's awfully drunk. I don't believe he knows what he hears!"

Pop leaned a hand on the table and balanced himself. "Who's drunk?" he said. "I tell you, I heard Mort's voice."

"Why don't they come up then?" Terhune said.

"I tell you they're looking around. They sounded like they might be going to the basement. That's why you don't hear anything now."

Edna said, "There's some stuff in the basement."

Terhune said, "Then you both slip downstairs. Quick, both of you. Don't waste a second. You can get out."

Edna didn't move. He leaned forward and gripped both her arms lying on the table. "For God's sake, don't be caught here! Get out!" he said.

She looked at him and then at Pop, and Terhune said,

"If Pop can't make it, leave him. I'll look after him. Get out!"

Edna got up slowly. She said, "Come on, Pop. Give me a hand."

Pop did not hear her. He tiptoed waveringly over to the trapdoor again. When he got there he hung on to the door, leaning forward to listen.

Edna came around the table and took Terhune's arm. When he saw what she actually intended he said in a low voice, "You damned little fool, leave me alone."

He jerked his arm from her and drew back. They looked at each other in a fury of anger. Then she fell on him, seized him under the arms and tried to lift him up. Her sudden weight forced him back against the table, but with one foot on the floor he braced himself, and he was stronger than she. He pulled her arms from him and held them against her sides. He held her in his arms, smelling a drugstore perfume, more poignant than the breath of poverty. He held her closer, and suddenly she was still. Her fury passed into a gentle submission, sad as the sadness of her young bones, delicately animal as the complete innocence of her young flesh. He held her like this and pressed his lips to her temple through the fine softness of her hair. Finally he kissed her on the mouth.

Then Pop's voice came faintly across the room. "Hey!" he said feebly, "hey! They're coming up."

Terhune let Edna go. She straightened and looked dazedly around. She went back to her chair and sat down.

Pop, as though he hung and supported himself by an

invisible cord stretched out to him, staggered back and sat in the other chair.

Then they waited. They listened to the men coming up. Heard their voices. Heard their voices stop as they saw the light.

Someone called, "Who's up there?"

Edna said. "It's me."

The steps began again.

CHAPTER XI

A MAN'S head appeared above the level of the floor, a decapitated head it seemed, turning slowly. Then it rose, supported by a large body. When the man was in the room a second man followed and stood beside him.

"Jeez," he said. "We got company."

Terhune knew the voice. This was Gus.

The other did not speak, but came to the table and stood holding the back of the chair where Terhune's foot rested. He was a heavy fellow with a red face where networks of veins showed, especially in the whites of his small, black eyes. It was a fattish face in which a correctly modeled nose and mouth were lost, somehow. He pushed his hat back on his head, showing a little cluster of damp, black curls pressed to his forehead like a miniature of the flat curls between the horns of a bull. Terhune knew at once he had been a pink and white baby, all curves and dimples. When his mother left him outside the A. and P. tired housewives would have stopped to coo over him.

This must be Mort.

Gus slipped around him and peered down at Terhune. He turned to Edna. "Who's the boy friend?" he asked.

Terhune, afraid some recognition, or at least some preknowledge, would show in his face, looked away and did not answer.

Gus, he had seen at the first glance, was not as he expected. Physically, he was like Edna in color, but in nothing else. Everything about his face was slightly out of line, the nose, the mouth, one eyebrow—except for this he would have been a beautiful boy. As it was his good looks were disturbing, as though there had been a crazy and evil intention against him from the start.

With what must have been a characteristic gesture he shook a pale gold lock out of his eyes. The pupils of his eyes were pinpoints. "Who's the boy friend?" he repeated.

Mort gave a backward flip of the hand. "Get going," he said. "You got work to do."

Gus said, "Why, the boys aren't even here yet."

"I told you to get going."

"Listen," Gus said, "you know they won't be here for an hour yet. And I want to know what goes on."

"I'll find out what goes on," Mort said. "On your way."

Gus looked at Edna. "You better tell a good one," he said.

Then he turned and went to the trapdoor. The uneven step Terhune had heard turned out to be full of grace. It was a dancing step, made by a half-blind dancer. At the trapdoor he turned and gave a salute with one finger, the gesture Edna had made. It was a sort of family signal, perhaps. He disappeared, and they heard him going reluctantly downstairs.

Mort looked around at the occupied chairs, and Pop instantly got out of his and staggered over to the wall under the windows. Here he leaned, shaking visibly, and saying nothing. That rabid exhibitionist, Terhune thought, now wished to shake himself into the walls and disappear from view, probably because a greater exhibitionist had come. Already Mort made them all seem to be drained of half their color and substance, though he had really said little and scarcely moved.

He looked at the chair where Terhune's foot was. "What's the matter with him?" he said to Edna.

"He broke his ankle," she said.

"I'm the one to talk to," Terhune said. "What do you want to know?"

Mort didn't answer him. He pulled the chair vacated by Pop toward him and sat down. Then he examined, with an attention which was meant to be a part of his rebuff, every object on the table, the radio, the sterno, the can of beans, the coffee, the remains of the food, the newspaper. The tube of shaving cream and the razor had gone back to the pocket of Pop's coat, still on the back of the chair. *That* was good luck anyway, Terhune thought. It would have given much too much of a house-keeping air. As he watched Mort's manicured finger touching each object he felt a strong repulsion for his finger, though there was nothing wrong with it except the high glaze of the nail. Then he realized it was because he'd unconsciously connected it with Edna. She had probably given him the manicure. It was odious to think of her bending over that plump, muscular hand.

Mort said, "You weren't expecting me, baby, were you?"

"Yeah, I was expecting you," she said.

"Is all this for me?" he asked.

Edna nodded.

"Well, that's nice," he said, "that's very nice. Looks like we're having a celebration—a regular clambake."

It was hard to tell yet whether or not he was angry. His face was solid and expressionless. And even looking at Edna, Terhune couldn't tell for she also looked only calm and perhaps just a little wary. He couldn't tell whether or not this was their usual manner with each other or if there was a constraint they would recognize that he didn't.

"Quite a clambake," Mort said, "only I don't like the company. First, you got that old bum, then a guy I never seen before. You can do better than that, baby."

Edna didn't attempt to answer. She simply shrugged and waited for him to get down to the point. She must have expected he'd take his time about it.

Mort was not handsome but Terhune saw that he cared for himself as though he were. He was a fancy dresser. He wore a tan suit with padded shoulders that looked expensive, except that it was cut a bit too closely. He wore a silk shirt; his foulard tie and a handkerchief showing at his breast pocket were matched. He had two disadvantages making for disorder—hairiness, and an inclination to fat. His wrists were furry, black hair showed in his nostrils, his shaven chin was bluish, and

his stomach bulged slightly over his belt, but in spite
of these he managed to look neat and well groomed, and
this showed he spent time on himself and preferred to
present a pleasing appearance. Indeed, there was something pleasing about him, a physical ease and a volup-
tuous well-being left over from the handsome baby.
Nothing yet suggested the savage killer described by Pop,
though that "bounce," that muscular drive, were visible.
And another of Pop's observations was beginning to be
borne out, which was that when he got hold of a joke he
liked to hang on to it.

He said to Edna, "I see I got to keep my eye on you.
Soon as I turn my back and you're on your own, you
make all the wrong social contacts."

Edna smiled for the first time, a very faint, small, and
perhaps only dutiful, smile. It showed, however, that
there had been a constraint but that it was beginning to
lighten.

"Don't you think you can get down to cases?" Terhune asked him.

Mort gave a glance in his direction. "Don't try to
crowd me," he said. "I'll get around to you in a minute."
Then he turned toward Edna again. "Come on, baby,"
he said. "First we have your story."

"Well," Edna said, "I came up here and found this
guy."

Mort waited for more. Then he didn't actually smile
but he looked amused.

Terhune thought, everyone is getting back to his
natural behavior. This means that Mort considers a
laconic reply an accepted part of Edna's character, and

he finds it, as always, amusing. They have formed a habit of admiring each other's peculiarities. That is the atmosphere between them.

"I thought I told you to stay away from here," Mort said, amiably.

"That was this afternoon," she said; then she added impudently, "You said then you'd stay away yourself. What *you* doing here?"

"I heard something to change that," he said.

"Well, I did, too."

"Yeah? Where?"

"I heard it on the radio. Where'd you get it?"

"On the radio. Just as we were halfway to that place I told you about."

"Well, I heard it, so I figured you'd come back."

Mort's look of amusement deepened. "You got out of that all right," he said.

The atmosphere between them, Terhune thought, was not that between lovers. If he hadn't known a moment ago, holding her in his arms, he'd have known now. It was a more subtle balance, with many nuances he couldn't guess yet. And absorbed by that innocence and what it meant to him, he thought, one factor in their relations was precisely her innocence, and Mort found her innocence funny. But also he valued it. It was a point of secret, obscure vanity with him: he could keep around him a kid, a woman, almost, and she was innocent.

He said, now, a little less amiably, "I see you got some liquor here. Where'd you get it?"

"It belongs to Gus," she said. "I found it in his room. He always keeps some there."

"But you know I don't drink."

"Yeah, of course. I just thought some of the boys might be with you."

He said, "Now, I like people to think of things like that. It's thoughtful. And then I see you got beans and coffee and sandwiches. That's thoughtful, too." He lifted the bottle to the light and shook it slightly. There was obviously very little in it. "Pop must have got at this," he said.

Hearing his name Pop took a few scraping steps out from the wall. Mort did not turn, and Pop spoke from behind his back. "You know me, Mort," he said.

"Yeah, I know you."

"I like a little drink every now and then."

"Sure—you're a lush."

"Now, not a lush, Mort—just convivial." He smiled and winked at Terhune over Mort's head. "Just friendly, always ready to help a friend celebrate. I crashed the party."

"Remind me to laugh sometime."

Mort's voice hadn't changed much but Pop evidently noticed a new note was beginning to come into it. "What seems to be the trouble, Mort?" he asked quaveringly.

"I told you to keep away from here, too."

"That's right, you did!" he exclaimed. "You did. I remember it. But I was just coming along the street and I met Edna and she asked me up."

Mort said to Edna, "That right?"

"Yeah, that's right."

But Pop couldn't let well enough alone. "She was feeling awfully pleased," he said. "She was feeling so pleased, that's why she asked me up."

"Oh, she was pleased, was she? She tell you why?"

Edna said, "I never told him a thing. But I guess you know why I felt so good. I was going to give him a quick one and send him on his way."

"You both came up here together?"

"That's right."

"Did you invite this guy, too?"

After a moment's hesitation she said, "No, we found him here."

Mort took out a cigarette case that might have been of gold. It was the sort that would be presented to him at a dinner by admiring friends. It would be inscribed, "To Mort. A prince of good fellows. From the Waterfront Benevolent Association." He took out a cigarette, closed the case, and put it back in his pocket. Then he got out a match, struck it on his thumbnail, and lighted his cigarette. All this time he seemed like the dealer in a poker game, dealing out silence. Everyone watched him.

"You," he said finally, jerking his head toward Terhune, but looking at the tip of his cigarette, "what's your story?"

"It's very simple," Terhune said. "I was in New York for the day and I had some time on my hands. I came down here to look up a house I used to live in years ago. It was this house. I saw the door unlatched and I came in."

"The door was unlatched?"

"Yes."

Mort turned toward Edna. She said, "I don't know who left it open. Maybe Benny. He don't see so good."

"Maybe—" He turned back to Terhune. "What'd you do then?"

"I looked around a bit. The place wasn't as I remembered it. I came upstairs because this attic used to be my room. I didn't want to go without seeing it. But it was dark by that time and I fell over something and broke my ankle."

"Then what?"

"Then I was knocked out for a while, and then this girl and the old man came in, just as she says, and found me."

He wondered what Mort thought of it. He himself was so used now to being in the attic that he might never have been anywhere else. It was his permanent shell, it was himself. His explanation of how he got here seemed as frivolous to him, though for entirely different reasons, as it must seem to Mort. He represented, found like this, a curious problem in what to believe, and Mort, he saw, was not quite as stupid as Pop had said. The unexpected fact hadn't at all thrown him off balance and, more than that, his instinct told him there was something even more unexpected hidden in it. There was something of motive, of emotion, that touched more or less everyone in the room. This instant realization of strangeness was what had made him cagey from the beginning. He had to move cautiously but thoroughly, overlooking nothing.

They had to be cautious, too, and match his thoroughness. Unfortunately, they were several and had to have a story in agreement, but they weren't prepared for that.

"You say it was dark when you came?" Mort asked.

"About sunset. It was dark inside the house."

Mort held up his hairy wrist and glanced at his watch. "This happen tonight?" he asked.

Terhune, after a second's hesitation, said, "Yes, tonight."

Mort looked thoughtfully at Edna. Terhune realized why he deferred constantly to her, the young, the naïve, participant. It was because he knew her and would be able to detect in her more quickly what was strange, especially that obscure emotional involvement that he felt in them.

"Tonight," Mort repeated. "And you, baby, what time did you get here?"

"Ten, twenty minutes ago, I guess."

"Must have been a surprise," he said, "you coming in with beans and coffee, and sandwiches, and whisky, and finding him here."

"Yeah, it was."

"What were you going to do about it?"

"Get in touch with you," she said.

"You were pretty sure I'd come."

"Yeah, I was."

The puzzlement showed more clearly on his face. Terhune knew why now. It was because of Edna's calm. Even for her it was too much. There was a lack in her. There should have been a spontaneous curiosity and alarm in finding a stranger here. Her manner had the effect of having been deliberately controlled and prepared in advance. There was a lack in himself, too. Even in the drunken old man. They were all too controlled.

They had all prepared, if not a story, a manner. Even as he thought of it Edna also seemed to realize it, for she tried to turn Mort's attention to a subject where she could be more lax and at ease.

"Aren't the boys coming tonight?" she asked.

"Yeah," Mort said slowly. "They're coming, but it's kind of awkward, isn't it, having visitors?"

"I'm not a visitor," she said.

"No, but this guy is, and Pop is."

"Oh," she said quickly, "Pop's screwy. He don't know from nothing. Why don't you let him go and forget it?"

"Listen, now listen," Mort drawled, "supposing you let me say what to forget, and what not to forget."

"O.K.," Edna said, "I guess I spoke out of turn."

"I guess you did."

He looked at her soberly, shaking his head very slightly, and she said, "You aren't sore, are you?"

"Yeah, I am sore. But not at you. You're a good kid. Only I got a feeling maybe I ought to keep an eye on you. I been spoiling you a little." With a face still sober he doubled up one fist and made a phantom jab at her jaw, barely touching it. She smiled. Evidently this, too, was a playful routine of theirs.

Then he said, with no change in his voice, "What's the guy's name?"

Terhune answered, "My name's Terhune."

"I didn't ask you."

"I'm the one to ask. Why should she know?"

"Didn't you ask him who he was?"

"Oh, sure, I asked him," Edna said. "That's what he told me, Terhune."

"Did he tell you how he came here?"

"Yeah, just like he said."

"Believe it?"

"Yeah, I believe it. He sounded so kind of screwy that I figured it must be the truth."

"You think everyone's screwy," Mort said. "That's getting to be a bad habit of yours. Everyone's screwy but you. Only you're smart. Now I don't think this guy is screwy a-tall. I think maybe he's crazy like a fox."

"What do you mean by that?" Terhune said. "I've told you the truth."

Mort's voice suddenly snapped at him like a whip. "Nobody's told me the truth yet," he said. "I've only heard a lot of craperoo and I don't like it."

Edna said, "Well, I just told you what happened."

"No, you didn't, and I'm awfully afraid I'm going to have to do something about it. You mustn't get to thinking *I'm* screwy."

"Why, Mort!" she exclaimed. "You *are* sore." She opened her eyes like a child unjustly reproved. Her whole face showed a reproach, and at the same time a subservience that with the least encouragement would become comical. Terhune thought she overdid it grossly and he wondered if Mort, who probably was accustomed to his satellites overdoing things, was accustomed to quite this much parody from her. In any case he apparently accepted it, not as parody, but as the real thing. That he should be so easily deluded, even in the midst of his suspicions, showed, Terhune thought, that her attitude simply answered a real need in him to believe her.

He shook his head seriously but his voice was mild

again. "Don't try to put anything over on papa," he told her. "You can't get away with it."

He dropped his cigarette on the floor, leaned forward, and folded his arms on the table.

"Now," he said, "I'm going to tell all of you what happened. No one came here like they said. You," he looked at Terhune, "you didn't come in this evening. You been here quite a while. Long enough to get good and hungry. You couldn't get food for yourself, so you sent someone out. The food's been here a couple hours, maybe. Someone's had time to lap up most of the liquor. It must have been Pop went for it, and that means *he* came in and found you. Right? And I know it was Pop and nobody else, because Edna and me had a little talk around four o'clock this afternoon. That was when I told her not to come up here. We had quite a talk about the place, and she never mentioned anything about a guy hiding out here, so I know she didn't come until a while ago, like she said. Only she lied about Pop. She didn't bring him in, she didn't buy this stuff to celebrate. Well, that's about how it went. You came last night. Pop found you. He bought the stuff for you. Edna came in tonight. Right?"

Pop had been listening and as he listened he made soundless words, smiling to himself. His face was dark red and his eyes watered. Now he took another step toward the table and answered promptly, "Right. Yes, you sure sized it up all right. It was me found him. I came in and found him, and he asked me to get him some food, so I went out and got it."

"Come out here where I can look at you," Mort said.

Pop moved sidewise like a crab till he stood by the table. He leaned one hand on it, breathing through his open mouth.

"I told you to stay away from here, didn't I?"

"That's right, you did. But you see, lately I've had this pain, in the chest. I had pneumonia last winter and they took me over to Welfare, so I don't feel so good in wet weather."

"I don't give a damn how you feel," Mort said, "I told you to stay out of here."

Pop looked indignantly at Edna for support, but Edna only looked back at him warningly; then suddenly she dropped her eyes. She didn't want Mort to see the strain in them.

"I was hunting for a place to sleep," Pop said, more distinctly. He made a dignified gesture that sketched briefly roofs, shelter, the inclement weather. "But they're tearing everything down. This is about all's left." His voice slurred again. "If you don't get your sleep," he said, "you can't keep in condition."

Terhune saw with a sick sense of unease that he was so drunk he could scarcely stand. He kept his balance only by a continuous shifting of weight, which was what made him seem to be trembling. Also, all his edgy wits were dulled, all his briskness had become lethargic. He saw also that Mort was beginning to feel that Pop was the weakest spot in the combination and that he was preparing to concentrate on him, leaving Edna for the time being.

Before Mort could speak Pop stumbled and made a sudden snatch at the whisky bottle and Mort struck his hand down. It was a light blow but Pop cried, "Ouch!" and stared at his hand in astonishment. Then he held it against his chest, covering it with the other hand. He said indignantly, "Why, you damned near broke my hand!"

Mort watched him and his eyes became so calculating that Terhune decided to divert him if he could. If Mort really made up his mind to concentrate on the old man, to put him to an inquisition, it would be the worse for all of them. Pop would never hold out.

Terhune said, "You've got it straight now. I did come in last night. I don't know why I said what I did, except that I knew you wouldn't like my being here and I thought the shorter the time I'd been here the better. The old man came in today, the girl, as she said, about twenty minutes ago."

"What did you lie about Pop for, baby?" Mort asked.

"I was afraid you'd be sore at him," she said.

Again she was laconic, but this time it didn't go over. He took out his case and got another cigarette. When he had lighted it he narrowed his eyes against the smoke. "As to your being so anxious to cover for Pop, we'll go into that later," he said. "Now I got a few more things to clear up. I want to ask, for instance, what Pop did all day besides go out and buy things."

Terhune answered for him, "He didn't do anything. I asked him to call an ambulance for me but he told me he couldn't do that."

"Did he? What about friends? You didn't maybe ask him to call up some friends for you?"

"He wouldn't call anyone."

"Did he say why not?"

"No."

"Maybe you guessed?"

"Well, yes. It's pretty obvious, isn't it?"

"So you just let it go at that?"

"I had no choice."

"You didn't maybe offer him a little something to get in touch with your friends?"

"See here!" Terhune said, "I think you ought to know more about me. I'm afraid you have a totally wrong impression. I told you I came here by chance, but I can prove it, that is, I can prove I am someone who would have no possible interest in you, who had never heard of you, and doesn't care if he never hears of you again. Look at this." He took out his passport and laid it on the table.

Mort said, "Let's see what else you got." So he took out everything that was in his pockets, driving license, his wallet, a bunch of keys, the bottle of sleeping pills, his cigarette case, two letters addressed to him at the steamer, a handkerchief, a clip of matches. When they were all before him Mort got out a pair of horn-rimmed spectacles and put them on. They fitted his nose badly— it was too small and classic in shape, not meant for glasses—but he looked rather like a judge wearing them. He examined all the objects, lingering over the cigarette case as though surprised that it was not nearly as handsome as his own. He studied the driver's license, counted all the bills in the wallet, and compared the passport picture carefully with Terhune's face. Then he pushed everything back. Terhune returned each object to his pockets. Mort took his glasses off and put them away. "I see you been in Germany," he said.

There was a difference in his voice, a muted note of greater perplexity. His problem had been, in effect, that a man, a fellow he didn't know, had come into possession of knowledge dangerous to himself. But now that Mort knew who the man was the possibilities were even more complex. If the fellow really was here by accident, and a big shot—in his way—what could he do with him? He'd already let himself in for pursuit by the implacable government, with all its resources. The fellow didn't know this (Terhune almost read in his eyes that exact thought as it came to him), or did he know? That could be only because Edna had talked too much, and that, if only because of the time element, was scarcely possible. Or the old man? But then, the old man would hardly know himself. He might, though. In any case, the fellow had seen all this stuff here and he knew what it meant.

And besides, what if his passport and the rest were phonies after all? As he thought all these things his eyes grew bright and then narrowed into greater thoughtfulness. For beneath all this there was, as he had at first realized, something else, phonier perhaps than a set of phony papers, some happening that had brought this unlikely three together, some relationship that had already formed between them, some understanding. And as the suspicion grew that they, the three of them, might be putting something over on him, or trying to, his eyes suddenly glazed, looked blind, like china eyes. Terhune followed his suspicions and his fears. And he knew this was his own sole advantage—that he guessed what Mort was thinking but Mort couldn't guess what he was thinking.

The silence lasted a long time.

Then Mort said casually, "Government job?"

"Yes. It had to do with education. I'm the president of a college."

"I see. A professor, then."

"Not a professor. The president of a college doesn't have to be a professor."

"No? That's a new one on me."

He took his cigarette case out again but instead of opening it he held it in both hands, looking at it and shaking it up and down lightly. His flattish, classic face looked serious. He squinted through the smoke of the cigarette still in his mouth. They could all feel his indecision.

After a moment he said slowly, "Well, so everyone's come clean finally. And now we know who you are and when you got here. And we know Pop's the one found you. But I got just a few little details to settle with Pop. And Pop better answer for himself this time."

"O.K.," Pop said, "go ahead. Shoot. Anything you can think of to ask, I can answer it."

He still nursed his hand against his chest, but he was smiling idiotically. He seemed to think everything was going better and probably he ascribed it to his own handling of the situation.

Mort said, "You figured to give this guy the shake, didn't you?"

Pop laughed cacklingly, "Now see here, see here. You

know me. Why, I'm a man you can trust." He made another elaborate gesture, this one of candor, holding one
hand, palm up, toward Mort.

"Yeah. Well, now I'll tell you about how I can trust
you. I already heard your story, how you came up for
a drink with Edna, and I already told you you're lying
and that you spent the day here. Now I'll tell you what
you did all day. We leave out all question of who this
guy really is. So far as you're concerned that don't
matter, because no matter who he is or what he wants
here, there's just one thing certain—he wants out. The
quicker the sooner. But what do *you* do? You figure
here's your big chance. You figure you can put the
screws on him, shake him down for a couple hundred
bucks, maybe more—whatever you think the traffic
will stand.

"But he don't fall for it right away. Maybe you ask
for too much, or else he's got other ideas. And so you're
here all day, because you figure he'll have to give in
sooner or later. You even go out and get him food and
liquor, and you even lap up the liquor yourself because
you're so sure of the answer."

Pop said, "Now see here." He leaned his hands on the
table and his voice rose. "I never did any such thing. I
told you I'm a man you can trust. Why, I've got more
sense than to try a double cross on you. I knew it wasn't
right to let him out, no matter what he was to give me.
Even if he was to swear to keep his mouth shut. Why,
I was intending to get in touch with you. The only trouble was I didn't know where to find you and I didn't like
to leave him long enough to look for you."

"You went out, didn't you?"

"Well, yes, I did do that." Pop leaned forward to look at what he had bought and then said, airily, "Oh, it was only a few minutes."

"Then why didn't you try contacting Edna? You know where she lives. Why didn't you step into Louie's and leave the word?"

"I just thought I'd wait here until someone turned up. I thought you'd turn up. Or maybe Edna. She *did* turn up," he said, triumphantly.

"Yeah, she did, and she's explained why, though I'll be interested to hear later how *she* sized up the situation." He turned and looked steadily at her. "I'll be interested to know what *she* expected to do about it."

"Why, I was going to do just what Pop was going to do," she said. "If you didn't come like I thought I was going to get in touch with you."

"Everyone was going to get in touch," he said. "But no one did. Funny, eh?" He took Edna's hand and held it in both of his. "It's a good thing I know you like I do," he said. He seemed to speak earnestly and even warmly. "Because I believe you. Otherwise I might begin to get ideas. I'd begin to figure out that a kid like you was pretty easily influenced. That even old Pop must have influenced you, since you were so ready to cover up for him. And maybe even the professor here. It's true he hasn't had more than twenty minutes or so, according to what I hear, but still, even in that time, he might be able to give a kid like you a snow job."

"Oh, nuts," Edna said. Her face flushed and she closed her mouth tightly. Mort let go of her hand abruptly.

"Now about you," he said to Pop, "let's get back to you. I've told you what you did here but I didn't get to the best part. The best part is that you thought you could take your time. You had two days and two nights to work in, till the house came down. And if it hadn't been for the wreckers you'd have figured you had more time than that. You could starve the guy out if you had to. And why? I'll tell you: because you thought I was out of town."

"Out of town!" Pop exclaimed. He forced an expression of indignation to his face, then his own slyness spoiled it. He's a rotten actor after all, Terhune thought. But it wasn't that. He just couldn't resist being himself. He could act only himself. Now as he drowned in silliness, as he swam in it in slow motion, each gesture revealed by the very lethargy of the pace more malice, more vanity. "Out of town," he said craftily. "Now why should I think *that?*"

"Suppose you tell *me.*"

"What's there to tell? Maybe you were. Maybe you weren't. You think *I* care where you spend your time?"

This slowness of his seemed to infect Mort, too. He didn't answer right away but fiddled with his cigarette case, spinning it with one finger in circles on the table.

Edna fixed her eyes anxiously and compellingly on Pop but he was too far gone to give her more than a fatuous frown, telling her to keep out of this.

Mort said, "You like to snoop. You like to find out things. Like that tip you gave me. How'd you pick that one up?"

"It don't matter how I picked it up, does it? Anyway,

I passed it on to you. And little thanks I got for it, too.
Two busted teeth, that's what."

"You got five bucks."

"Five bucks!" Pop cried. He ruffled one hand through
his sparse hair and a few hairs remained indignantly on
end. "What's five bucks to a big racket man like you?
You might as well have given me five cents."

"Oh, so I'm a big racket man, am I?"

Edna said sharply, "Watch it, Pop."

He waved her aside with his hand.

"Yes, that's what I said, a big racket man, a great big
racket man. Anyway, you like to think of yourself as big,
don't you? Well, if you're so big you have to expect
people will take a certain interest in you from time to
time."

"Then you did know I was out of town."

Mort said this so quietly that Pop seemed offended
by his lack of emphasis. He drew himself up. Then he
winked at Terhune as though to say: Listen, this one
will be good. He held up one finger. "There's a big
noise when you're around," he said. "Suddenly there
seemed to be a silence."

"Pop!" Edna cried. Then she said to Mort, "Don't pay
any attention to him. He got away with most of the
bottle and he don't know what he's saying."

"No, no, he's very inter-esting," Mort said. He threw
his cigarette onto the floor. "I like to hear him talk. Go
ahead, Pop, and tell me about what you know. And tell
me about *how* you know it, too."

"What's it worth to you?" Pop demanded, hectoringly.
"Another five bucks? Nothing doing."

"Maybe it's worth more."

Pop started to laugh derisively. Then he caught the anguished message in Edna's eyes, and this time a gleam of caution came to him. He hiccoughed, embarrassedly. "I didn't say that," he said.

"Maybe you think it's worth a couple hundred. A grand, maybe. You wouldn't want to put the bite on a big racket man like me for less than a grand."

"Oh, come now," Pop said. He made a vague gesture of reassurance toward Edna. "Why don't we quit all this foolishness? You know I'd never try to put the bite on you, no matter what I knew."

"No matter what you knew. But you are hep to something, aren't you?"

"Quit it, Mort," Edna said. "You're just driving him crazy. He don't know what he's saying."

"Who says I don't know what I'm saying?" Pop's caution struggled with his vanity. He bent over Mort and mouthed recklessly at him, but with no sound coming, then he began to talk in slow, slurring words, his voice gradually rising, and every now and then a hiccough interrupting. "Now, see here. I'm getting sick of this. People think they can say anything to me, or about me. They act like I'm not there. They don't care *what* they say about me. And that's just how I find out the things I do, that's just exactly how. You're wondering if I really know anything or am just bluffing, and if so, how I know it. I'll tell you. I pick up a word here, a word there. A look passes between two mugs in a bar, say, Louie's. A plainclothes man comes in to Casey's and asks a certain question. All the time they're not noticing me.

If they do, they say: never mind, it's just the old bum. Things no one would put together *I* put together. Why, before I even heard it on the radio I knew what had happened, and I guessed it was *you* did it.

"And then, another thing you don't know, and that is what goes on in here." He tapped his forehead. "It isn't only what I know. It's what I think about it. Anyone can guess the lowdown. But what does he think about it? That's what you don't know about. Why, I got in here something you can't touch, something that watches, something that judges."

He rapped his forehead with his finger. All his gestures were becoming ever more absurdly histrionic. "Yes, something no one can touch, but least of all you, Mort, because, to tell the God's truth, you're nothing but a big schlemiehl. I said to Mr. Terhune just a while back, I said, 'He's a racket man and a killer, and he's got a sort of style to him, but inside his head there's only soup.' Why," he said, and his voice sank suddenly to a confidential lowness, "if you'd even had half a brain would you have come back here like you did? No. You'd have seen those government guys were putting something over on you. You didn't see it, but I see it. I'm tipping you off like I did before. They never picked up anyone at Newark airport. If they picked up someone they never thought for a minute they had the fellow killed their man. They know *you* killed him, and that piece on the radio was a plant. They knew it would make you feel easy in your mind, and instead of lamming out you'd stick around. And do you know what's going to happen to you? They're going to come here in a little while and pick you up. What a schlemiehl!"

Well, Terhune thought, that tears it. He's done it up brown, for all of us.

Edna clasped her hands to her chest. "He's tight," she whispered, "don't listen to him."

Mort sat motionless, with lowered eyes. Terhune felt that if Mort raised his eyes they would see his china stare. But he didn't look up. He leaned back and seemed to forget Pop. And Pop, after a few abortive gestures, a few words formed but not spoken, passed, himself, into a reverie that seemed to be almost as peaceful as sleep. And in it he also forgot them. He supported himself by his hands, and his head nodded gently and his eyelids fluttered, and Terhune thought at any moment he'd collapse into complete unconsciousness on the table.

The silence grew heavy, and again it was Mort who imposed it on them and they had to take it.

Then Mort reached out and patted Edna's arm. "Baby," he said, heavily, "I want you to go get me some aspirin, and on your way down tell Gus to come up, will you?"

Edna looked at him pleadingly. "Don't do that, Mort," she said. Her voice, still husky, sounded suddenly younger and thinner than any of theirs, it had a treble note that made it seem to have less weight than before. "Don't do it," she said.

"Don't do what?"

She hesitated, afraid to say the word. "Anything," she said.

"Who says I'm going to do anything? I tell you to get me some aspirin."

"I'll get it, Mort, I'll get it. Can I take Pop along?"

"No. Leave him. He's too tight for you to handle."

"I can handle him."

"Quit worrying. Gus'll look after him."

But still she didn't move. "He won't remember a thing," she said. "He gets like that, then he's O.K."

"Shut up about Pop," he said. He turned around and looked at her, putting the whole weight of his will into his eyes. "I got a headache, I tell you, and I want some aspirin."

Edna held her still clasped hands toward him like a suppliant. "Oh, please don't be mean to him," she said. "He's so old."

Suddenly Mort's eyes seemed to soften. He gave her hands a little pat, pushed them away.

"Oh, sure I know he's old. I just don't want him around. I'm going to have Gus take him away some place where I don't have to look at him."

"I wish you'd let me take him."

"Now don't be like that," he said. "I don't like it. Sometimes you talk back and I get a kick out of it. Hell, I don't want nothing but yes-men. But don't do it now. Go get me a box of aspirin."

"I won't go unless you promise," she said.

Terhune expected his anger, but Mort only looked at her, thoughtfully. Finally he took a deep breath, like a sigh, and patted her shoulder.

"Run along, baby," he said. "Everything's O.K."

"You mean about Pop?"

"Yeah."

Edna also took a deep breath. She said, "You promise?"

"Sure, I promise."

"Cross your heart?"

"I said, I promise."

"You're a swell guy," Edna said.

"I'd do a lot for you, baby."

Edna suddenly leaned over and for an instant pressed her forehead against Mort's shoulder. It was the gesture of thanks of a child, or a puppy. Mort held himself very stiffly.

Then Edna got up and said, "O.K., I'll get your aspirin."

"Here," Mort said. He took a roll from his pocket and peeled off a ten-dollar bill. "Keep the change," he said.

Edna took the bill, put it in her purse, and snapped it shut.

"Don't forget to tell Gus," Mort said.

"I won't."

She was smiling now, a confident smile, like the one she reserved for Mort's grand sense of humor, except that it showed strain. She went around to Pop. He roused himself, smiled idiotically at her, and nodded his head.

"You do just what Mort tells you," she said. "Take it easy. And I'll be seeing you."

Pop answered easily, "Be seeing you."

Then she gave them all the little flicking salute of the finger and walked over to the trapdoor. She turned to go down the ladder.

Never once had she looked directly at Terhune, and she didn't look now. On her face he saw only the strained, confident smile. Then she disappeared.

When she reached the lower floor she started to walk slowly, but suddenly she broke into a run. Her high heels clattered like a shower of pebbles down the stairs.

CHAPTER XII

WHEN they couldn't hear her any more Mort got out his glasses and put them on. He picked up part of the Sunday newspaper and held it in front of him. Terhune and the old man might not have been in the room, except that to make space for the spread of the paper Mort pushed Pop's hand as though it had been something inanimate, like the can of coffee. It was only a moment the three of them were in this silence together, but Terhune had time to be thankful that Mort had sent Edna away.

He saw her moving off into the night. He saw her moving toward safety. That was what Mort had intended. He had deliberately sent her out of the range of his anger, his immediate anger. And he had meant her to stay away. When she thought of it she would know that was what he meant. She would think over his promise and probably she would believe in it. She had had a long trust in him. She might be right. In any case she had done all she could and there was no reason for her to come back.

Not for me certainly, he thought. Why should she

come back for me? She has done all she can for me, too, and what have I done for her? Nothing of good. I have only brought her into the extremest danger. I have only deluded her. (I have kissed her, and that kiss, for all she knows of me, might be a Judas kiss.) No, she won't come back for me. Even if she wanted to, any plea such as she made for Pop would only make my end more certain. I think she doesn't want to know my end, just as Mort doesn't want her to know it. So his will, so familiar to her, will envelop her once more and she won't come back.

Good-by, Edna, he thought, good-by, little ghost of myself, my little darling. Stay away, stay away from me forever.

When Gus came in Mort went on reading. Gus waited, balancing first on one foot and then on the other, a handsome, spoiled young man getting ready to start a tap dance. His look shifted from Mort's paper, hiding his face, to Terhune. He gave Terhune a queer, nervous smile. He took out a pack of cigarettes, thought better of it and put it back. Then, this use of his hands reminded him of something, he held them outspread and looked at them as though some sensation reached him through them, as though they were organs of sense. He smiled at them. Suddenly he gave a start that made his whole body jerk. He put his hands in his pockets.

"What'd you want me for?" he said.

Mort laid the paper aside. He took his glasses off and put them away. "Did Edna go out?" he asked.

"Sure she went out. She said she was going to get you some aspirin. She said she'd be right back."

"She won't be back," Mort said.

"So what?" Gus said, teetering on the balls of his feet. "So you got rid of Edna."

"I didn't want her around," Mort said. "I want you to do something for me."

"Yeah, and you didn't want Edna to know. Someday," he said, gloomily, "she'll bring you plenty trouble."

Mort looked contemptuously at him. "I heard somewhere that she's your kid sister."

"Sure she is. But I'm no fall guy myself. I know how to handle Edna."

"You think I don't?" Mort asked.

Gus shrugged his shoulders. He looked disinterested. "She can always give you a line. But I guess you can handle her. What was it you wanted?"

Mort's eyes hardened as he looked at him. He waited a long, cold moment before answering. Then he said, "I want you to take Pop downstairs. To the basement. You can show him what we got down there."

Gus took his hands out of his pockets and looked at them again. "You mean I should show him the basement?" he asked quietly.

"That's right."

"Like we showed it to Nelson?"

"That's right."

Gus began to smile again at his hands. "No foolin'?"

"No foolin'."

"Well, O.K. then. I guess I better get going."

"Yeah, you get going."

Suddenly everything in Gus broke into a little dance, into one graceful movement that carried him across to

where the old man stood. He tapped his shoulder lightly.
"Come on, Grandpa," he said, "you and me are going
places."

The old man very slowly turned his head toward Gus.
His arms slowly raised and rested heavily on Gus's
shoulders.

"Come on, Grandpa."

"Listen," Terhune said. "Don't do anything to him.
It's my fault."

"It don't make any difference whose fault it is," Mort
said. "Besides, you didn't *ask* him up here, did you?"

Terhune couldn't say who had asked him up. "No,
but it's my fault for being here. He was loyal to you. I
tried to offer him money but it was no use."

"Well, so what?" Mort said.

"Let him go. He'll never talk."

"That's what *you* think. I know him."

"One word from you—" Terhune began.

"One word from me and it'll be all over town. No,
leave it alone."

"Can't we at least talk about it? There ought to be
something else possible. If money would make any
difference—"

Mort looked at him with pity. "Get going, Gus," he
said.

The old man's mouth moved. He spoke to Gus without sound.

"What's he want?" Gus asked.

"Maybe he wants his overcoat," Mort said.

"He won't need it," Gus answered.

"Take it anyway," Mort said. "It smells."

Gus slipped one arm away and reached for the greenish overcoat on the back of the chair. He put his other arm around the old man and led him across the room. They moved, trancelike, with pauses and sudden arrestings of movement, as in a ballet. When they reached the trapdoor Gus twisted in front of him and with one hand held him bent over and with the other guided his feet down the ladder. The last Terhune saw of Pop was his bald spot, with the flyspecks on it.

Mort again took out his glasses and put them on. He opened the paper and turned several pages. He pretended to be reading again. Presently the whole house was quiet.

CHAPTER XIII

AFTER a few moments Mort shifted to lean on one elbow and Terhune saw he was not reading at all. His eyes did not move. They were set in the stare that saw nothing. But Terhune saw in their blind ferocity exactly what it was that Edna had escaped from. And he saw what he himself was moving to, as he had for a long time been moving, called from a distance, choosing it out of all things to be chosen.

This storm now centered around the old man's death, but presently it would center around his own. He and Pop, he thought, two men barely met together, disliking each other to the core, were meant by Mort's will to die a fraternal death.

As he watched him he had also the curious impression that he saw the moment when the old man died. Mort's expression changed, relaxed, as though he knew that particular concern was over. Perhaps he could estimate, out of his experience, the time it took, or he had a sort of barometer in himself, delicately adjusted to record the carrying out of his will. In any case, he became once more conscious of Terhune.

He yawned and put the paper down and took off his glasses. Then he crossed his arms and scratched his armpits.

"Well," he said, "it seems to boil down to you and me."

"It was you and me from the start," Terhune said.

"Think so? Well, I don't agree. There're other angles, and it don't pay to be hasty. You got to get the whole picture." He folded his plump, muscular, well cared for hands on the table. His face, because of its organization of curves and the cruel twinkle of his eyes, again reminded Terhune of a bull's face. "See what I mean? Basically, it's a question of security."

"You mean you're still not sure who I am, or why I'm here, and you don't know whether to take a chance on me."

Mort said, "Yes, that's about what I mean."

"So you're not going to take a chance."

Mort smiled. "I see you don't like to stall. But frankly speaking, I haven't made up my mind yet."

His voice had no finality and Terhune gathered he was meant to feel there might still be a deal. But how could there possibly be? Terhune now knew about the stolen liquor, the G-man, and even the old man, at this moment dead in the basement. What did Mort intend then by his uncertainty? Was it going to be a morbid pleasure to him to prolong Terhune's hope? Did he just want to make a fool of him? Terhune angrily decided this wouldn't happen. A man can face death with many sensations, and one of them might even be hope, but he won't, if he can help it, be made a fool of. And yet, Terhune thought, the consent to be made a fool of might contain a secret similar to death. That consent is itself a death for a great deal that encumbers our understanding. Many times I've been made a fool of, he thought, and always refused the secret, so what do I hope to learn from death itself?

But then, he thought, even if Mort intends to make a fool of me that isn't all he is after, that will be only by the way. He wants more than that. He wants to find out not what happened, because he knows that now, but why and how it happened.

Mort said, "You see, you got to get the whole picture." He spoke in an almost friendly voice, or one that would have seemed friendly in other circumstances.

"How about you?" Terhune asked. "Have you got it?"

"Listen," Mort said amiably, "just because I didn't latch on from the start you mustn't think I'm dumb from here in. From here in, pal, I not only get the picture but I make the picture."

"I knew I was right," Terhune said. "The old man seemed the paranoiac but then you came along and you outclassed him."

"That so? How do you figure that one out?"

"Because everything went on in his head and nothing came out. You put it into action. That makes you a more advanced case. Also, it means your position is more precarious."

"Precarious?" Mort repeated.

"More easily spoiled."

"Yeah, I know what it means. Pop's got spoiled though pretty easy, didn't it?"

"Not really. He never knew what hit him."

"Maybe."

"He lived a long, fairly happy life, believing in the superiority of his intellect. And not only that, believing in intellect above all other things."

"Sounds like a bum steer," Mort said. "All he ever did was high hat people in his own head—is that fun?"

He took out his cigarette case and started to pick a cigarette, then with a quick movement of ostentatiously remembered politeness offered one to Terhune.

Terhune shook his head.

"Sore?" Mort asked. "Don't be that way. We're just a couple of guys, aren't we, having a social talk."

"Thanks, I'll smoke my own." But when he got out his case he had none left. He snapped it shut. Mort smiled, lit his own, and blew two smoke rings at the ceiling. He looked up at the ceiling with his twinkling eyes, and Terhune knew he wasn't really getting more than the slightest incidental pleasure out of this. He was too intently occupied by the probing, the search, and it wasn't in his line, this sort of thing. It was one thing he didn't know how to go about and he was beginning to feel the strain of it, and even to show the strain.

"I should think," he said, "that a guy that's lived as long as you have would realize you can't have all the breaks all the time. Some people never get any breaks at all. Ever look at it that way?"

"You call what's happening here a break? But you said you made it."

"A break," Mort explained, "is the *chance* to make it. Now like tonight. I come here and find you and that old bum in my place here. If I don't come it isn't so good for me, and if I come and don't do anything about it, it isn't any better. But I do come and I'll figure what to do and then I'll do it. See?"

"You put your trust in 'to do,' " Terhune said. "The old man believed in mind. You believe in will. It may be interesting to see how *you* end. But I imagine, so far, your life has been a series of what you call breaks. Happy meetings of opportunity and your special talent."

"Talent?" Say, that's artistic stuff, isn't it?" Mort opened his eyes with exaggerated simplicity, partly to live up to the famous sense of humor, partly as defense against the superior classiness of his adversary. "What you mean," he said, "is I know how to look after myself."

"Perhaps that's what I mean."

"You're right," Mort said. "And I've got a kind of a philosophy about it, too. I guess you got a philosophy. Everyone's got one." He looked inquiringly.

Terhune said, "Mine doesn't work."

"Mine does," Mort said. "Maybe you better change over to mine."

"What is yours?"

"I can tell you in a few simple words. It goes like this: know what you want—that's not so easy to begin with, most people don't—but when you know, go after it. Don't take your eye off the ball. When the breaks are good, play 'em, play 'em hard, for all they're worth. When they're bad, play 'em for laughs. That way you can't lose. That's my philosophy."

"It sounds very hearty and jolly. Is that all there is to it?"

"Yeah, that's all."

"You don't seem very exacting. I mean you don't expect much from it."

"Don't expect much from it! Say, what do you expect from *your* philosophy? Think it'll clean the car and do the housework? Maybe you expect *too* much, maybe that's why it don't work."

"Maybe. But I don't believe in that last part of yours either, that about the laughs."

"You're wrong there, pal. I get a kick out of pretty near everything. Sometimes I get one even when it goes against me."

"That's fine," Terhune said.

"Oh, I'll bet you're like that, too," Mort said indulgently. "I'll bet you're a good sport when it comes down to it. Now listen—better take a cigarette." He held the case out again and this time Terhune took one and lit it. "Listen, you got your ideas and I got mine, but you and I are not so different after all, maybe. Why, you said something about living down here once. So you were a kid here, right?"

"Yes, I was."

"Then you didn't start with much, either."

"No more than you did, probably."

"See? That's what I mean." Mort looked at him blandly. Then his gaze wandered off and became apparently reminiscent, though it still sparkled with the effort behind it. "Why," he said in a false dreaminess, "I'll bet you dove off a coal barge hot summer days same as me, coming up in that oil slick and banana peels and the rotten water smells. Gee, I can remember it! And

didn't you ever hang around pool parlors or play the
numbers with a buck you'd lifted out of the old man's
pants? No? Or borrow a flash tie off some Yid's pushcart to wear on a date? And then maybe get the girl
between you and the wall in a dark hallway? Well,
maybe you don't like to think of those things but I
do. I like to think of them because they remind me that
I've come a long way. That I got finally all I ever wanted
to get."

"What was that?" Terhune asked.

"Why, what do you think it was? Say, aren't you a
man, too? What does a man want?"

"Well, what does he want?"

Mort shook his head and smiled. "You're kidding me,"
he said. Then he put his elbow on the table and made
a gesture with his clenched fist. He grew solemn.
"Power," he said, "that's what a man wants."

"Any kind of power?"

"How many kinds are there? I mean just what I said
before. *You* make the picture."

"You mean you make people do what you want. If
they don't do it you bully them. If that's no good then
you kill them."

"No," Mort said thoughtfully, "no, that's not what
I mean. You have to do that sometimes but it's what I
call cheap. Yes, that's what I call cheap. It doesn't cost
anything. Any mug, you give him a chance, he can do
the same. No, what I mean is better than that. I mean
make 'em *want* what you want."

"Oh," Terhune exclaimed, "that's it!"

He spoke with reserve and unconsciously he drew

away a little. The true object of all this delay and shilly-shallying talk had been, though Mort didn't realize it, very baldly stated. He knew Mort wanted to know what Edna's part had been in what had happened in the attic. He knew Mort suspected an understanding between himself and Edna. He might even suspect they had seen each other before this, and that the understanding was a long one. Their caution, their preparedness, might suggest it. They never even looked at each other, as two people naturally would. What did all this mean? Mort couldn't find out now from anyone but Terhune. Edna he'd sent away, in case he should get sore, really and truly sore, and go off half cocked. Sometimes that happened. Sometimes it was a mistake. So he had only this guy to work on, this fancy egg, who if he gave him half a chance would talk circles around him. But he intended to keep him here till he found what he wanted to find. And in the meantime he was tormented, and the crux of his torment was exactly in that will to power he had just acknowledged. He had to know if Terhune had made Edna *want* what he wanted.

Then, even as Terhune guessed what was in his mind, he saw his intention harden toward him and his patience abruptly shorten. To hell with all the soft soap, he seemed to say. His clenched fist relaxed, clenched again harder on the table.

"No," he said slowly, "maybe we *are* different, after all. Anyway, you got a kind of a nasty manner, like you thought we were. Why, sometimes you talk to me like I wasn't human, like I didn't have any friends like other people, or brush my teeth in the morning." He spun the gold case around on the table with one finger. "You don't know a thing about me," he said, "not a thing. But that don't mean I don't know about you. Want me to tell what I know about you?"

"Go ahead," Terhune said.

"Well, as a starter, I'll tell you the kind of kid you were. You went to school and learned a lot of stuff. You got a prize. You never picked your nose. Teacher's pet! Maybe you went to Sunday school and sang in the choir. You carried papers. You helped with the wash. You put your money in a little iron bank. Every now and then some tough kid gave you a working over and then you cried and ran home to Mom."

"You sound as though you'd read it all in a book."

"Oh, I don't have to read a book. Maybe that's another difference. I got no time to read books. But I know human nature. *That's* my book. What's the percentage in knowing all about art and stuff if you don't know human nature? I'm telling you—I know it. Nothing gets by with me. No one puts anything over on me. No one."

His eyes started to freeze again into the stare, and Terhune could feel in him the ferocity of his will striking against that blank, frustrating wall, that doubt. Terhune felt the storm. But suddenly Mort controlled it by an effort so painful that his smile was like a grimace. Not yet, he must have said to himself, not yet. Watch it, take it easy; it's not time yet.

Mort bent his head and lighted one cigarette from another. The smoke streamed across his face. Then he leaned back, trying to relax. He clasped his arms behind his head and looked up at the ceiling.

"Life's a funny thing," he said. "I guess you never know what you're going to run into. Now take that kid that just went out of here, Edna. There isn't anything about that kid I don't know."

Here we are, Terhune thought. This is it. He drew all his faculties together for the crisis, and he thought, it's not my life. That's over. It's Edna's.

He said, "Yes, she seems to be a great pal of yours."

Mort looked at him from lowered lids. "Yeah," he said. For a moment there was a terrible sarcasm in his voice. "Yeah," he said, more guardedly. "Well, she knows me too. Now you get to talking to that kid sometime you might get a different angle on me."

"She seems to think you're all right."

"She's a bright kid," Mort went on, "a lot brighter than you'd think. Sometimes maybe too bright. She talks back. Edna's no yes-man. She talks back so much sometimes people might think she puts something over on me. Maybe she does once in a while. Hell! It's nothing but kid stuff. I know. Only some people might not understand."

"I think I understand."

"Maybe," Mort said slowly, "maybe you understand. You see," he said, "that kid came to me nearly four years ago. I'd never seen her before in my life. She was some sight. She had on a pair of Gus's pants cut down, and a man's shirt hanging to her knees. She must of weighed no more than sixty pounds. She looked like a sick cat. It seems she'd been in an institution and then on a farm down in Jersey, and now she was working nights in a hamburg joint. All this time no one paid her a dime. So, she was twelve and a half years old and she was looking for a job." He was becoming genuinely reminiscent in spite of himself, and he smiled as he remembered this. "I said to her, 'What do you think you can do, kid?' and she answered right back, 'You got a button off your shirt. I could sew it on.' And it was off, too; it had just come off account of some lousy laundry or other. Well, I let her sew it on. Then pretty soon I got her a job in a beauty shop with a friend of mine, and from then on she got her three square a day. She never did grow much but she changed. Only she didn't change much either, come to think of it."

For a moment he almost forgot Terhune. Then he looked at him and said, "And don't get me wrong, pal. I never got a thing out of it, not a thing. Know what I mean?"

"Yes," Terhune said. He thought, he wants me to know that. Why? Wouldn't he normally want to say the contrary, even when it isn't true? (The you-know-what-men-are line—yes, even *you*, you poor sap.) And because of his present doubt of her, wouldn't he want to make me at least think that he owned her, that I had not and never could impose any part of my will on her? But since he's just said what he has it means one of two things: either he's trying to make me think she isn't really important to him so I'll be tempted to talk more freely—and this seems likely—or else in that very special way of his, he loves her. He doesn't want to think of her or speak of her as he would of Gloria or those Atlantic

City floozies. She is precious to him. He must keep her that way. If *this* is true, Terhune thought, the strangest part of all would be that he doesn't know it.

He looked at Mort with a flash of wonder. "I believe you," he said, "and I also believe she's very fond of you."

"Yeah," Mort said. "Yeah." But it didn't please him. Terhune saw, too late, that it didn't please him because it implied understanding.

"What makes you think she's fond of me?" Mort asked.

"Intuition, that's all."

"Intuition? That's what you have when you got no way of knowing. Like *you* got no way of knowing—or have you?"

"I have no way of knowing."

"Is that so? You sounded pretty sure."

"What do you mean? You've just been telling me yourself. You've made it clear enough for anyone to guess."

"Have I? I only said the kid asked me for a job and I gave it to her."

"You also said she'd been in an orphanage, and in an all-night hamburg joint. You helped her to get away from that."

"Anyone who helped her would be the same then? You think she wants to better herself?"

"I have no idea. I should imagine kindness was what she most wanted."

"Kindness." He rolled the word derisively on his tongue. "You think what women want is kindness?"

"Maybe not women. Children, certainly."

"Who says Edna's a child?"

"God, man, you don't listen to yourself! You've just said she was twelve years old when she came to you, and you've known her nearly four years."

"How long have *you* known her?"

Terhune saw he had said too much. He had been too ready to reassure Mort. If he wanted to reassure him this was not the way. He shrugged his shoulders.

"I have no idea what you're talking about."

"I said, how long have you known Edna?"

"Known her? I don't know her at all."

"You've talked to her."

"Maybe ten minutes."

"That all?"

"Don't be a fool!" Terhune said.

"Don't you be one, either! And don't you try to give *me* any runaround." He lurched forward and Terhune braced himself. But then Mort drew back. He struck his cigarette case violently with his finger. It rang on the table, spun, and slowly came to a stop. Then he gave a short, self-conscious laugh.

"I don't give a damn whether you know her or not. Only I can see you got ideas about her. You got plenty ideas. Maybe you better tell me some more of your ideas. I'd like to hear them."

Terhune thought, which is better? To go on obscuring what is already obscure or, since I've already said too much anyway, to try to clarify some one point that might be clarified. Either he'll go on butting his head against the wall till his rage gets beyond control, or he might be made to think he saw one thing exactly. It would have to be something his mind is all ready to receive. Then he might credit himself with insight, be appeased, diverted.

"I have an idea," Terhune said slowly. "Maybe I'm wrong, but I don't think so."

"What is it?"

"It's that Edna is very valuable to you."

"Yeah," Mort said. He looked blank. Then he said, suspiciously, "Just what do you mean by that?"

"Well, it's hard to explain what I mean. I don't know whether I can or not."

"Keep trying."

"I haven't really very much to say. It's all guesswork. Remember I've had more talk with you than with Edna. But you've given me a certain picture of yourself, you've told me what you've done with your life and what you've wanted to do, and you've given me a picture of Edna, too."

"Stow all that," Mort said. "What's your idea?"

"Why, my idea is that Edna is valuable to you because without her you'd always be doing the same thing."

Mort gave a low exclamation. He didn't know what it meant, and yet he knew Terhune meant him to know something. "What same thing?" he asked intently.

"Actually it doesn't matter what the thing is. You know, though, and I don't need to tell you. The point is that there would be no change. There was an old story about a man who had to push a stone up a hill in hell forever. It was thought that the worst punishment of hell was to do the same act over and over."

"So what?" Mort said.

"So we all have our act, the one that can easily become our only act. It doesn't matter what it is, but when we get to that point we're the man pushing the stone. Finally we're the stone itself. That's the true death. There is no other death. It's always easier to die in that sense than to live. It's always easier to go on being whatever we are than to change. It's easier to stay in hell than to get out."

Mort's small black eyes scarcely showed in the slits of his lids. But their concentration never wavered. "Where's Edna come in?" he asked.

"Edna, I'd guess, is your charm against never changing. She breaks up the pattern when it needs to be broken. Without her you'll roll the stone in hell. She's your charm and your luck. I think you know that. I think you'll never want to be without her."

"Very inter-esting," Mort said. His eyes were unreadable. He picked up the gold case between thumbs and forefingers and balanced it, looking for himself in its shining surface. "Very inter-esting. I see you got all kinds of ideas. You understand all kinds of things. Maybe you understand Edna, too. Now tell me," he said, looking up suddenly. "Edna went away just now. You think she'll come back?"

"No."

"Why not?"

"Because you don't want her to. She knows it."

"So she'll do what I want?"

"I think so. But not always. Because that isn't what

you really want of her. That's what I've been trying to
tell you."

"Still, you think this time she'll do it. She won't
come back."

"I think so."

Mort put the case slowly in his pocket, drawing back
and staring at Terhune.

"I don't know yet whether you're a smart guy or not;
whether you know all this stuff or not. But we're going
to find out in just a minute. I thought I heard the front
door a while ago. Maybe it was one of the boys, but
maybe it was Edna. And now someone's coming up.
Maybe it's Gus. But maybe it's Edna. I hope you're
right, pal, about what you say, because it better not be
Edna."

Terhune heard the steps. They didn't sound like hers.

Don't let it be, he thought. He could feel his face
growing tense as the steps grew nearer.

CHAPTER XIV

I T WASN'T Edna. It was Gus. Even before he appeared Mort recognized the quick, agile climbing of the ladder, and he began to smile. He gave Terhune a long look, as though to say: You were right, pal; I'm still boss man around here. Even after what he had just heard from him Terhune was surprised by the vehemence and complacency of his triumph. Perhaps Mort himself was surprised. He stopped smiling and set his mouth in a businesslike firmness.

Gus crossed the room languidly and sat down. His face was greenish-white, the gold lock hung in his eye, and he looked sleepy.

"What'd you come up for?" Mort said.

Gus shook the lock out of his eye.

"What'd you say?"

"I said, what'd you come back up for?"

"I thought you wanted me."

"You finish what I told you?"

"Yeah. . . . That's O.K."

He slumped in his chair, with his legs straight out in front of him, his hands hidden in his pockets. After a minute he got out one of his reefers and lit it.

"The boys come yet?" Mort asked.

"Not yet."

"No? I thought I heard someone come in. They're late. Wonder what's keeping them?"

"I wouldn't know. But they were coming in an hour. It's over that. Want me to go out and phone?"

Mort lifted his arm and looked at his wristwatch. "Give 'em ten minutes," he said, "then maybe you better go over to Louie's and phone."

"O.K."

Gus sank into a sleepy waiting. His shirt was damp and stuck to his body. Sometimes he twitched his shoulders to loosen it. His only other movement was the slow lifting and lowering of his cigarette. Then he stopped even that, letting it hang from his lip and drip ashes on him. He stared into the smoke, lost in a succession of pictures. Once in a while he smiled, and sometimes his face contracted as though a pain pricked him.

After several minutes of silence he yawned and said, "Oh, another thing: Edna's down there."

"What!" Mort stiffened in his chair. He did not look at Terhune this time. "When did she come back?"

"About ten minutes ago. She brought your aspirin."

He took the box out of his pocket and skidded it across the table.

Mort picked it up slowly and put it down again.

"She was asking about Pop," Gus said.

"What'd you tell her?"

"Oh, I stalled around. I told her he'd gone."

"She believe you?"

"She said you promised her."

Mort drummed his fingers on the table. "Yeah," he said, somberly.

In a minute he said, "What's she doing down there now?"

"Sitting on the basement steps."

"What's that?"

Gus made an effort. He looked as directly as he could at Mort but his eyes didn't focus.

"Can I help it?" he said. "She was set to believe me, all right, but the old guy's overcoat fell off, it was lying there in the hall. And then she said he'd never go any place without his overcoat."

"So you told her," Mort said.

"Not right away. I stalled some more. But she was wise as soon as she saw the overcoat. She pushed right by me to the basement."

Mort said, "You god-damned cluck."

"What the hell!" Gus said. "She'd of found out sooner or later. But anyway, she'll get over it. I told her she better go home. I told her you didn't want her around any more."

The muscles in Mort's bluish jaw worked as though he were chewing something. There was a fine, greasy film forming on his forehead.

"Tell her to come up," he said.

Gus never got anything right away. There was always a pause between what happened and his reaction to it. After a second he said, "What for?"

"I want to talk to her," Mort said.

"Well, you won't want to when you see her."

"Why not?"

"Because she's putting on a show. I finally had to slip it to her."

"What's she doing?"

"She's just sitting down on the steps and won't move. I told her to go home. But she won't move."

Terhune thought: Go, Edna, for God's sake, go.

"She won't go?" Mort said. "Well, tell her to come up."

"Are you nuts!" Gus exclaimed. "You went and promised the kid, so she says. You know she liked that old guy. Him and her were friends. She was always fussing about him. But you promised her. Now you want to explain. Both times you're wrong."

"Tell her to come up."

Gus frowned and blinked his eyes. He took his gilded lock in his fingers and twisted it.

"If I was you—" he began. Then he said, "Well anyway, she must of gone now. I told her to go."

The three of them listened, hearing only the silence of the house in which perhaps Edna sat huddled on a step—or from which she had run away in fear and horror.

Mort put his finger inside his collar and loosened it.

"Yeah," he said, "I guess she's gone. I guess that's what she'd do. Forget it."

But then Edna came up. They heard her in the lower hall, walking slowly. She climbed the stairs slowly. Every now and then she stood still. When she reached the floor just below she stood a long time. Terhune saw the fine, grease-paint shine getting heavier on Mort's face.

At last her head appeared above the level of the floor, and she came into the room. She stood there, looking at

the floor, not moving. Mort made a brusque motion toward the empty chair, but she didn't see him.

"Sit down," he said. His voice was harsh and loud in
the quiet of the room.

As she heard his voice her face wrinkled as though
she were about to cry, but only two tears formed in her
eyes and slowly spilled down her cheeks. They left
gleaming lines, like the paths of snails, in her powdered
cheeks, reached her chin, and slid off. There were no
more.

"Come, sit down," Mort said again.

Edna walked obediently to the chair and sat down,
with her hands folded in her lap, her eyes looking
straight ahead. Her body was queerly tilted to one side
in an attitude that seemed involuntary, so that she
reminded Terhune of those staring, flaxen-haired dolls,
set always a little askew on the shelves of toy shops. And
even more painful to him than her tears was this air of
an inanimate object, picked up, put down, moved
around at will.

"Thanks for the aspirin," Mort said.

She gave a shake of her head and said nothing.

Mort twisted his collar and loosened his tie, and
suddenly his appearance of neatness and grooming disappeared. The cluster of curls on his forehead had been
flattened by his hat. They were curlier now, damp with
sweat, ruffled and disorderly.

"You came back," he said.

Edna nodded. "You told me to."

Mort took a long breath. "You ought to of gone
home," he said thickly.

Then for several moments no one spoke. Mort turned his cigarette case, catching gleams of light, sending them to the corners of the room.

"If people are smart," he said finally, "they know what people want them to do."

Edna didn't answer.

"You used to be like that," he said, "you used to know."

Edna nodded absently.

"That's because you wanted to know," he said. "Now you don't give a damn."

Edna opened her bag and took out a lipstick and a pinkish gray puff. She began to make up her face. Smearing her lips together she wiped off all the lipstick and made a smaller outline. With the puff she smoothed away the tear trails on her cheeks. Then she pulled her hair, first backward, then down again, lower on her forehead. She looked quite different.

Mort watched somberly her almost symbolic gestures, her attempt to make a new thing out of herself. He was helpless. For once there was nothing he could do. All his relations with Edna had grown and taken shape in the climate of her unquestioning admiration. This was so fixed that he wasn't able even to imagine her disapproval. If occasionally, as just lately, he questioned her behavior, it was because he saw her as a child, deeply dependent on his judgment and incapable of looking after herself with others older and smarter than she. Terhune thought Mort might even have tolerated her disloyalty, because he would think it sprang from jealousy and a natural desire to get even with him, because of some neglect on his part. This could still have sweetness in it. But when he saw her now he realized vaguely that she had wanted to destroy all he had ever seen of her, all she had ever been to him, and he sensed he had lost her forever.

"You go home," Mort told her. "You go home." He waved fumblingly toward the door.

Gus roused himself to repeat, "Yeah, kid, you better go on home."

But Edna did not go. She rearranged the objects in her bag and shut it with a snap. Then she sat still.

Mort slumped in his chair. His will, for once paralyzed, left nothing of him but flesh. His flesh took over. He was fat. He sat like the fat boy waiting to be told what to do. Hesitantly he picked up the aspirin and unwrapped it, shook out two tablets, put them in his mouth and swallowed them. Then he rubbed his fingers wearily across his eyebrows.

Gus watched him. He said wonderingly, "The guy's sick." Then, with a spirit of clowning, he added in falsetto, "Is there a doctor in the house?" He looked around for laughs. Then he seemed to see something. He snapped his fingers in front of his eyes. "Like Edna," he said distinctly. "She was sick."

Terhune's heart gave a heavy lurch. He thought, maybe Mort didn't hear that. Mort had not moved. And Terhune saw that Gus at once forgot, because he could not really remember. Memory is selective. Gus saw only unrelated pictures as they came cloudily into his head.

Mort said without emphasis, "Sick?"

He wrapped the aspirin up again, snapped the elastic

around it, and put it in his pocket. This might be a moment like all the others, or it might be *the* moment.

"What's the matter with Edna?" he said. "When was she sick?"

It *was* the moment.

Gus said, "Oh, she was sick last night. Edna was sick."

"Where? . . . Up here?"

"Yeah, up here."

"Last night?"

"Yeah, last night."

Mort closed his eyes and pressed his fingers into the inner corners. When he took his fingers away and opened his eyes the change was terrible. His fat seemed to fall away, leaving only muscle and bone. Even the black curls changed, became his badge once more, his crest.

"You and Edna came up here last night," he said.

"Why, yeah. Didn't you know?"

"How would I know? Who told me?"

Gus straightened and looked earnestly at him. "Say, what is this?" he complained. "Didn't you tell us to come up here and wait?"

"No."

"But you phoned Edna."

Edna said, flatly, "You told me to locate Gus. I looked all around for him. When I couldn't find him I left word at Louie's he should meet me here. I don't like to wait around Louie's."

"Why not?"

"Sometimes they get fresh."

"So you came here and waited. How long?"

"Maybe ten minutes."

"Ten minutes. Alone. . . . Only not alone."

"She didn't see me," Terhune said. "I was lying behind those cases over there, right under the shelf where
they're all piled up. I was looking for something on the
shelf and I fell there, just below it. She couldn't see me."

"Why didn't you speak to her?"

"I was knocked out. Before I could do anything, *he*
came in. Then I was afraid to."

"You see him?" Mort asked Gus.

"I didn't see him."

"Notice anything queer?"

"N—o, I guess not." Gus began his wandering search
of the room again. Terhune saw the room as it must be
reflected in Gus, pictures shaken by water. "Only the
window," Gus said.

"What about the window?"

"The tacks were out, that's all."

"I did it," Terhune said. "There was no light when I
came in so I pulled the blanket back to see."

"You pulled it back so you could see what you wanted
to see on that shelf?"

"Yes."

"Then you fell down and broke your leg?"

"Yes."

"And got up and pulled the blanket back in place and
then went and lay down under the shelf again."

"The blanket must have slipped down by itself."

"Yeah, it must."

Oh, get this over with, he thought. I can't stand it
any longer.

Gus still didn't know what it was all about. He only saw those pictures, distorted and wavering and separate, that would not be still nor come together.

Then suddenly everything fell into its place.

"It was account of the nylons," he said. "I told her to get them, and then Edna was sick."

"Where were the nylons?"

"Why, on the shelf."

But even then it took Mort a moment to get it. He looked at the shelf and the cases still piled below, and the opening in them where Terhune had pushed them aside. He looked at Terhune, then at Edna.

Under the fresh coat of powder Edna grew pale, but she looked back at him stonily. Then all that Terhune had seen in Mort, in glimpses, came baldly out. He saw Mort's true face. The other faces of Mort had been like Hallowe'en masks of painted scrim, humorous, solid, good-fellow, sentimental masks, from which his secret, glazed, ferocious eyes sometimes looked out. But this was the whole of him, the evil and the terror of his true self, bare at last.

He suddenly threw out his arm and caught Edna's neck in the crook of it. He jerked her half across the table, holding her against his slightly bulging stomach like a passionate, oafish lover. He seized her jaw in his hand and forced her head back against his shoulder.

"So that's what my baby did," he whispered hoarsely, holding his face close to hers. "Let me look at you. Let me see you once—before I fix you for good."

Terhune started up, but half out of his chair he stopped, because Mort didn't move. He held Edna close to him and stared into her face, and Edna stared back.

Then, as suddenly as he had seized her, he let her go. The blood that had rushed to his face drained away. He shuddered all over, like a dog coming out of water. Then he leaned back in his chair, put his hands in his trousers pockets, and began to laugh. He laughed until his eyes filled with tears. He pulled out his silk handkerchief and wiped his eyes. Gus gave a few accompanying nervous titters.

Finally Mort carefully folded his handkerchief and put it back. He laid his hands flat on the table, still chuckling. "What a laugh! Eh, baby? What a laugh!" He doubled his fist and gave her the phantom jab on the jaw.

Edna straightened out her suit, and did not smile. She looked sullen. Mort's anger had apparently gone over her, leaving her with only a sulky humor and a rumpled suit. She had not been afraid.

Then Terhune knew that Edna had not been afraid from the moment she found him. Whatever she had felt —anxiety, doubt, an awe of life, a longing—craven fear for the safety of her own body she had never felt. He remembered that when he first saw her he had sensed a curious hollowness in her, as though one ingredient, which in that circumstance should have been there, was lacking. This was what it had been: she had lacked fear. For a moment this knowledge of her made her seem monstrous, more monstrous even than Mort. It seemed to take away her natural physical attributes, and turn her into a fragment of some other order, a snow crystal, magnified and terrible, an intricate, fragile form precipitated into an immense hostility it would not recognize.

And he saw that the lack of physical fear was another of the things Mort had loved in her. One was innocence, one was her unclouded acceptance of him. Those were destroyed now, and because they were he wanted also to destroy her fearlessness. But there was only one way to destroy that. Terhune felt a great, enveloping terror for her. Edna!—he wanted to warn her with his whole being—Edna! Be afraid! It's all that will save you.

"Well, baby," Mort said, "you sure gave me a laugh. You sure did." He flipped his hand toward Terhune. "What did I tell you, pal? Sometimes you got to play it that way."

He held the cigarette case, still chuckling and shaking his head humorously. He was like the man in the smoking car whose funny story hasn't gone over very well and who keeps up the signs of mirth out of embarrassment and to reassure himself.

He lighted a cigarette. "What a story!" he said. He leaned his elbows on the table and let smoke trickle upward from his mouth. "Edna," he said, "a kid I picked up out of the gutter. And gave her all she ever had. And watched her grow up. And along comes some punk she never saw before, who hands her a line. And she falls for it. She falls so hard she tries to double cross her best friend.—God! You never really know people, do you? You never really know."

"What happened?" Gus said foggily. "What did the kid do?"

"She did plenty," Mort said. "She finds this punk

here and she hides him. First she hides him from you. Then she's all set to hide him from me, only I go away and she don't have to. It was sure tough I came back!"

"You mean he talked to Edna last night?"

"That's right."

Gus leaned forward and his eyes wavered all over Terhune.

"He was here all the time?"

"That's right."

Gus knit his brows in a weak imitation of Mort's ferocity. "Well I'll be damned," he said.

Then he couldn't keep it up. A half-clowning, half-admiring look came into his face. It was sure a joke on Mort, all right. Little Edna put it over on Mort this time.

He held up one finger. "What'd you promise her?" he asked. "Come on, Jackson, tell us. We could do with some of it too."

"Cut the comedy," Mort said. "He never promised her a thing. He didn't have to—unless you'd say he promised hearts and flowers."

Gus lost the thread. He said plaintively, "Why, everyone's nuts."

"Leave the girl out," Terhune said. "You'd better try to get her to go home. Then you can settle it with me."

Mort shook his head. "She won't go," he said between his teeth. "Not when *I* tell her. Supposing *you* tell her. Maybe for you she'll go."

Terhune said nothing.

Edna did not move. She looked down at her hands in her lap.

"You know she won't go," Mort said. "Not so long as I got you here. You know that because you know so much about her. You even told me some of what you know. He did, Edna. He told me lots about you. You'd be very inter-ested to hear sometime. Only he didn't tell me just one little thing. He didn't tell me how you feel about him. I had to guess that. I had to guess how crazy you were about him."

Edna raised her eyes and let them brush over Mort quickly. What had been fixed and inward and even resigned in her became external. Her eyes showed a contempt more volatile than hate, a contempt already so close to indifference it seemed to come only from her body, from the surface ends of her nerves.

"You're a dope," she said. "You don't know anything. You never will."

"I know this," he said, "I know you'll never get a thing out of it."

"What you mean," she said, "I won't?"

"What I mean!" he jeered. All the curved lines in his face formed a mask of emotion somehow comic by its distortion. "I'll tell you what I mean. You might as well have a wall twenty feet high between you. You might as well be at the North Pole and him at the South Pole. You might as well be black and him white. What I mean, you'll never come together, no matter how hard you try."

"Yeah, I know," she said.

He leaned toward her and the veins in his eyes showed up like red rivers on a map. "But for you it's the real thing," he said, "the real thing—right?"

"Right."

"Christ!" he said. "What do you know!"

Edna looked away from him. She looked at Terhune and smiled. He smiled quickly back. Their smiles met and became one smile. They looked at each other and then their faces grew slowly grave. They both knew what separated them. Everything separated them. All that he was, all that she was. They would never come together as man and woman. Now he would live without her always, for whatever years he had, for whatever minutes. He had not come to find her. His search had another end, and there was no sign that their brief meeting had any part in it. But just at this moment she gave him, without doubt or fear or grudging, what had never been given him before. And he knew that any search for a plan and an identity is no more than an arid and fatuous illusion, unless its root and its spring are in the love of man.

When Mort spoke finally he heard the sound but not the words. Then the words, repeated, grew insistent, and he heard them.

"You know, don't you," Mort said, "you know what's going to happen?"

"No—yes—I suppose so."

"What?"

He turned then to Mort and saw what Edna's look had done to him.

"You're going to kill me," he said.

Mort gave a short, barking laugh.

"Not a bit of it," he said, "not a bit of it. Why'd I do a thing like that? . . . I don't have to."

"No? What then?"

"See that?" Mort raised his eyes to the ceiling and they rested on the beam over their heads. Terhune's eyes followed his. There was a spider hanging directly over them, at the distance that a man's head might be if he were standing on the table. It hung there on an invisible thread but its shadow on the ceiling was larger than itself and on the ceiling the thread was like a cord. As he looked it grew larger and became the shadow of a boy with a red sash dangling from a trapeze. Then larger still, and it was the shadow of an old woman swaying at an end of rope. Finally it was another, heavier shadow.

"That's what you came back for, isn't it?" Mort said. "You wanted to come back to where you used to be once. That good kid I told you about. You wanted to come back, and maybe you thought you wanted to begin all over again from scratch. But I'll tell you—when a man feels that way the fact is he don't really want to begin all over at all. He just don't want to live."

"I see what you mean," Terhune said.

"Well, it's true, isn't it?"

"No."

"Why not?"

Terhune looked again at the beam. The spider, conscious of them, had started to climb back. He could not see the boy on the trapeze now. He could not see the old woman either. Both were gone out of him. The other figure didn't matter. It was only a darkness without shape.

Mort said, "Maybe I'm wrong. Maybe you want to live. Yes, I see you do. You want to live on account of

Edna." He moistened his curly, small lips several times. "Gus," he said in a soft voice, "go down to the basement and get me a piece of rope."

Gus' eyes widened slowly. He frowned. "Say, is that smart?" he asked.

Mort said, "On the feet. Start moving."

Gus got up shakily. He held up two fingers and repeated with earnestness, "Is that smart? *Two* of them?"

"We'll get rid of 'em. Get going, I tell you."

"Sure, sure. But maybe you two better talk a little more."

Mort said, "Don't make me say it again."

"Sure, sure." He started across the room and stopped. "Listen," he said, "if it's Edna—"

"Get out!"

He danced nervously across the room. At the trap door he looked back at them. "Say, what is this?" he said. "Is everyone nuts?"

Then he made a little salute to Edna with one finger and let himself down like a monkey.

Edna watched him go. She gave a small nod in answer to his salute. Then she listened intently to his footsteps. When she couldn't hear him any more she straightened up in her chair and put her hands flat on the table.

"Listen, Mort," she said, "I gotta tell you something."

Her hands on the table looked large and capable. They were still grimy.

"That so? What is it?"

He spoke lazily. He put his cigarette out and, taking hold of the table, tilted himself on the back legs of his chair. Now that his will was released once more he was ready to be at ease, to relax, almost to be genial.

"I called the cops," she said.

It was a lie. A lie so brazen it blazed in her eyes as she looked at him. It was like a sword striking him across the eyes. Doomed, Terhune thought: oh, poor Edna! Doomed.

And yet not really doomed. Where there is one truth everything takes a reflection from it, and the truth of her sudden blazing hatred almost gave truth to the lie. Mort recoiled a little before the reality of her hatred.

Then he smiled. He rocked his chair, holding onto the table. "That's a hot one," he said. "You want to give me another laugh, don't you?"

"No. I called them. When I went out to the drugstore to get the aspirin. I called the station house."

His jaw muscles worked under the bluish skin. The fine, greasy sweat began to form again on his forehead. He still smiled.

"You hate me, don't you, baby?" he said.

Edna looked at him and didn't answer.

"O.K.," he said. "I'll play along. So you called the cops. What'd you tell them?"

"I told them Mr. Terhune was here. I didn't tell them about Pop because I didn't know that then."

"You called the cops," he said. "Jesus, what a laugh!" His smile became a grimace. "Aren't they kind of taking their time?" he asked. "What's keeping 'em? They ought to be here by now."

"I didn't tell them exactly. I just said one of these houses. I said I wasn't sure of the street, and I didn't

know the number. It'll take a little while. But they'll
be here."

"It's a good gag," Mort said, "but it won't work."

A drop of sweat rolled down over his eyebrow, struck
his fine, small nose, and slid down his cheek. It might
have been a tear.

"It will in a minute," Edna said.

Mort leaned a little to one side. He stared intently at
the table as though something were written on it. There
was a terrible doubt in him. Such hate as he saw was
capable of anything. Even of this. He struggled with the
ancient dilemma in its most primitive, most urgent
form: what to believe, what of all this was true.

He was no better off, Terhune thought grimly, than
a baffled metaphysician.

"Did you tell 'em I was here?" Mort asked.

"No."

"Why not?"

"I was going to come back and give you and Gus a
chance. You had time to make a getaway."

"But you didn't."

"No," she said. "I saw Pop downstairs. Then I didn't
care what happened to you."

Mort leaned his chair forward. He put his face close
to Edna's. "But you cared what happened to this guy
here," he said, "you cared about him."

She nodded, her shining eyes fixed on him.

Suddenly Mort screamed at her, "Quit lying to me!"

"It's the truth," she said.

"It's a god-damned lie!"

Edna shrugged. "O.K. Sit on your can then. And wait."

Suddenly his rage overwhelmed him. It was all that mattered. The truth no longer mattered. He wrenched himself to his feet. He could barely walk, but he staggered across the room like a drunk, holding one hand in front of him. He reached the trap door and leaned on it.

"Gus, oh, Gus!" he called hoarsely.

No answer came from below.

Then he straightened up and looked back at Edna. His look was like a drunk's look, crafty but utterly befuddled.

She didn't say she told them about me—and she wouldn't have done that, so that makes it true. But no one's come—the cops would have hopped on it. Then: *She hates me. She'd do anything to save him—and maybe all along she hated me—maybe she hated me that much when she went out.*

He started back, his hands groping before him.

When he reached them he swayed between them, and his hands began to tremble. He couldn't decide where first to let loose what was now centered in his hands. He hated them both, and his hate, drawing two ways, immobilized his hands.

Then suddenly he bent his head and listened. Terhune thought he heard far off in the night a long, thin wail. It was blown, whipped like a scarf, toward them across the wasteland. It might have come out of interstellar space, the eerie sound of a world wrenched loose, screaming to death at the far side of ten billion years of light.

It might have been a fire engine, careening up the avenue. Or it might have been a police siren. Or it might have been the ghost of a shrill, admonishing cry echoing from a long-gone, red brick parish school.

But Edna, whether because she heard it or because she saw it in Mort, jumped up and ran to the window. She jerked at the blanket.

Mort came around the table and struck at Terhune. Terhune ducked and fell half out of his chair. He caught the table with one hand and with the other struck upward to Mort's stomach. He felt the softness of it over resistant muscle, felt the breath go out in a thump. Mort reeled backward, but Terhune couldn't right himself in the second allowed him.

He heard breaking glass at the window.

Mort, swaying forward, swung at him, and this time caught him on the jaw.

The darkness sang with lights for another second. Then the lights went out.

CHAPTER XV

IN THE dark Edna was with him. He could never
see her but he felt her hands and heard her voice.
Sometimes he talked to her. "Are you all right?
Are you sure you're all right?"

She always answered, "Oh, yes, I'm all right."

They said this to each other many times.

Once he was stricken with fear and strangeness. He
said, "What am I doing in this place?"

"Don't worry. It's nearly morning. They'll come
pretty soon."

"But Mort," he said, "where's he?"

"Gone."

"What'll he do to you?"

"He'll never find me. They'll get him first."

Finally she said, "You know I have to leave you."

"Don't go," he said. "We mustn't be separated."

"But we are," she said. "We are separated."

Then she was gone. And it was dark again.

Then it was light.

And a new voice said, "He's coming around now."

He opened his eyes, seeing only sunlight. Nothing

hurt very much. His jaw was sore and his head ached. At the ankle he felt only something heavy, weighting it.

"How are you, old man?"

This voice seemed to be Charlie's.

There were people all around, some in white, one in a uniform. And one was Charlie.

"Pretty good, thanks."

"Why, that's fine, that's just fine."

"Where's Edna?"

Silence. The air was very bright and aseptic. There were no dust motes in it and every object was astonishingly itself. But no one answered, except that Charlie cleared his throat in the familiar, bleating way.

"The girl—Edna—where is she?"

A low murmur from the nurse, very professional and discreet, meant for the special ear of the doctor in white. "He kept talking about someone named Edna."

"She's the girl who was there. Where is she?"

A dry hand on his forehead. "Now try not to get excited. Remember, you're with your friends."

"Listen, old man   "

"But you must find her. For God's sake, Charlie, she was there. Don't let them waste any time."

Another voice, with a slight brogue. "There wasn't any girl, Mr. Terhune."

"But there was. She was there with me."

"Well, sir, I'll have to ask you a question or two."

"Just a minute, officer. Give him a chance. He's just coming out of it."

"Edna was the one who telephoned the police."

"No one telephoned the police, sir."

"She lied, then. I knew she was lying."

"Well, take it easy, old man. Take it easy."

"But why did the police come to the house? How did you find me?"

"The wreckers found you, Monday morning."

"The wreckers?"

"Yes, sir."

"And they didn't find a girl?"

"No, sir."

"But there was a girl in the house."

"There was plenty in the house, sir, but no girl. . . . And the house is gone."

"Gone!"

"Yes, sir."

"Already?"

"Yes, sir. That whole row is gone now."

How red and brilliant the roses and carnations were in the glass jug. And a sheaf of telegrams, like autumn leaves.

"What happened to Mort?" he asked.

"Mort? Now if you don't mind we'd like to have a description of Mort."

"Officer, I must insist. My patient is not up to this now."

"Haven't you found Mort either?"

"I'm not sure. This morning a man was fished out of the river. Heavy-set fellow, expensive suit. Couple of holes—in his back. No complete identification yet, but he may be your man."

No identification yet. Nothing but an expensive suit. Nothing left of Mort but an expensive suit.

"Now just a minute, officer. This is all very interesting but I have one or two really important things to say. Cass, the Secretary wants to talk to you as soon as you're well enough."

"He does?"

"I said the Secretary, Cass. *The* Secretary. I said he wants to talk to you."

"What about?"

"Well, I don't like to discuss it here. It's very, very confidential. He asked me to offer you his sincere sympathy for your accident and to tell you they all think you did a swell job over there. The last report you sent in before you had your illness was swell, simply swell. So he's got something very interesting lined up for you that he wants to talk to you about."

"That reporter is still outside, doctor. Shall I tell him to go away?"

"No reporters today. Sorry, absolutely not."

"How would we like a nice cup of soup?"

"Everyone must leave, I'm afraid. Even you, Mr. Bates."

"Just a minute. I only want to say, Cass, you'll be hearing from the Secretary shortly. I'll be seeing him sometime tomorrow and I'll tell him how you are. By the way, don't worry about the telegrams. I've answered the important ones, and I'll drop in again this afternoon."

"Thanks, Charlie." A silence, not long. "Better bring a stenographer with you when you come, will you?"

"That's the stuff, Cass. You bet I will. Doctor, I think our patient is back to normal."

"Oh, yes. A little rest is all he needs."

"So long, Cass."

"So long, Charlie. Thanks."

"I'll get the soup right away, and maybe if we drink it nicely we can have a rare piece of sirloin for our dinner."

"It would be a good idea to get some sleep now."

"Well, Mr. Terhune, sorry to stick around but you know the police do have to ask a few questions. As soon as you feel able we'll want to know all you can tell us. Now you spoke of a girl. Couldn't you give us a brief description of her?"

"Of Edna?"

"You say the name is Edna?"

He didn't answer. He looked at the face before him. Then he said, "Perhaps I just imagined her."

"Well—" The Irish voice was reproving but the Irish face became indulgent. "Well—sometimes we dream things," he said. "Good morning, sir."

"Good morning, officer."

Then he was alone.

There was nothing left. The house was gone. The old man sitting on the stoop. The room where Madame Golden sang. The Morellis' room. The attic where he read his books. The stolen whisky. The radio piano playing boogie-woogie. Mort. And finally, Edna. Even she was gone. Last night she had bent over him and then left him. And she would not come back. She would live her life somewhere unknown to him. Like all the rest, she might never have been. But like them she was in himself, where all things had their reality—the sight of the sun, the long search, the experience and memory of love.

Set in Linotype Baskerville
Format by A. W. Rushmore
Manufactured by The Haddon Craftsmen
Published by HARPER & BROTHERS, *New York*